BURDEN OF POOF

JULIE ANNE LINDSEY

Cozy Queen
PUBLISHING

Dedicated to my Cozy Queens.
The readers of my beloved genre. The collectors of clues. I couldn't
do this thing I love without you.

A NOTE FROM THE AUTHOR

Hello Lovely Reader,

Thank you so much for joining me on the first Bonnie & Clyde adventure! I've dreamed of sharing these characters, and the many humorous wonders of Bliss, Georgia, for *ages,* and the day has finally come!

There will be eight novels in the Bonnie & Clyde Mysteries, along with additional, spin-off series, as secondary characters rise to the front and insist their stories be told. So, if you have a favorite, be sure to let me know!

You can keep in touch between the books via my Cozy Club newsletter.

And if you enjoy BURDEN OF POOF, don't forget to grab your copy of SEVEN DEADLY SEQUINS.

Now, it's time to meet your new favorite furry little outlaw!
  -Julie Anne Lindsey

CHAPTER ONE

"Welcome to Bless Her Heart!" I called, thrilled at the sound of jangling bells against my new boutique's glass front door. Bless Her Heart, a second-chance dress shop and retailer of all things pretty, had been brewing in my heart for a lifetime, and finally, at age thirty-nine, I'd pushed that dream into existence. It seemed almost poetic that my failed marriage had prompted my major move into entrepreneurship because I identified with my products more than ever now. This was, after all, my second chance too.

Hope burst in my chest at the possibility of another actual, honest-to-goodness customer, which had been few and far between since I'd opened for business six weeks ago.

I spun away from the petal-pink taffeta dress I'd been hemming, eager to greet the shopper with a smile.

The woman I found smiling back wasn't a shopper. She was something better.

My best friend, Cami, shook her head at the sight of me. "I should've known I'd find you working."

I grinned and went for her with open arms because I was a hugger.

Camilla Rose Swartz, on the other hand, was a force of nature, in energy and in presence alike. I'd adored her from the moment we'd met while feeding ducks at the lake in preschool, and nothing would ever change that.

"What are you doing here? I was just about to meet you on the square."

Spring had sprung right on time in our neck of the woods, and the square was full of locals enjoying the weather.

She accepted my hug with a tight squeeze, then released me with narrowed eyes.

"I thought I'd come over here and see if you'd gotten lost. I'm willing to draw you a map if that's the case." She cast a pointed look through the door behind her, to the town square across the street.

The square was where most of our community events took place, and oddly enough, actually a large grassy oval. Little shops and businesses, like my own, lined the streets on each side, and a massive octagonal gazebo stood near the southern end.

Basically, I'd have to be blind and headless to miss it.

Since I was neither, I rolled my eyes, then checked my watch, stunned to see the time. I'd spotted her when I opened the shop at ten, and called out to say I'd be right over, then I'd gotten wrapped up in my work. One thing leading to another, the way it always did. "Oops," I said, raising apologetic eyes. "I'd thought for sure it was barely after ten. It feels like I just opened for the day."

"You did," she agreed with a nod. "A half hour ago. Now, tell me what smells like heaven in here."

My smile returned, immensely thankful for the pass she'd given me. Losing track of time wasn't one of my best qualities, but I was working on that. "I baked again last night," I said, answering her question. "Help yourself." I pointed to the small table I'd arranged beside the register. "How's your day going?"

"The landscapers are out. Spreading fresh mulch and hanging large baskets of flowers in the parks, as well as outside schools, the library and a few other locations, like the sheriff's department and fire station. Their efforts are making a huge difference already," she said with a prideful gleam. As chairwoman of a new beautification taskforce, meant to generate commercial interest in our hometown, Cami was turning the little haven, and everything in it, into something worthy of a Hallmark movie.

I imagined movie cameras pushing in on an image of the square, while a rich, southern voice-over announced, "Welcome to the historic village of Bliss, Georgia, tucked peacefully away from the hustle and bustle of big-city troubles, where folks know their neighbors, community spirit abounds, and visitors can expect a heaping helping of Deep South charm."

Cami sauntered toward my small refreshments stand, her black capri pants perfectly accenting a robin's-egg blue blouse. She was lithe and graceful without intention, and had been five inches taller than me since puberty, when she'd shot up overnight, while my body had tapped out at five-foot-two. "Bless your grandmama for teaching you to love baking," she said, lifting a napkin and adding a pair of pecan sandies to it.

Nostalgia and pride bloomed in my chest, along with a thousand memories of baking beside Gigi. I'd unintentionally given the little nickname to my mama's mama when my little toddler tongue couldn't quite manage the mouthful that was *grandmama*.

Cami nibbled on one cookie, then brushed crumbs from

her ruby-red lips, while her dark eyes raked over me in evaluation. Her warm brown skin was sun kissed from a long morning outside, and looked as dewy and blemish resistant as it had in high school.

My skin, on the other hand, was so fair it would've been classified as translucent if not for the thick mass of freckles trailing across my nose and cheeks. Add in my hazel eyes and red hair, and I was a walking argument against the luck of the Irish. In fact, thanks to my genetic heritage, I burned faster than Dracula in a shaft of sunlight. Not ideal for a lady in southern Georgia.

"Tell me, Bonnie Balfour," Cami said, polishing off her second cookie. "If you truly came home for a fresh start, how are you going to do it if you stay holed up in here all day, every day, alone with your work."

I averted my eyes. "I can't afford to hire anyone yet," I said, hoping to cover my cowardice with rationale.

"Uh huh," she said, not buying it for a minute. "You close up at seven. Then what?"

"I bake." And I sulk a little, still licking the wounds of my not-quite-official divorce. It didn't matter if I knew in my heart I'd done everything right in the relationship. A failed marriage felt a lot like a direct reflection on both parties, and I didn't like to fail at anything. Especially not something so important. "Baking helps me think," I said. And mostly, I tried to think about what I could've done differently, but it only made me more upset because I'd been alone in my efforts for at least a decade.

"There's only so much to think about before it becomes obsession, or depression," she said, her gaze jumping to the taffeta gown I'd been hemming. "I understand that you're going through some big things, and that you need time to process and acclimate, but Bonnie." She paused, leveling me with her gaze once more. "You've been here for months. Your shop's been open for weeks. You didn't leave Atlanta to reinvent yourself in Bliss as a hermit or a workaholic." She hiked a perfectly sculpted brow in challenge. "Did you?"

"Of course not," I said a little defiantly, though I knew she was right. "I just get caught up in the details."

I'd spent the first eighteen years of my life in Bliss, Georgia, population 3,128. A quintessential southern small town situated just far enough off the beaten path and highway to attract little more than a handful of tourists each year. Now, two decades later, I was home and figuring out how this place worked as an adult. The trouble was that everyone I'd grown up with had spouses and families now. They juggled jobs and housework with their kids' homework and extracurricular practice schedules. They'd bonded with one another, and I'd become the odd woman out. I had my folks, my cat and Cami. Why couldn't that be enough? "I thought starting over would be easier," I admitted, frowning as I realized how ridiculous I sounded.

"You're thirty-nine and single for the first time since college. You've got to live a little," she said, selecting a mini pecan pie from my container of sweets, then helping herself to coffee as well.

I spun dramatically, then collapsed onto a floral tufted chair and groaned. She was right. I hadn't been single since my sophomore year at University of Georgia. Then I'd met a grad student finishing his MBA and fell for him, meaty hooks, cheesy lines and life-altering sinker. We were married within months, and he'd stopped loving me sometime mid-ceremony, it seemed. I'd spent most of my days afterward trying to reclaim the feeling we'd had during our too-brief courtship. Now, being home and alone was new and weird, but I was working on it. "I'll try."

"That's the spirit," she said, nibbling her way around the little pie. "You know, I don't understand why you opened a dress shop when you can bake like this." She bit into the gooey filling and flaky crust with an audible moan. "Why not open a bakery?"

"Baking is Gigi's thing," I said, pushing myself up straighter on the seat. "I've always wanted a boutique where old things are made new again. Something about it just feels magical. Don't you think?"

Cami smiled, then nodded. "I do."

At Bless Her Heart, I gave outdated and castoff items a chic new look, then sold them at affordable prices. I specialized in women's clothing and household décor. From dress*es* to dress*ers*. A few adjustments to seams of the former. Fresh paint and new knockers for the latter, and suddenly the item that had been discarded and undesirable was fancied once more.

I frowned as I realized how much I resembled the proverbial dresser, right down to the need for revitalized paint and knockers. Gravity hadn't been as kind following my thirty-fifth birthday, and it seemed to get a little ruder each year.

Cami spotted Clyde, my sleek black kitty, curled up on a chair, then went to say hello. "Look at you," she said in baby talk while Clyde sized her up. "You're so handsome in your little green bow tie."

Clyde yawned, as if to say she'd declared the obvious, and was, perhaps, a bit slow to just now be noticing.

"How do you get him to wear these collars all the time?"

"He likes them," I said. "I think he enjoys being dapper."

She turned back to me, another question forming on her wrinkle-free brow. "Are you planning to bring him to work every day?"

I wasn't sure how to answer because I hadn't decided. I'd gotten used to bringing Clyde with me to work in the weeks before I'd opened. We'd spent long hours together while I cleaned and decorated the empty shop. Now that the store was open for business, I never knew how long I'd be gone, and it seemed unfair to move him to a new house, then abandon him every day. "I don't know," I admitted. "He might have separation anxiety if I left him home. I wouldn't want him to worry for hours on end."

Cami frowned. "I've watched enough Dr. Phil to know projecting when I hear it. So, I'm going to take that as a yes, every day is Bring Your Cat to Work Day. I suppose it's a good thing you didn't open a bakery. The health department would take issue."

I smiled, then poured myself a cup of coffee.

"What are you working on over here?" she asked, running an appreciative fingertip over the neckline of my petal-pink dress. "This is charming."

"Thanks. I'm prepping as many fancy gowns as possible. Last-minute and tightly budgeted prom shoppers will thank me. I found that dress in a trunk at an estate sale. What do you think?"

"I think it's gorgeous and you're incredibly talented. And I can appreciate your dedication, as long as you aren't using your work as an excuse to hide."

"I'm not," I said too quickly, unsure it was completely true.

Instead of giving the idea further thought, I worked up a warm smile and changed the subject. "I remember what it was like to want pretty things, when the family budget only provided for necessities. I'm excited to make more things financially accessible for everyone in the community."

My parents' flower farm had taken off in the years I'd been away, but while I was growing up, that hadn't been the case. I'd missed more than one middle school dance for lack of an appropriate dress, which had motivated me to learn to sew and get creative with a needle and thread before prom rolled around. I'd enjoyed the empowerment, and I hadn't stopped with sprucing up dresses.

Cami moved on to a rack of newly acquired ball gowns I still couldn't believe were mine. "Where on earth did you get these?" she asked, pulling a sequined number away from the rest. "Oh, my stars. This is some serious couture."

I glided across the floor in her direction, excited to share the news she'd barely believe. "Viola Abbott-Harrington stopped by first thing this morning and asked me to help her unload them from her car."

Cami straightened, then turned slowly to face me, mouth agape. "Shut. Up. The same Viola Abbott-Harrington who yelled at you in public last Christmas when you asked her to consider donating?"

"The same one," I said, cringing internally at the memory.

"She's barely been seen in public since that night," Cami said, checking over her shoulder for potential eavesdroppers in the empty store. "Everyone says she's gone batty and thinks people are after her money. The latest rumors about her make Scrooge McDuck sound like the greatest philanthropist alive."

"They're just rumors. She seemed nice enough this morning."

Cami stared. "Huh. I wonder why she had such a big change of heart?"

I shrugged and returned to my coffee.

"She was just so awful to you," Cami said, sounding as baffled now as I had been then.

The annual holiday parade had brought crowds of locals to the square. I'd just signed a lease for the new shop when I'd approached Viola about donating. Most people had been thrilled to let me haul away the things they no longer had use for. Viola had been offended that I'd asked.

"She lectured you on your presumptuousness until you basically ran away," Cami continued.

"Well aware," I said, with a roll of my eyes. "But thanks for the reminder."

The worst part about the encounter had been when I'd returned to Mama and Cami outside the café where we were seated. I'd recapped Viola's harsh refusal to them, while fighting tears of shocked humiliation, then said I could absolutely kill Viola for embarrassing me like that. A few people overheard, and my comment had been passed around on the lips of gossips for weeks. I'd only been home a couple of months at the time, and being caught badmouthing an old lady wasn't the impression I'd hoped to make on anyone.

I'd wondered more than once if my unfortunate slip of the tongue that night had contributed to my lack of foot traffic since opening Bless Her Heart.

"She told me I can stop at her house tonight and get the rest," I said, a flutter of excitement returning.

Cami poked her head through the neckline of a royal-blue beaded mermaid dress, wearing it like a big necklace while she admired herself in the mirror. "I suppose I should be happy with her change of heart, but I still think she owes you an apology."

I shrugged, catching Cami's eye in the reflection. "Maybe this is her apology."

"And maybe it's finally time you throw a proper grand-opening party like we talked about," Cami said. "You can showcase these gowns. Invite the whole town. Hand out invitations. Put an ad in the paper. Oh! You can get Mirabelle to cover it."

I sighed. Mirabelle was the octogenarian reporter who showed up at every event, took pictures and got one liners from the guests. "I'm not sure I'm ready for a grand opening."

"You've been up and running for weeks," Cami said,

tapping a crimson fingernail against the corner of her mouth. "Trust me, it's time. But now that I think about it, I'm pretty sure Zander Jones is covering town events. Mirabelle moved to covering crimes." She wrinkled her nose. "She wanted to retire, but they couldn't find anyone to fill the position. This way she at least has most of her time off."

It had only been six weeks since my shop had opened, but she was right. I could use the sales and exposure that a grand opening would bring. In fact, the highly unfortunate truth was that until I sold at least a few things, I wasn't sure I'd have enough money to keep the lights on through the summer.

"I'm thinking about it," I admitted.

"That's all I ask. Meanwhile, why don't you participate in one of the community events this weekend? I'm sure your mama would love to do the Shop Hop with you."

The Shop Hop was a Friday night affair that happened on the last week of every month. Shops stayed open late and set up displays on the sidewalks. Local vendors sometimes came to display their wares. There was music and games and plenty of time to mingle and laugh with other locals, while snacking and shopping and enjoying the perfect Georgia nights.

"It'll be fun," Cami said. "And a great way to support your fabulous best friend."

"You're playing dirty, using the best friend card."

"Hey." Cami put her palms up. "Desperate times."

I snorted, and she smiled.

"I've got to get going. Call me later? Maybe we can meet somewhere for dinner?"

"After I pick up those dresses from Viola," I promised.

I'd be counting the minutes until I got a look at the rest of her fabulous collection.

I closed the store at seven sharp, then tucked Clyde into his soft-sided carrier and headed out, locking up behind me. A cool April breeze whipped down the sidewalk as I hurried to my car.

"I'm going to leave you for a few minutes when we get to Viola's house," I told him. "Her place is on our way home, so the drive won't be any longer, and I'll just pop in and out. I'll crack the windows for you while I'm gone so it doesn't get stuffy in here."

I slipped behind the wheel of my blue Mercedes convertible, top up, in case of rain. The car had been the only thing I'd taken from Atlanta that wasn't specifically mine. I'd packed my clothes and personal items but left every other marital asset for the attorneys to sort and divide. The car, however, was special. It had held me through many long cries in our dark cavernous garage, beyond listening ears. And taken me safely to see my parents a hundred times in the last few years. Back when I knew my marriage was crumbling but had no idea how to stop it. The car, at least until I'd met Clyde, had been my only friend.

Clyde blinked long and slow as he tucked all four legs beneath him in the carrier, green eyes glowing in the shadows.

"All righty." I gripped the wheel, suddenly nervous about seeing Viola again. She'd blindsided me earlier with her generous donation, and left within a few minutes. This time, I would be the one calling on her, and I wasn't sure how to make proper small talk with someone I'd only met twice. Especially someone who'd had a completely different mood each time.

I said a silent prayer that she wouldn't change her mind about the dresses, then shifted into drive.

The growl of a black sports car startled me into slamming my brakes just as I'd eased onto the street.

The offending car flew past in the opposite direction, at probably double the posted speed limit, music pumping through the windows as it shrank in the distance.

"Jeez!" I complained, working to get my heart rate under control.

I removed my foot from the brake as I turned back to the road ahead of me, then squealed when something landed on my hood with a thud.

"Glory!" I jammed my foot against the brake and worked to focus my eyes on the problem.

A man wearing a crisp white dress shirt and gray slacks stood at the front of my car, one palm pressed to the hood, and a menacing scowl on his face. The lid from his disposable cup had popped off and landed near his palm. Dark-brown coffee soaked through his shirt and clung in droplets from his scruff-covered chin.

I lifted both hands to my mouth as he stepped back onto the sidewalk, actively murdering me with his stare.

A car behind me honked, and I jumped again.

"Sorry!" I said, shaking internally at the realization I could've killed a complete stranger.

I waved to the car in my rearview mirror, then to the man on the curb. "Sorry," I mouthed.

The car beeped longer in response, and I released a shuddering breath, taking one more look at the man to be sure he was okay.

"Go!" he hollered, motioning me to leave and scowling as if I was a moron.

I bristled, then gunned the engine and glared back at him as I zoomed away.

I could only hope my visit with Viola would go more smoothly.

CHAPTER TWO

I turned away from the square, then wound along the rural two-lane road toward Viola's home and mine. The Abbott-Harrington estate was several miles closer to the shop than my inherited cottage, which was seated at the edge of Bud's and Blossom's, my parents' flower farm. The fact that my mama and daddy—two desperate flower nerds respectively named Bud and Blossom—met, fell in love, then opened a flower farm, was basically proof that the stars sometimes aligned in love and business. I was just thankful to have been named after my paternal grandma, or who knows what my folks might've paired with my unfortunate middle name, which I was careful never to speak.

I adjusted the volume on my radio, while I watched for Viola's property to appear in the distance. I'd passed the estate a thousand times in my life and always wondered what the home looked like up close. No one I knew had ever been beyond the stone pillars near the road. Despite the wrought iron gate always being open, the driveway and land beyond had felt forbidden.

I slowed to take the turn onto her ambling driveway,

ignoring the sense of foreboding that hit as I rolled past the lion-topped pillars. Rows of ancient oaks lined the way. Their mossy, reaching limbs created a canopy overhead, dappling the path in shards and streaks of moonlight.

Clyde made a low mewling sound, and I slowed our roll further.

"It's okay," I told him, lifting my hand to the mesh door of his carrier in comfort.

He sniffed my finger through the material, then gave a low, gurgling yowl.

"Shh," I soothed, my muscles tensing in response to the sound.

Clyde was a reformed alley cat, tough to a fault, and never afraid.

I decided he was just hungry and pressed on.

Still, the world seemed darker after Clyde's complaints, and I shivered. I'd missed the relentless peace and stillness of the country while I'd been away, but Clyde was right. Something about the moment felt ominous.

Maybe I was hungry too.

A historic Greek Revival home stood regally at the end of the long drive, where the towering oaks gave way to a circular expanse of concrete, complete with a central fountain.

"What must it be like to live here?" I wondered aloud, shifting carefully into park.

The grand white structure was a tribute to an architectural style that had been wildly popular at the turn of the last century. Four massive pillars supported a wide, triangular roof and showcased an equally grandiose front door.

Clyde stretched in his carrier, watching me closely with big luminescent eyes.

"Wish me luck," I told him.

All I had to do was accept the gowns, smile, thank her, then leave.

I forced my chicken feet forward in measured steps, willing myself to stay the course, and resolving to be quick about the visit. The sooner I toughened up and rang the bell, the sooner the whole thing would be behind me, and I could get Clyde home for his dinner.

I pressed a fingertip to the illuminated doorbell button, then listened as the low gonging echoed inside the home.

I clasped my hands behind my back and tried to be still.

My phone began to ring as I waited, and I stole a glance at the screen, just in case it was Viola announcing she was running late. Or canceling.

My divorce attorney's name and number glowed in the eerie night. Martin Ross from a law firm with more partners than I could accurately recall, back in Atlanta.

I bit my lip, then stepped aside and answered in a hushed voice, to avoid being overheard and perceived as unprofessional. "Hello," I said quickly, hoping for good news. My husband had filed for divorce nearly a year ago, and at this point, I needed closure like I needed oxygen.

"Hello, Bonnie," he said. "I was wondering if you have a minute to talk."

I evaluated his soothing tone and knew instinctively it wasn't good. "I'm sorry. This isn't a good time. Can we talk tomorrow?"

The stretching pause made me wince.

"Okay," I said. "Never mind. Let me have it, but if I hang up on you, I'll call you tomorrow."

"Very good." He cleared his throat. "I wanted to let you know I've had to file additional paperwork," he began. And I was certain the distant sound of my money blowing out the window could be heard throughout the land.

"Why?" I asked. At our most recent meeting, everything

had finally been agreed upon. All that was left to do was divide the retirement funds and pay the attorneys. And that last part was going to hurt.

"It seems the balance in the retirement account has dwindled significantly since your initial paperwork was filed," he said.

I took a beat to process the words along with his tone. Grant's 401K was a benefit offered through his company. I'd never had any direct access to the investment, and the market was fairly stable, which meant Grant was the only likely cause of the deficit, and any withdrawals should be easily tracked. "Define dwindled."

Mr. Ross cleared his throat. "I suppose the most accurate term is depleted."

I took a long, slow breath and reminded myself it was useless to be upset. I couldn't change whatever was happening. And I definitely couldn't deal with it at this moment.

"I'm sorry, but I have to go," I said, seeing a shadow pass over the window before me.

I disconnected, then rapped a little more heavily than intended on the window. I pushed the bell again as well.

"Come on," I groaned. Viola might not have heard me ring or knock the first time, but she had to hear me now. The shadow I'd seen had to have been made from someone on this floor.

I leaned forward at the hips, peeking casually through the narrow sidelight window from a foot or two away, willing Viola to appear.

A pile of silks and crinolines drew my eye to the ground at the base of the stairs.

And I screamed when Viola's twisted, unmoving body appeared among them.

I yanked my phone free as I grabbed the door knob and

turned. The barrier swung easily inward under my command. Thank heavens she hadn't locked the door.

"Viola!" I called, dropping into the mass of fabric at her side.

I dialed emergency services, then pressed my fingers to her already cool throat, searching hopelessly for a pulse I knew I wouldn't find. The slack expression on her face and pooling blood beneath her silver hair were evidence of the horrific truth.

"Nine-one-one. What's your emergency?" a distant tinny voice asked from the other end of my call.

I fell back, onto my bottom, against the cold marble floor and inhaled a shuddered breath. "This is Bonnie Balfour," I croaked. "I'm at 1811 Pecan Lane. Viola Abbott-Harrington is dead."

CHAPTER THREE

*H*alf an hour later, I'd been relocated to a chair in a formal dining room fit for thirty and left to stew. The sideboard along one wall was large enough for me to crawl into and hide. A possibility I'd been considering for at least fifteen minutes.

Clyde was sleeping contentedly in his carrier at my feet, delivered by a woman in a Bliss PD windbreaker after I'd asked if I could get him from the car.

Men and women in similar jackets and uniforms were visible in the foyer, along with members of the coroner's department and the first EMT on scene with me. Even more officials milled around outside. The crew of volunteer firemen, who had been dispatched when I'd dialed 911, were playing security guards at the end of the driveway, stopping lookie-loos and concerned citizens from coming to see what was going on and if they could help.

I recognized Sheriff Miller immediately. He was a friend of my dad's, and the comfort in that association had gone a long way when he'd arrived. If my entire body hadn't felt both numb and leaden, I would've hugged him. He'd offered to call my parents for me, letting them know what had happened before they heard it from the gossip mill. I'd accepted gratefully with a nod, not yet able to speak.

My stomach churned and knotted as I imagined poor Viola, tripping and falling. Her feet and legs tangled in silk and chiffon. The fear she must've felt, knowing she was alone. All because she'd tried to carry those gowns down the steps for me.

Did that make me responsible for her death somehow?

My mind scrambled with a new, horrible thought. Was I complicit in the untimely death of another human being?

I pressed a shaking hand to my middle, hoping I wouldn't be sick.

The coroner moved methodically around her in the next room, poking and prodding. He'd spoken to Sheriff Miller shortly after his initial evaluation, and both men's eyes had drifted to me. Probably feeling awful that I'd found her this way, or maybe they were thankful she'd been discovered tonight, since she lived alone. I wasn't sure when someone might've come across her otherwise.

A fresh flash of lights drew my gaze to the driveway where a late-model Jeep Wrangler, masquerading as a mudball, rolled into view.

I watched intently as the driver climbed out. How many people had to see her this way? The whole process had already gone on far too long, and I suspected that Viola would be utterly horrified if she knew her body was splayed on the floor while a half-dozen people traipsed around her, as if she was the equivalent of a human coffee spill.

Mirabelle, marched up the driveway with a fireman escort. She wore a camera on a long black strap around her neck and curlers in her short white hair.

The Jeep's door opened, and the driver climbed out. He was dressed in jeans and a T-shirt, while everyone else, except Viola and me, seemed to be wearing some kind of uniform. Was this a family member or caregiver? The man turned toward my Mercedes for a long beat, adjusting a black ballcap low on his forehead, before turning toward the house.

Light washed over him as he approached, and I swallowed a painful groan. I'd seen the man once before, barely more than an hour ago, when I'd nearly made him my hood ornament.

"Sheriff Miller," he said in greeting, shaking the older man's hand before scanning the scene. "Sorry I'm late." His gaze turned to me, as if he'd already seen or sensed me there. "I got your call when I was on my way home to change my shirt."

I tried not to stare at his recently changed top or his pretty eyes. My attention caught on something I hadn't noticed the first time I'd seen him, a shiny badge clinging to his black leather belt. Directly beside a gun and holster.

My gaze met his, and my cheeks flared hot. I'd nearly run over some sort of lawman. And based on his expression, he definitely knew it was me.

"We're just glad you're here, Detective Wright," Sheriff Miller said. "It's been a long while since we've dealt with something like this. So, I'd like to turn it over to you."

The detective nodded. "Who found the body?"

Sheriff Miller swept an arm in my direction.

I lifted Clyde's carrier onto my lap and wrapped my arms around it like a shield as the newcomer approached.

He sized me up before pulling out a chair and taking a seat at the table with me. "I'm Detective Wright."

"Bonnie Balfour," I said, shivering unintentionally as a wave of misplaced adrenaline attempted to burn itself off.

He leaned forward, resting muscled forearms on the table and appraising me with ethereal blue eyes. His jaw was square, nose straight, and his cheeks were dusted in a mix of light-brown and gray stubble. He was clearly closer to my age than the sheriff's, but I didn't think I'd ever seen him before today.

My gaze dropped to the lines of dark ink peeking from beneath the sleeves of his T-shirt, more visible with each flex and shift of his arm.

"How are you doing, Bonnie?" he asked, his tone smooth and incredibly comforting.

"Terribly." My voice cracked on the little word, and I felt instantly guilty, yet again, for being the indirect reason Viola had fallen.

"Why don't you tell me about it," he encouraged. "You've been through a lot tonight. I'm a good listener."

"This is all my fault," I said, a sob breaking on my lips.

Detective Wright glanced to the sheriff, who'd positioned himself in dining room's open doorway. "Did you do something that caused her to fall?" he asked, turning carefully back to me.

"I don't know," I said, covering my trembling lips with one hand. I didn't know what had changed her mind about donating the dresses, but it had been me who'd approached her all those months ago.

"Bonnie," Sheriff Miller warned. "Think carefully about your answers."

The detective shot him a frown.

I waved a limp hand. "Of course. Sorry."

"Why don't you start from the beginning," Sheriff Miller suggested.

I nodded, then wet my lips. My gaze drifted to the coroner behind him, who was finally allowing Viola to be loaded onto a gurney.

"You said this was your fault." The detective's voice drew

my attention back to him. "I'm going to need you to elaborate."

I batted heavy tears from my lashes as a pair of EMTs piloted Viola through her front door and into the night. Then I wiped renegade drops from the corners of my eyes. "What?"

"How did you kill Ms. Abbott-Harrington?" the detective asked flatly, searching me with cautious eyes.

"What?" I looked to the sheriff, then back, confusion muddling the words.

The sheriff shifted, drawing my eyes his way once more. "Bonnie, Detective Wright is on loan to the Bliss Sheriff's Department. He's been with the FBI for eight years. Before that, he worked homicide with Cleveland PD. He's still getting settled here, but I thought this was the right place for him tonight. I'm afraid I won't be able to stay unbiased in the matter. I've known you far too long, and your daddy and I are going fishing in the morning."

I balked. "Unbiased about what?"

The detective shot a disbelieving look in my direction. His brows furrowed and forehead wrinkled. "Your presence at the crime scene, for starters," he said, cocking his head to one side. "And the fact you said that woman's death was your fault."

"I didn't mean that literally," I scoffed. "I feel guilty because she'd offered me those dresses, not because I hurt her. She clearly fell while trying to carry the gowns downstairs by herself."

"Is that what it looks like to you?" he asked.

I tented my brows. "Obviously. What does it look like to you?"

"Suspicious."

"How?" I snapped, utterly baffled. I turned to Sheriff Miller for support, but he only stared back.

The detective's lips twisted into a deep, ugly frown, and he laced his fingers on the tabletop between us. "For starters, a rich old lady appears to have fallen to her death, but the person who found her body had no business being present. And she already claimed responsibility. I'd say that's the definition of suspicious."

My jaw dropped, and a little flame blazed to life in my core, heating me from the inside out. Whatever else I'd been feeling went up like kindling and blew away on the storm of my temper. A temper I'd had firmly in control for years. "That's completely ridiculous."

"Is it?"

I blinked. "Yes!"

"So, you're recanting your confession?" he asked.

"I never made a confession." I hugged Clyde's carrier tighter and narrowed my eyes.

Clyde meowed in response to the disturbance.

"Why on earth would I kill Viola?" I snapped. "I barely knew her." My intuition spiked, and my eyes narrowed. "You're still mad about the coffee. Aren't you?"

"What coffee?" Sheriff Miller asked. "Did the two of you have coffee?"

"No," the detective nearly growled. "She almost hit me with her car," he tattled. "I spilled coffee all over my clothes and had to go back to my rental and change. I can't help but wonder why she was in such a big hurry. Maybe trying to get over here and take care of business before the estate manager returned?"

"I wasn't in a hurry. You walked out in front of me. And not in a crosswalk."

His eyes widened, and it spurred me on.

"I was on my way over here to pick up those gowns," I said, pointing to the mess on the floor. "Viola was donating them to my store, and I volunteered to come and get them." I paused, then mentally backpedaled. "What's an estate manager?"

A pair of men walked into the foyer, as if on cue. One fireman. One old man in a tweed jacket. "Sheriff?" the fireman prompted. "This is Theodore Runsford. Ms. Abbott-Harrington's estate manager. He's here reporting for work."

"Teddy," the small white-haired man corrected gravely.

The sheriff shook Teddy's hand, then led him to the other end of the room.

I leaned forward in my chair to listen.

"I can't believe this happened," the older man said. "It doesn't make any sense."

"I know, and I'm very sorry for your loss. The two of you have worked together a long while," the sheriff said.

"I was just here," Teddy told him, heartbreak clear in his milky blue eyes. "I come by every night at seven to check on things. Door locks and whatnot. I bring in the mail and see to whatever she needs. Everything was fine a little while ago."

"Is there somewhere we can talk more privately?" the sheriff asked. "Then we'll take a look around. See if anything's been bothered or is missing."

The men swung their gazes to meet mine.

I turned my eyes away.

"Sure," Teddy agreed. "My office is in the basement."

"Anyone else have a key to the home?" the sheriff asked as they moved back toward the foyer.

"Only Emma and I," he said.

Detective Wright cleared his throat, and I jumped, having forgotten he was there.

"Mercy," I panted.

"Ms. Balfour, I'm going to have to ask you to come down to the station with me. I have a few more questions, and I'd like to get your written statement." He slid his chair back and stood, then motioned for me to go out ahead of him.

I stood on wobbly noodle legs and hefted Clyde up with me.

A woman in a Bliss PD windbreaker was dusting the door handle for prints as we entered the foyer. She'd soon discover my prints were there. Another deputy was packing the pile of gowns into a large container marked as evidence. I stared at the sheer number of dresses, astounded by Viola's ability to carry them anywhere, let alone down a staircase.

I bumped into an antique table in the hall as I rounded the corner, not watching where I was going. I pressed a hand to the table to steady it, holding my breath as a tall white candle, dish of potpourri and framed black-and-white photograph of Viola wobbled, but thankfully didn't fall. Viola was at least sixty years younger in the image, and wearing a white ball gown. She was surrounded by other young ladies dressed the same. Presumably debutantes being introduced to society.

I frowned at a small crescent-shaped scratch in the table's finish. I could fix that scratch with a little TLC, but there was nothing I could do to help Viola, and it gutted me.

Outside, Detective Wright paused beside my car. "You're obviously shaken. Can you make it to the station safely, or would you like me to drive you?" he asked. "I can bring you back for your car."

I eyeballed the muddy Jeep, then opened my passenger door to secure Clyde and his carrier. "I'd like to drop Clyde off at home, if you don't mind. He's had a very long day and it's past his dinnertime."

"No problem. I'll follow you." He moved toward his vehicle, then turned back, suspicious stare renewed. "Bonnie and Clyde, huh? Interesting choice."

I climbed behind my wheel, refusing to take his bait. I hadn't chosen Clyde's name, or intended for our names to match a murderous couple from the Great Depression, but the combination had seemed right anyway. Clyde had been a stray when we met. As lost and alone as I was. I knew we needed one another, and when I bought a carrier and offered my home to him, he climbed aboard for the trip. Grant had denied me a pet, among other things, throughout our marriage, but the loneliness had won out that day, and I'd taken a stand. Adopting Clyde was the first in a long line of brave steps I'd taken since then. Steps that had brought me back to myself, and I'd never regret any of them.

Though I did feel a little like an outlaw as I imagined ramming the muddy Jeep with my shiny little convertible.

CHAPTER FOUR

*T*he sheriff's department was housed in an old white church, complete with bell and steeple. It'd been there as long as I could remember, but I'd never had reason to step inside. I'd heard my dad say there were less than a dozen deputies on the force, and he thought that was twice as many as we needed.

Bliss was a safe town. *But accidents*, I realized, *happened everywhere*. And my heart broke again for poor Viola. She'd tried to do a good thing, and look at what had happened.

Detective Wright led the way to the front door, then held it for me. I paused inside, waiting as he took the lead once more, striding confidently through the empty waiting area. He flashed his badge at the woman behind the desk, who quickly buzzed him in.

She waved shyly as I passed, an inquisitory look in her eye.

"Janine," I said, recognizing my old Sunday school teacher after a beat. I hadn't seen her in ages. She was slightly rounder now, with a fuller face, and her kind, brown eyes were accented by a full head of gray hair. She looked the part of a grandma, but I supposed was around the same age as my folks. "How's your mama and them?" I asked, thankful for her warm, familiar smile on an otherwise awful night.

"Good." She struggled with a smile, then leaned in my direction. "Your daddy was just in here steaming up the place, but I sent him home. Told him you'd give him a call just as soon as you could."

"Thanks," I said, already regretting the conversation ahead. As daddy's only child, it didn't matter if I was closer to forty than fourteen. He'd defend me to the death, as readily today as he had when we were both half our ages. And I loved him all the more for it.

Detective Wright sighed, drawing my attention.

I waved goodbye to Janine, then hurried on.

The detective ushered me into a small room with a wooden table and two matching chairs. "Do you know everyone in town?" he asked.

"No." I puzzled over the bizarre question. "Did you know everyone in Cleveland?"

"That's hardly the same." He said, dropping a notebook and pen onto the table. "I'll be right back. Don't go anywhere."

He left, closing the door behind him.

I stewed, then took a seat in one of the chairs.

The room smelled like fresh paint and furniture polish. For an interrogation room, the space was fairly welcoming. Nothing like those cold, intimidating spaces in cop shows, with the beat-up old folding chairs and metal tables. This table set appeared to be made of maple and had probably been donated or picked up at the local bazaar.

The detective, on the other hand, was a conundrum. I'd never given local lawmen much thought, but if Dad was right about twelve being too many deputies, then why was Detective Wright on loan from Cleveland? Did it have something to do with his homicide and FBI experience? Was something big secretly going on in Bliss?

And how could a man who was so pleasing to the eye be such a sour pill? Maybe all the years spent working major crimes had cracked him. Maybe he'd become angry and bitter like those cops on television who'd been undercover too long.

I checked my watch twice before the detective returned, nearly ten minutes later. My mind had run the gamut of questions in his absence, then returned to the snide question he'd asked before disappearing.

"Bliss might have a limited population," I said when the door reopened, "but there are several thousand residents, spread over a generous amount of land. Geographically, we're hardly small at all. I know a completely normal amount of people, like the folks I grew up with and their families. Friends of my folks and friends of friends."

He took the seat opposite me with a smirk, then set a manila folder and two bottles of water on the table. "So, if I get to know ten percent of the population, I'll have a link to everyone in town?"

I wasn't great at math, but that sounded right. "Basically." I nodded. "Why? Thinking of staying?"

"Not if people keep looking at me like I'm going to accost them."

"Have you tried not making that face?" I suggested.

His eyes widened by a fraction before he resumed his usual unpleasant expression. "What face?"

I raised an eyebrow in challenge. "You have to know you're scowling."

"I'm not—" he started, then stopped, composing his features. "This is just how I look." He pushed the pen and paper in my direction, before pulling the folder closer to him. "I need a written statement from you about the events leading up to your phone call for emergency services tonight."

"How much lead up?" I asked, staring at the paper, and feeling as if I was about to fail a very important test.

"Start after you nearly hit me with your car, but before you entered the victim's home without invitation."

"You were jaywalking," I muttered, lifting the pen and refusing to meet his eyes.

I neatly printed the date at the top of the page.

"You would've known I was there if you'd been paying attention to where you were going. Eyes on the road is driving one-oh-one. You were turned completely around."

I dropped my pen, ready to tell him that what he'd described was impossible, but decided to focus on him instead. "Are you justifying your crime, detective? Jaywalking is punishable by a fine."

He glared.

I froze as something else whipped into mind. Another law had been broken only moments before he'd stepped into my path. "A black sedan flew down Main Street right as I pulled out. It had to be going fifty in a twenty-five. It startled me, and I watched until it was gone. That's what I was looking at. Figures you didn't notice that."

"I was probably in the coffee shop." He sent me a pointed stare. "I'm surprised you don't know the driver."

"I don't know everyone," I repeated.

"I guess a lot's probably changed in the nineteen or twenty years since you left this town."

My mouth opened, and I forced it shut. "Were you out there talking to Janine?"

"About what?" he asked, casually opening his folder so that only he could see whatever was inside. "About the fact you went to University of Georgia, married young, then apparently spent the days since then as a fundraiser and media liaison for your husband and his company?"

"That's none of your business," I said, the word *husband* landing like a slap to my heart. "You don't know anything about me." Or the fact that I'd volunteered at Grant's company for the first ten years of our marriage, trying to be closer to him. Those were also the years I'd struggled with the physical and emotional exhaustion of trying to get pregnant. Eventually, I'd stayed home, hiding from the heartbreak and loneliness, while Grant pulled further away.

"Married almost twenty years," the detective continued, "but you just moved back to town. How does that work? Will your husband be joining you soon?"

I crossed my arm and pursed my lips, hoping the tears blurring my eyes didn't show.

"Downsizing from a fifty-two-hundred-square-foot home in North Buckhead to a twelve-hundred-square-foot cottage in Bliss is quite the move. Caught embezzling company money? Or is there trouble in paradise?"

I gasped, shocked at how he knew so much and sounding more like my mother than I had in my life. I clutched my collarbone, thankful I wasn't wearing pearls, and certain Detective Wright would've laughed in my face if I had been. "My life has nothing to do with Viola's accident, and I would appreciate you sticking to the point."

"You are the point," he said, closing the folder. "You came from this little town, raised on a flower farm." He glanced at me, brows furrowed, as if to say, "what the heck is a flower farm?" before carrying on. "You married into money. Lived the high life for a long while, then here you are again. Back in Bliss, alone, and set up in a home that's probably smaller than your previous pool house."

"It was my grandparents' home. And I prefer it to the house in Buckhead."

He opened his folder again, appraising me more closely. "Bonnie Buttercup Balfour. Anywhere else, I'd assume that was a typo. Your middle name have something to do with the flower farm?"

"Obviously," I said, shifting my gaze.

The detective made a strange, amused sound, drawing my eyes back to his.

"Organic flower farming is a growing industry," I insisted. "People love flowers, but not everyone has the time, space or know-how to cultivate healthy, vibrant blooms. My folks provide plants and bouquets for stores and chains all over the state. They've worked hard for decades, and they're proud of what they do. And I'm proud of them."

He watched my rant with interest, lips twitching, as if my anger entertained him.

I picked up the pen and began to write. Something told me I needed to finish this conversation and get away from the loaner detective before I opened my mouth and said something I might regret.

CHAPTER FIVE

*C*lyde and I arrived at work an hour early the next morning. My parents had been waiting at the cottage when I returned home from the sheriff's station. We'd talked until I was nearly asleep on the couch, wrapped in a warm blanket by Dad and filled with chicken noodle soup and toast by Mama. I hadn't been able to stay asleep after they left, so I'd baked until nearly dawn in a failed attempt to push the image of Viola's slack face from my mind.

I wanted to do something for her loved ones. To pay respects or give condolences, maybe even deliver a casserole to soothe someone's grief. But Viola didn't have any family in town, and an online search had revealed her only heir was an estranged son named Nathan Harrington, living in Nashville.

With no one to comfort, I dove headlong into my work on an alabaster ballgown. As exquisite as any wedding dress, it had been crammed into a box marked FREE at an estate sale a few towns over, and I had hit the proverbial jackpot. I'd repaired the torn seams and replaced the zipper, but other than that, the dress was sublime and clearly something from the 1940s. I moved the hanger onto a hook I used when steaming, then arranged the deeply creased material over an extra-full petticoat and got to work de-wrinkling.

Clyde leaped onto the nearby bookcase, dropping a feathered hair barrette from my window display before stretching out.

"You sneaky little kitty," I said, going to collect the pretty turquoise accessory. "That isn't yours and you know it. What's the rule about stealing?"

He ducked his head behind a collection of sky-blue hardcover classics I'd stacked on their sides. Each spine was embossed with golden letters and a small insignia that reminded me of a fleur-de-lis. His shiny black fur stood out on the white shelf like a sore thumb.

I stroked his back and sighed. "I'll set out some more things to hunt in a few minutes," I promised. "I know you're bored inside and miss running free, but I don't want anything to happen to you."

He huffed a breath and began to groom himself.

"I'm glad you're here," I told him. I wasn't sure I could've done all the things I had without him. In the days since his adoption, Clyde had stuck by my side, giving me comfort and purpose as I made some of the toughest decisions of my life. Even now, he seemed to say, "You've got this. And I've got you," with every lick of his furry black paw.

I returned the barrette to the window display, then hummed and admired my shop as I returned to the gown. A few weeks of late nights and elbow grease had gone a long way to turn my portion of a former bank building into an uber feminine boutique, showcasing clothes and accessories, for shoppers and their homes, in a broad palette of pastels and florals. I'd painted the walls a shade of white called rosewater, with a hint of pink so subtle, it was just enough to accent everything in the store. I'd used golden frameworks with glass shelves to display costume jewelry and make the space look bigger. I placed a variety of pretty rugs strategically over damaged hardwood floors, then topped them with fancy end tables and an array of reupholstered armchairs. I'd even sewn lengths of muslin fabric to hang in sweeping tufts over the ceiling, giving an air of the outdoors while pulling double duty to hide water spots in the plaster. The shop had needed more work than I could afford to do at the time, but I'd hoped that would soon change.

After the call I'd received from my attorney, I wasn't so sure.

To make matters worse, if folks had been slow to visit Bless Her Heart before, they'd surely avoid it like the plague now that I was associated with a woman's death. The whole thing just made me seem like bad luck, and Bliss was nothing if not superstitious. I blamed that on our founding father, Father Frances Flanigan, the priest who established our village about two hundred years ago. Flanigan was an ancestor of mine, and the reason my mother's family had wound up in the United States at all.

Flanigan named the land Bliss after stumbling onto a waterfall four days into a trek by foot through the relentless Georgian heat. He'd claimed it was the most beautiful sight he'd ever seen, and that the water was restorative. As I'm sure it was for someone who'd probably been close to death by dehydration. But he'd also claimed the land was enchanted, blessed and special. Nearly two centuries later, his claims had left a mark on the fabric of our town. Villagers still searched for and believed in good vibes and positivity. Bad luck, on the other hand, was equivalent to leprosy.

I couldn't afford to have leprosy.

A small shadow fell over the front door, and my mama appeared.

I waved when I saw her, then set my steamer aside and

went to let her in. I flipped the CLOSED sign to OPEN while I was there.

"Baby," she cooed, wrapping me in a tight hug, careful not to crush the bouquet in her hands. "How are you holding up? Your dad and I worried all night after we got home."

I sighed, hating that I'd worried them. "I'm sorry."

"You have nothing to apologize for. It's just what parents do. We worry."

I smiled, knowing she was right on both fronts.

I looked like my mama. From her wild red hair, hazel eyes and abundant freckles, down to her small stature and pointy elf nose. A nose I'd never change because I liked looking like her. Even if that meant I also resembled a fairytale forest creature from certain angles.

Today, we'd dressed alike too. Both in black shift dresses, hers in an A-line, and mine in a sheath. Each donned in respect for the loss of a local.

Mama cradled the bouquet in one arm, then pushed flyaway hair behind my ear with her free hand. "I'm sorry you're going through all this," she said, fixing me with a meaningful stare, as if to confirm she wasn't just talking about last night. "But your dad and I are here for you, whatever you need. Just ask. Okay?"

The warmth of her touch soothed the tender corners of my heart, and I breathed a little easier with her there. "Okay."

"Good." Mama presented me with the bouquet. "For your counter."

I found a wide-mouthed milk-glass vase and set it near the register, beside a row of other vases, already full of mama's beautiful blooms.

"Perfect!" She unfastened the paper and arranged her gift, then plucked wilted petals from the previously delivered flowers. "A little something to brighten your day."

"Thank you. They're beautiful."

Mama inhaled deeply, then floated to my refreshments table. "Look at all this. I guess you weren't able to sleep either."

"Nope." I returned to steaming my dress, nervous energy fizzing through my veins. "Help yourself, and pack some up for Dad. I've got more than I can eat and no one to give it to. There aren't any shoppers, and I'm already outgrowing my pants again." In fact, I'd been outgrowing my pants regularly for several years now, since I'd started a steady routine of late-night baking to distract my mind.

It was too hard to let any sweets go to waste afterward.

"I hear you're going to attend some of Cami's events," Mama said, pouring coffee from the pot. "I think that's a marvelous idea. It's good to put yourself back out there. Ripping off the bandage and all that."

I shot her a sad smile. Mama had always hoped I'd find someone to love me the way Dad loved her, and vice versa, but I'd tried that when I was young, and I'd failed. Now, I was less than two years from forty, and I didn't have the energy to date again. "I just want to support Cami and maybe have a great time with my mama."

She smiled, apparently approving of the idea. "Fine, but remember. You're a catch, and Grant was the exception, not the rule. When you're ready to seek your soul mate, it won't take long for every eligible man in town to see how special you are, but what matters most is that you see it."

I gave up the steaming. "Thank you."

"Speaking of single men, every woman in town is talking about how attractive the new detective is," she said, her voice going light and singsong as she selected a cookie from the container near my coffee pot. "That's interesting. No?"

I grimaced. "No. That man is trying to arrest me. He thinks I killed poor Viola or that I had a hand in it somehow. He's maddening."

"You mentioned that a few times last night," Mama said. "Hello, Clyde." She crouched to rub behind his ears when he leaped from the bookcase to greet her. "Don't you look smart in your paisley collar."

He skidded across my checkout counter to her side, then offered her a headbutt. He swatted her charm bracelet while she stroked him. If she didn't keep an eye on him, he'd Houdini the charms right off her, but she already knew that, so I pressed on.

"I think the detective actually enjoys arguing," I continued, my feathers ruffling all over again. "I snapped at him. Multiple times. And I never snap at anyone anymore," I complained. I'd worked very hard to overcome the stereotype of temperamental redhead. Grant had used it against me anytime I was upset, and over time, I'd broken the habit of getting worked up.

Or maybe he'd intentionally manipulated me, tricked me, into becoming compliant, and I'd accepted my new doormat status willingly. I wasn't sure, which only made me madder, and I didn't want to think about Grant anymore.

I was ranting about Detective Wright. "He hadn't known me five minutes, but he made all sorts of assumptions. And faces," I added, trying my best to recreate the handful of angry and disinterested looks I'd received.

"You mentioned that too." Mama's lips curled into a tiny cat-that-ate-the-canary grin. "You haven't mentioned if the rumor was true. Is he as good looking as everyone says?"

I groaned, his ridiculously handsome face flashing into mind. "I don't want to talk about him," I said, averting my eyes. "I'm still trying to get past feeling as if I'm the cause of someone's death." The words left my mouth like whispers, and the pressure built in my chest once more. "Viola was carrying all those dresses down the steps for me when she fell."

"Not your fault," Mama said. "Imagine if the roles were reversed. What if she'd asked you to carry them down for her because she was having trouble, so you did, and you fell, and you died. Would it be her fault? Even if she'd asked you to do it?"

"I guess not."

"See." Mama helped herself to coffee and smiled. "You didn't even ask her to carry them. She was just going about her life, and there was an accident. Awful and tragic, yes, but still an accident."

"Bad luck," I said, and Mama gasped.

She craned her neck for a look around the store, then outside, as if someone might've overheard me from the sidewalk. "Don't say that. This has nothing to do with bad luck. When it's a person's time to go, they go. That's it. She could have just as easily gone in her sleep or choked on a chicken ball."

"But she didn't. She was carrying gowns down the steps for me."

Mama widened her eyes. "It was an accident, and you weren't even there when it happened."

I inhaled slowly, then wet my lips, preparing to say the other thing that had been on my mind. "Do you think there's a chance it wasn't an accident?"

Mama blinked her wide cat eyes at me. "What do you mean?"

"Detective Wright thinks I'd had a hand in her fall," I said quietly. "Now, I can't stop wondering if it's possible someone else did." The memory of a shadow moving across Viola's window raced back to mind. I'd seen the shadow before I'd seen Viola's body. So, what had caused the shadow? Or had I imagined it?

Mama shook her head. "You can't start thinking things

like that. It's dark and you're nothing but light," she said. "If it'd been up to me, we would've named you Sunshine."

I nodded. "You're right. I've got plenty on my plate already. Sheriff Miller and the detective will figure this out."

Mama finished her cookie with a flutter of her lashes, then refreshed her smile. "You should bake a few of your pecan pies for the cake walk. Gigi always brought her cakes for events like these. You can make the donation in her honor. I know she'd love that. I can try to call her and tell her, if you like the idea."

"Sure." I nodded. I liked the idea of honoring Gigi, and of giving some of my pies away, instead of eating them.

Mama clapped silently. "Excellent. Now I can brag to the ladies at Auxiliary Club. They all think their daughters are the best, but none of them can touch your pies with a ten-foot pole."

I laughed. "I'll let Cami know."

"Perfect." Mama approached again, then kissed my cheeks. "I've got to run over to the historical society and see about getting my hands on a few of the plants in Viola's greenhouse before some knucklehead throws them out because they don't understand the value of good botany. You know Emily Dickinson was known for her gardening long before her poetry saw the light of day. Nowadays, no one cares about the plants," she huffed, eternally irked at this truth. "Viola understood."

"Is the historical society in charge of the estate now?" How quickly had the property changed hands? Viola hadn't been dead twenty-four hours.

"They will be if the council has anything to say about it. Then who knows what will happen. I've heard rumors they'd like to turn her home into a satellite office. Rent it out for events and rake in the dough."

I frowned, unsure how much truth was at the kernel of

that rumor. "You should reach out to Theodore Runsford about the plants," I suggested. "It's unlikely the historical society has any authority over things so soon. When Mr. Runsford came to the house last night, Sheriff Miller called him the estate manager. He's probably still in charge enough to make decisions like that for you."

Mama beamed. "Teddy Runsford?"

"Yeah. You know him?" I nearly grimaced at the small town connection the grumpy detective had practically made fun of.

"I know his wife, Evelyn. She sometimes plays bridge with the ladies and me," she said. "You are a flower-saver. Viola raised orchids, something her mama had taught her. Do you know how much folks love orchids? They're so hard to grow, but if your father and I can get a crop going, we can corner a new market." She shimmied her shoulders. Nothing excited Mama like a rare flower.

"Good luck," I said.

"You always were good with the details," Mama praised. "I'll give Evelyn a call right away."

I waved as she headed out. "Be careful," I called after her.

Because now that I'd said it aloud, I couldn't get the possibility Viola had been murdered out of my head. And that would mean a killer was at large in our village.

CHAPTER SIX

*B*y lunchtime, a number of shoppers had come in to peruse the store, and several had stayed to try something on. They all adored Clyde, and one woman even asked about him after peeking under two dress racks. Apparently Clyde had fans.

He also had a satin hair ribbon between his teeth that didn't belong to my store. I could only hope it didn't belong to any of the shoppers. Having a black cat could easily be seen as bad luck, but so far, everyone seemed enamored with Clyde and his adorable little bow ties.

I wasn't sure they'd feel the same way if they caught him running off with their things, but for now, he was working wonders at drawing folks in from the sidewalk by curling in the window display for his naps.

Maybe my black cat was a good luck charm.

I reveled in the possibility, until a few braver folks asked questions about what had happened at Viola's house last night.

Then I saw the influx in guests for what it was. A reconnaissance mission for the local grapevine. They hadn't come in to see Clyde. They were after information. I'd been on a few similar outings of my own at one time, sent by a friend to determine if a cute guy was single, for example. Or making nice with HOA board members to get the scoop on upcoming rule changes so folks on my block could beat the clock and be grandfathered in. I'd managed to add a small wildflower garden and inappropriately tall picket fence back in Buckhead using that tactic, and my yard had looked fabulous.

Maybe Mama was right. I was good at getting details.

The door bells jingled again, and I brightened my smile. "Welcome to Bless Her Heart," I chimed, before catching sight of the newcomer.

My expression fell when I recognized Detective Wright, darkening my doorstep in all his grumpy glory.

He'd chosen another dress shirt today and rolled the unbuttoned sleeves to his elbows again, exposing his forearms. He'd traded last night's jeans for dark dress pants, but the badge and sidearm were ominously visible on his belt.

He scanned the room, nodding at each shopper, then dragged his attention over every display.

"You can come in," I said, watching him waver two feet inside the door. "You aren't going to lose your Man Card, or wind up in a committed relationship, or whatever you're thinking, if you stick around too long."

"I was thinking I'd accidentally walked into a pile of cotton candy and rainbows," he said. "Thought I'd hang back to see if a unicorn galloped by."

"Funny." I narrowed my eyes. "I'm sure you meant to say you were taken aback by my beautiful shop, but maybe they didn't teach you manners up north. It's too bad you'll be headed home soon," I guessed, hitching a brow in question.

"Not until my case is solved," he said. "Sorry about your luck."

Heads swung in our direction, and the shop seemed to still.

I waved a dismissive hand, then worked up an eye roll for show. "No, no," I explained to stunned shoppers. "It's fine. He's from Cleveland."

Detective Wright frowned. "What?"

I marched closer and grabbed his elbow, then tugged him several feet away from the nearest set of ears. "Folks take luck seriously here. We don't joke about it."

He snorted a little derisive laugh.

I shook my head slowly and folded my arms.

"Oh, you're serious," he said. "Right." Detective Wright released his next breath with a puff of his cheeks.

"What brings you by?" I asked, tracking him as he walked away, headed directly toward my little refreshments table.

My handful of shoppers began to whisper as their wide eyes travelled the length of him. Little did they know, he was only fun to look at. Once he opened his mouth, the effect was ruined.

"Where did you get all these cookies?" he asked. "Rob a bakery on your way to work?"

"I made them. They're meant for shoppers, but help yourself, I guess."

He loaded a little floral napkin with pastel macarons.

"Oh, my word. What are you doing?" I darted around the table to get him a small paper plate. "It's like you've never seen sweets before. You're not one of those people who avoids everything with carbs and calories, are you? Then you see free cookies and lose your mind?"

A no-carb diet would certainly explain his physique. He had to be in his late thirties or early forties. The shocks of gray in his light-brown hair and beard said as much. But his lean, muscled build screamed twenty-five. "Here. Give me those." I tugged the napkin away from him.

He grabbed the top cookie and pushed it into his mouth. "I can't bake," he said. "I love cookies, but I don't like the prepackaged stuff at the store."

I set the cookies on a plate and passed it back. "That's because those are terrible."

"And I'm hungry," he said, taking another cookie from the table. "I didn't have time for more than coffee at breakfast."

"Well, no wonder you can't resist my cookies."

Someone nearby giggled, and my cheeks began to burn.

"Maybe we should talk in my office," I suggested.

Whatever had brought the detective to my shop must've had to do with Viola, and I didn't need that conversation twisted and passed around town by a game of telephone.

He nodded, then followed me down the short hall to my private space and stopped, once again, in the doorway. "Wow. This is a mess."

I leaned against my little pink desk and tried to remember what I normally did with my arms. "It's not a mess. These are boxes of unsorted donations, categorized by content. Once I have a chance to evaluate which items I can give new life, those things will move into the storeroom until I can get to them. The rest will go to another place accepting donations. Until then, everything stays in here, where I can't be tempted to ignore them. It's my system."

"So, hyper-organization feeds your obsessive tendencies," he mused, waltzing through the cramped space, passing judgment on the stacks of boxes against one wall. "Makes sense."

"I'm not obsessive," I said, fibbing a little. "I just like to have a plan." Plans were far better than simply free-falling through life. All that romanticized talk of spontaneity in movies and on television led to chaos and complications. Which was why troubleshooting was the right way to go.

Not that he would understand any of that. "What?" I asked, realizing he'd been staring.

"Have you seen your shop?" he asked, looking a little confused. "Or a mirror?"

I stole a peek at my outfit, which was fine. "I don't know what you're getting at."

He moved back in my direction. "You know which kinds of people keep things in fanatical order like this?"

"Conscientious, business-minded problem solvers?" I guessed.

"People who like to be in control," he said, practically cutting me off. "The kinds of folks who are wound too tight. The ones most likely to lose their Cool-Aid if something doesn't go their way. Maybe take that out on an unsuspecting victim."

I ground my teeth. "Please just tell me why you're here so that you can go. I don't want to feed the rumor mill by spending too much time alone with you. Not after what happened to Viola."

He took a seat in the tufted periwinkle armchair before me, apparently letting me know he wouldn't be rushed. His knees angled up in front of him, too big for the newly uphol-stered, low-sitting piece I'd worked so hard on.

My lips twitched as I suppressed a laugh. He looked like a giant on doll furniture. "How tall are you?" I asked, amused with his struggle to maintain superiority from down there.

"Six-three."

I nodded. "That explains it."

"What?"

"The attitude," I said. "Tall guys are always so proud. As if they had anything to do with their genes."

"All I did was sit down." He smirked. "You're the one talking about my enviable height."

I circled a finger in the air, indicating he should get on with it. "You were telling me what brought you by today."

"Couple things. I've been asking around about you, and it seems several people distinctly recall you saying you wanted to kill Ms. Abbott-Harrington a few months ago. Funny you left that out when we spoke last night. Don't you think?"

I felt the blood drain from my face. "That comment was taken completely out of context. I was upset and talking privately to my mother. You can't use that against me."

"I can. I'm not a court of law. I'm just a humble servant, and I consider everything I see and hear as evidence." He flashed a devilish smile, and humble wasn't one of the words that came immediately to mind.

"Then you've considered the fact I had nothing to do with what happened to Viola? Because I keep telling you that. If you haven't heard it yet, I'm happy to say it again,"

He patted the velvet arms of the chair with his massive palms. "It's interesting that she embarrassed you publicly, you threatened her verbally, and now she's dead, isn't it? I mean, I think so. Especially after allegedly changing her mind about the very thing the two of you argued about."

I pressed my lips together and concentrated on my composure before responding. "I never threatened her, and we didn't argue. I made a donation request, she shot me down at the Christmas parade, and I complained to my mother. That was months ago. I have no idea why she showed up yesterday with a donation and asked me to come by last night and pick up more dresses, but that's what happened."

"That's a big change of heart. Doesn't it strike you as odd? It can't just be me."

"It was unexpected," I admitted. "But I'm a firm believer in apologies and second chances, so I simply thanked her and left it at that."

"Second chances?" One of his thick eyebrows rose. "Interesting word choice."

"Not really," I said, dismissing his attempt to find dirt where there was none to be found. "I was just glad she'd decided to donate. Prom season is here, and those dresses will make it possible for some girls to say yes, when they might otherwise might not have. Bridal parties on a budget will appreciate the gowns too."

"So, you're like a little pocket-sized Robin Hood," he said, grinning at his offensive and incorrect assessment.

I took a seat behind my desk and leaned on my forearms in his direction. "Anyone ever tell you it's rude to discuss a woman's size? Better yet, that size is irrelevant? And I am not a Robin Hood. I don't steal from the rich and give to the poor. I accept donations from whoever is offering, then I work to revive those items in an appealing way. Bless Her Heart sells pretty things to people who appreciate high-quality on a budget."

"I see." He shifted on the too short chair. "So all those folks who told me you were over here doing a good thing were wrong."

"People think I'm doing a good thing?" I asked, instantly distracted and hopeful. "Who?"

"That's not really the point here. Is it? I think what's most important is whether or not what you're telling me makes more sense than my theory."

"Which is?" I held my tongue and my breath when he eased forward to answer.

"That maybe you've been simmering since your run-in with Ms. Abbott-Harrington at Christmas. You finally reached your boiling point, and you went over there to tell her off. You got into a scuffle and things went south. She lost." His blue eyes flashed with interest as he awaited my response.

"That was very dramatic," I said coolly. "And ridiculous. I've already told you she asked me to come to her."

"You said that, but did anyone see her come here yesterday? Or hear her extend an invitation for your visit?"

I thought of my usually empty store and the long days Clyde and I had passed alone. "No."

Detective Wright worked his jaw. "You see how that sounds? How the story practically tells itself?"

"The story of my murderous ways?" I guessed. "I'm afraid I don't have that much imagination, and you aren't thinking clearly. If I went over there to argue with her, then why did she have all those gowns ready for me? Why would I run upstairs and push her down when she was bringing me what I wanted?"

"Maybe you tried to take them from her closet, and she tried to stop you. Who knows why killers do what they do?"

"Killers?" I repeated, letting his unexpected visit and rude adamance settle in. Something in his tone indicated this was no longer a matter of due diligence and general follow up. "You have evidence to suggest her fall wasn't an accident?"

Had someone else been at Viola's home before me, like I'd suggested to Mama? Like I suspected I already knew?

"What would you say if I told you preliminary reports show no indication of impact on Ms. Abbott-Harrington, aside from her head injury?" he asked, keen gaze roaming carefully over my face, posture and hands.

"I'd say it doesn't sound like she fell. Even tumbling down a few of those steps onto the marble floor would've bruised her up like a peach."

His gaze flicked back to mine.

"Maybe she had a heart attack or stroke?" I suggested. "She could've hit her head on the floor when she collapsed."

"The coroner believes someone struck her. You know what that means?"

I slid the edge of my thumb against my lips and nibbled at the tender flesh along my nail. "Someone killed Viola." My mind working furiously over all the little details I had so far. "That explains why the door was unlocked when I got there. The killer probably left in a hurry." I thought of the ring of package thieves in my old Atlanta neighborhood during Christmases past. They'd eventually been caught and stopped by the popularity of home surveillance. "Did you check Viola's security cameras?" I asked. "The killer was probably caught on tape leaving the scene of the crime."

"No cameras."

I dropped my thumb away from my lips. "You're kidding."

"Not a single one. Apparently nothing ever goes wrong in this town, and the local-events reporter partially retired by shifting her job description to cover all the non-existent crime instead."

"Mirabelle," I said. "Mama and I were just talking about that."

"You already knew. Why am I not surprised?" he asked dryly.

I shot him a look, my knee bouncing and fingernails tapping against the desk between us. "I didn't hurt Viola. But I saw a shadow cross her front window last night, before I went inside. I've been trying to convince myself it was a trick of the light, a bird flying past another window, anything, but maybe someone was still there when I arrived."

My stomach knotted and churned at the possibility. Could I have been in the house with Viola's killer?'

The detective's expression flattened. "Now you're telling me you might've seen someone else in the home? Another fact you left out on your report and during our discussion at the station? What else aren't you telling me, Ms. Balfour? If I wait long enough will you confess again?"

I ignored his nonsense, concentrating instead on my

front teeth against my thumbnail. "People are going to hate this. It's scary, and we're a superstitious lot. Not me," I amended. "But a lot of folks."

"You have a black cat," he pointed out.

My attention flipped up to meet his eyes. "Clyde."

"Right. Your furry little outlaw."

"People love Clyde. And folks know me. If you want, I can ask around about what Viola was up to the last few days or weeks. Maybe uncover something you can use to find the person who did this to her."

"Pass."

My brows rose. "Pass? Don't you want to know the truth about what happened?"

He rose to his feet with a glower. "I've already got a pretty good idea, Ms. Balfour."

CHAPTER SEVEN

*T*he afternoon improved with the detective's departure. The man irked me to death, but I was admittedly thankful for his directness. If he insisted on viewing me as a suspect, then at least I knew it was on me to prove him wrong. Either that or hang out my closed sign and hope Mama could use another farm hand. Because who would want to buy anything from a killer? No one in Bliss, that was for sure.

I plastered a smile on my face, then dove back into my work. I sold a few things and saw some old friends. It turned out the folks who knew me from before I moved to Atlanta, and who'd been too busy to say hello before, found new motivation at the presence of my name in the morning paper beside news of Viola's death. Now, they were out in droves. Mostly proclaiming their support. A few seemed more interested in the details of Viola's death. All wanted information on the handsome new detective. I declined to comment on both.

I sold three prom dresses between bursts of online research, which meant I could keep the lights on a while longer. Two of the gowns went home with a pair of girl-friends, and the other with a teen who'd come in alone, looked at several price tags, then tried to leave with a small wave and cautious smile.

I'd recognized her disappointment and suspected I knew the reason. She confirmed when I asked. She couldn't afford the items, even at my rock-bottom, second-chance prices, so we'd struck up a deal instead. Lexi chose a dress, then gave me her number. She agreed to come into the shop and work for a few hours at a later date, in exchange for the dress today. It was possible she wouldn't uphold her end of the bargain, but I'd still know a girl whose family couldn't afford a dress had gotten one she loved to wear to prom. If she came back as promised, all the better.

My online research skills had been less successful. Though, in my defense, everything I usually needed to know was on Pinterest or Facebook. All I'd managed to dig up on Detective Wright was that he'd been somehow involved in a massive sting operation last year that had nearly killed two undercover officers but stopped a human-trafficking ring from moving women along the Ohio River to the Mississippi River, then out of the country.

It was a little harder to think he was a pain when he'd potentially saved so many lives from destruction.

Other than his alleged, undefined role in a major heroic event, I couldn't find any other mention of him online. Not even a single social media account. And it made me crazy. Even Gigi had a Facebook account, and she lived in a natu-ralist community without the internet.

Frustrated and pacing after I'd polished everything to death, twice, I caught sight of some commotion across the street on the square. "I'll be right back," I told Clyde, stroking a hand over his fur before heading for the door.

Cami and a group of women in matching yellow T-shirts

had pulled wagons of decorations across the lush green grass and begun to wrap everything in twinkle lights. The giant white pavilion was nearly finished, and several of the ladies had moved on to the antique lamp posts.

I put my little clock sign in the window, indicating I'd be gone a few minutes, then zipped outside.

"Hey, Bonnie!" Cami called, spotting me as I left my shop.

"Hey!" I hurried to meet her on the opposite sidewalk. "I saw you from the window. What are you up to? It looks like Christmas out here with all these lights."

She gave me a crooked smile. "I was going for enchanted. We've got lanterns and banners that might help."

"Banners?" I asked, craning my neck for a look at the nearest supply wagon.

"Yes, ma'am," she drawled. "Last month's quilting bee raised enough money to put an ad in a regional travel magazine about the history of our village, and the response has been fantastic. Fanny Jean said her phone's been ringing off the hook at the B&B. She doesn't have any more available rooms for the next two months! Now the town council's given me a green light to launch my new marketing initiative. Come on. I'll show you." She grabbed my wrist and pulled me toward the other ladies. Their shirts had large peaches printed on the front with the words Shop Bliss scripted over the fruit in teal. "Show her, ladies."

The group smiled, then reached into the plastic totes on their wagons and pulled out vinyl banners with logos to match their shirts.

"Shop Bliss is the campaign motto," Cami said. "I'm hoping it will increase tourism and encourage locals to support their fellow citizens. With a little luck, the ad will bring a lot of people into town, and I want to take full advantage of that."

"Smart."

"Thank you." She beamed. "I've also created a series of ads to showcase everything the Bliss community has to offer, from our cafes and diners, to our artisans, craftsmen and shops." She outstretched an arm, as if to indicate the businesses all around the square. "The bookstore, the matchmaker, Welcome Gnome." She paused on the store across the grassy patch from mine, filled with gnome-themed home décor. "Who else has one of those?" Cami asked. "And let's not forget the pet café. Being able to hang out on site with adoptable animals before taking one home is brilliant, and don't even get me started on the food at Pita Pan."

"All good points," I said. "Folks will visit town, take photos and share them as they fall in love with Bliss."

"Yes," she agreed. "While they're here, they'll also spend their money on high-quality, handmade items to take home and wow their friends. And those friends will come in search of their own Bliss," she paused, smile widening. "That should be our next slogan. 'Find your Bliss. Find bliss in Bliss.'" Her dark brows puckered. "I'll have to work on it."

Around us, the other women climbed up and down ladders, wrapping lamp posts in twinkle lights, before hanging the Shop Bliss banners from the tops.

"I took a poll while I was brainstorming," Cami said. "I was shocked by the number of our residents, especially those living on the outskirts of town, who drive nearly an hour to the next big metropolis to do their shopping instead of making the ten-minute trip downtown. Most of them said they hadn't been downtown in years. They remember this area as being boring and not having enough relevant shops to justify coming here instead of going somewhere else. They had no idea how much we've done to revitalize in the last few years."

"Bliss has come a long way," I admitted. "Much thanks to you."

Cami blushed and shrugged. "What can I say? I'm passionate about what I do, and about this town."

Across the street, Mirabelle, the semi-retired crime reporter, shuffled to the door at Bless Her Heart.

"Uh oh," Cami said. "Wonder what she wants. Didn't she get the whole scoop last night?"

I lifted my shoulders. I barely remembered her being there last night. But I was a little disappointed in the drab exterior of Bless Her Heart, something I hadn't really noticed before. I'd spent so much time making the inside bright and inviting that I hadn't bothered to rejuvenate the exterior as well.

Cracking brown paint lined the door and window frame, looking off-putting at best. Downright ugly, at worst. Definitely not representative of my abilities to make old things fresh and new again. My window display would benefit from some attention too. Clyde liked it, but it admittedly lacked pizzazz. The beaded dress on a form and crushed velvet chair were both pretty, but the pairing didn't make the kind of impact I needed to draw people in.

I'd have to see what I could do about all that.

Cami cocked her head as she watched Mirabelle. "Maybe she wants information on that hunky new detective I saw pay you a visit this morning." She worked her perfectly sculpted brows. "How'd that go?"

I puffed air into my bangs, then shoved them out of the way. "He makes me crazy. He called me pocket-sized. Like I'm some little piece of Halloween candy. And he thinks I hurt Viola, which is insane."

Cami grinned. "Sounds to me like he called you a snack, and from what I saw, he is also one of those."

I raised a palm, crossing guard-style. "Regardless. He's trouble," I said, careful not to let my voice reach the crew busily working nearby. "And if he doesn't start looking elsewhere for clues about what happened to Viola, folks are going to start thinking I'm dangerous. They'll avoid me, and my store, like the plague, and then what?"

Cami blinked. "Back up," she said, matching my hushed voice with hers. "Viola didn't fall?"

"Doesn't seem that way, but she had a definite head injury. I saw it." My stomach lurched with the flash of memory.

Cami's gaze darted as she processed. When her attention returned to me, the natural flush of her cheeks was gone, and she looked a lot like I felt. Horrified. Sick. "Does that mean there's a killer in Bliss right now?" Her lips parted, and she glanced at the ladies hanging lights and banners. "Are we all in danger?"

"I don't think so," I said. "Aren't murders usually personal?"

Cami's shoulders jerked up to her ears. "How would I know? You're the one obsessed with crime shows and mystery novels."

I pursed my lips. "I'm not obsessed. Why does everyone keep using that word with me?"

Cami scanned the streets, visibly rattled. "So, where's the killer now? Just out there living his life? Watching television or enjoying a nice cup of coffee? As if he didn't kill an old woman last night?"

"Shh," I told her. "But, probably. It would be in the criminal's best interest to carry on without drawing suspicion. Though, to be fair, we don't know it was a man."

Cami blanched, then eyeballed her crew.

I sighed. "It's less unnerving if you try to think of it as separate and unrelated to your life."

"Okay," she agreed. "I can do that. I'm a logical, educated woman."

"Great," I said. "Because I need you. I've been gone too

long to have the kinds of connections to Bliss I need right now. It'd be nice if you can help."

Cami stilled, and her dark eyes locked on mine. "Help you do what?"

"Find the real killer," I said. "Any idea who might've had a beef with Viola?"

"No, and are you kidding me? You can't look into this. Isn't that what the detective is doing?"

"One would think," I said, "but so far he seems to only be looking at me. Which means he's wasting precious time."

"Well, isn't the whole point of psychopaths that no one suspects them?" she asked. "No one knows they're deranged until they snap. Their neighbors always appear on the news, saying things like, 'He was such a nice guy, always kept to himself.'"

"Again," I said. "We don't know it was a man. And this probably wasn't the work of a serial killer or a psychopath. It's probably just someone who lost their temper. I need to know who that might've been. Because if I don't come up with someone else for Detective Wright to look into, he's going to keep prowling around me, making folks think I lost my gourd and hurt Viola. My reputation and my business will be ruined."

Mirabelle reappeared after ducking into the coffee shop beside Bless Her Heart, then went to wave at my shop window. She tried the door again, before staring through the glass a while longer, probably admiring Clyde. Eventually, thankfully, she moved on.

"Well, I should let you get back to work," I said when the coast was clear. I waved to the ladies as I stepped away. "Things look fantastic out here," I called. "I can't wait to see it in the morning." I walked backwards a few steps, returning my attention to Cami. "If you think of anything that might be helpful with that problem of mine, call." I mimed raising a telephone to my ear. "Oh, and please put me down for a pecan pie donation. I want to help with the cake walk."

"I've got you down for five," she said, as her lips twisted into her usual smile. "Your mama called this morning."

Of course she did.

CHAPTER EIGHT

$\mathcal{J}$ made a trip to the hardware store before heading back to my shop. I'd worked out a fast plan to spruce up the Bless Her Heart storefront for curb appeal, and it all started with a serious update to the exterior color scheme. It was time to reconsider the grand opening Cami had recommended, and maybe run an ad in the morning paper to boost awareness and attendance. Basically, I had to get my ducks together fast. I'd given up all delusions of putting them in rows.

I unloaded the gallons of bright white exterior paint from my trunk, then arranged them on the sidewalk, along with rollers, brushes and trays. I grabbed a bag with work gloves and a scraper from the trunk, then unlocked the store's door and turned the OPEN sign back around.

I doodled a quote from Coco Chanel about beauty onto a freestanding chalkboard and set it outside the door, beside an oversized planter of flowers I'd asked Mama and Dad to drop off while they were out running errands. Apparently I'd missed them.

I changed into a set of work clothes I kept in my office,

then scraped cracked brown paint off the door trim and window sill until the sun began to set. Hoping with every fatigued cry of my muscles that all the little touches were going to make my store inviting. And worth every bead of sweat on my freckled skin and, likely, bright red brow.

"Hey, there!" A woman with long dark hair called, as I opened, then drained, my third bottle of water.

I waved my free hand in response. "Hello."

"Hi," she said, reaching me a few moments later. "I'm Gretchen Meriwether. I run Golden Matches. This is my great-aunt Sutton. She's from Virginia, but staying with me for the summer."

The older woman smiled. She was dressed in a long, shapeless, floral muumuu and Birkenstocks with tan socks. Her lipstick was pink and a little crooked, but her eyes were bright and lively, as if she had a secret to tell.

"It's nice to meet you," I said, recapping the empty bottle. I wiped a forearm across my brow, then dried my sweaty palms on my jean shorts. Flecks of brown paint stuck to my arms, and piles of the same had collected at my feet. "I'm Bonnie Balfour. This is my shop."

Clyde strutted across the window display inside, tail up and chin high.

"And my cat, Clyde," I added with a laugh, before turning briefly toward the glass. "She sees you," I muttered. "Don't be such an adorable show off."

Gretchen laughed.

Sutton stared at Clyde. Her expression lit with pleasure. "Oh, dear. He's a handsome boy, isn't he?" Her shoulder-length gray hair floated in wild, unruly waves on the breeze. The style looked a lot like mine had before I'd drenched it in sweat

"Clyde is quite dashing," I agreed. "And boy does he know

it. I've been coordinating his bow ties with my dresses since I adopted him. He seems to like it."

Sutton watched him carefully another minute, probably noting his jade-green collar and little silver bell matched his eyes today, but not my work clothes. Then she nodded and turned to me, pleased. "He says he does. Matching with you makes him feel special. Like the two of you are a team in uniform."

I cast a glance at Gretchen, who grinned.

"Sutton talks to animals," Gretchen said. "And plants. She even brought you a gift. Isn't that right, Aunt Sutton?"

"Oh!" Sutton dug into her mammoth quilted handbag and unearthed a small potted succulent, tucked into a box with a plastic window. She removed the plant from the box and presented it proudly. "This is Judy. I heard you had an unfortunate experience last night, and knew Judy was just the plant for you. She's kind of a loner, but she likes flowers." She glanced at the large arrangement outside my door. "She makes a great protector too. Just keep her with you, and no one will give you any trouble." She lifted the little plant to her mouth and whispered to it, before handing it to me. "There you go. All your problems are solved." She shot a mischievous smile at Gretchen.

"Thank you," I said, hoping the unintentional inflection in my voice didn't sound like the question mark it really was. "She's lovely. Are you sure you can part with her?"

"You're welcome," Sutton said. "And yes. Judy's nice enough for me, but she's trouble for Franklin and Stew."

"Franklin and Stew?" I asked, looking to Gretchen for help.

She grinned. "Two flowering cacti."

Sutton shook her head, disappointed about something. "They're both so sensitive, and Judy's such a mouthy little broad. I can't seem to keep the peace when she's around."

I nodded, unsure what else to say.

Gretchen studied my freshly scraped shop face, then the supplies I'd lined neatly against the wall. "Need any help painting? Sutton volunteered to watch the store for me this afternoon. I was going to run errands, but they weren't pressing, and I'm an excellent painter."

Sutton flattened a palm between us then tilted it back and forth, as if to say Gretchen's painting skills were so-so.

"I'd love the help," I said. "As long as you're sure you don't mind."

"Not at all," Gretchen said, crouching to choose a brush from the bag.

Sutton clapped her hands together. "I'd better get back to the store. I love it when I'm in charge."

Gretchen passed her great-aunt a key on a lanyard, and the older woman hurried away.

"Thanks again," I called after her.

Gretchen rolled her eyes. "I love her, but she's nuts, and I mean that with all my heart."

"You don't think Judy's a troublemaker?" I asked, teasing.

"No way. It was clearly Stew that stirred up all the bad feelings," she said.

I set Judy on the ground carefully, then watched Gretchen to see if she was kidding.

The fact that I wasn't sure made me laugh.

In all the years I'd been married, Grant had only come home with me once, because he thought the people were weird. We'd spent a week visiting with my parents and exploring the village every day. He'd viewed quirky as crazy, curious neighbors as nosy Nellies, and genuine interest as general invasiveness. I'd been offended by his opinions and hurt by his comments, then devastated when he'd refused to return. Funny how hindsight makes so many things clearer.

He'd never understood me at all.

"I think you're ready for primer," Gretchen said, pulling me back to the moment.

We worked in companionable silence for a long while before another woman approached, then stopped to watch. She had a crown of short curly brown hair and wide dark eyes, adorned with chic vintage cat-eye glasses.

"Looking good," she said, nodding at the transformation of my dark peeling storefront to a clean white display.

"Thanks." I smiled, then stopped to admire the work so far.

Gretchen took one look at the newcomer, then rocked onto her toes with a broad grin. "Liz!" She set her paint brush down, then met her friend with a hug. "Have you met Bonnie?"

I set my brush aside as well, then offered Liz my hand. "Not yet. I'm Bonnie Balfour. This is my store."

"Nice," Liz said. "I've been meaning to get over here for weeks, but I was never sure if you were open." She wrinkled her nose at the window display. "There never seemed to be anyone in there."

I laughed. "That wasn't by design, though I'm beginning to realize the exterior appearance didn't help. I'm thinking of having a grand opening to celebrate the place. You should come."

"I'd love to," she said. "Just let me know when, and I'll put it on my calendar. If I forget, come and get me. I'm only a few doors down at the haunted bookshop, What the Dickens."

My smile stuck, and my brain spun its proverbial wheels. "You are?" I asked, thinking of the last time I'd shopped there. I'd been a regular as a kid, visiting weekly with my mama or Gigi, and I'd adored the owner. "Did Hazel retire?"

Liz offered a small, apologetic smile. "Grandmama passed last summer. She left the shop to me."

Her words were a punch to my core. "I'm sorry. I didn't

know." I took a minute to process, hating that I hadn't been there for the funeral or even known to send flowers. And as I considered the woman before me, suddenly the curly hair and wide eyes seemed more familiar, like the cat-eye glasses on her small, straight nose. "You look like her," I said. "Even the glasses."

Liz's smile widened. "They were hers. I had the lenses changed. I miss her every day, but running What the Dickens makes me feel close to her."

I nodded, hating the thought of one day doing things to honor Gigi's memory because she wasn't here to honor in person. "She was really special," I told Liz. "She fostered my love of reading as much as any teacher or librarian. She always seemed to know what I wanted to read before I did."

"The shop is like that," Liz said. "It practically runs itself."

I wasn't sure what she meant, or how it related to my statement, but I smiled anyway. Liz was pleasant and sweet. I made mental plans to revisit the bookshop I'd loved so much as a kid as soon as possible.

Gretchen grinned. "Sutton gave Bonnie a succulent today."

"Which one?" Liz asked, eyes flashing wide with interest.

"Judy."

Liz grimaced. "Good luck."

I laughed, then peeked at the little plant seated on the sidewalk by my supplies. When I returned my gaze to Liz, I couldn't help asking the question that had been waiting impatiently on my tongue. "Is the bookstore really haunted?"

Liz sighed. "It's something," she said. "I'll get it figured out. Probably a few obsessive readers who didn't go into the light because they were trying to finish the chapter."

I'd never related more to a hypothetical ghost in my life.

"I'll have to come by and check it out," I said, meaning it to my core.

"Please do," she said. "I guess I should probably get back."

We shook hands, then Liz went on her way.

The primer dried quickly in the sweltering heat, and both coats of bright white paint did as well. By the time twilight set in, I was ready to drop, but Gretchen seemed to be getting a second wind.

"Thanks for letting me help," she said. "This was fun."

"And incredibly productive," I added, admiring the bright, clean, new look. "I never could've made this much progress on my own in one day."

"What are friends for?" she asked, before turning her attention in the direction of her store. "Something tells me I should check on Sutton." Gretchen smiled apologetically at me. "I don't mean to paint and run, but she's not as good at matchmaking as she thinks she is."

"You really match people up over there?" I asked, packing up the supplies.

"Every day." She smiled.

"That must be an interesting job. Tough too. What do you base the matches on? Questionnaires and profiles?" I guessed. "Like the ones used on dating apps?"

Gretchen frowned. "No. Nothing like that. It's just a gift. I guess it's a little hard to explain."

"I think I get it. Trade secrets. There must be a lot of pressure in your line of work. I'll bet people get really angry when you're wrong."

"I'm never wrong," Gretchen said, expression bemused. "Sometimes the couple's timing is off, but that's not on me. Patience really is a virtue and timing is everything."

I could certainly understand that. It had taken me a very long time to come back to my hometown, but I was glad I had, and I was certain this was exactly when I was meant to do it.

Even if I had a cranky Cleveland detective to deal with.

CHAPTER NINE

I changed out of my paint-spattered clothes, packed Clyde into the car and headed home a few minutes later. The time had passed quickly, working with Gretchen, but it had passed, nonetheless, and the moon was making its nightly appearance among the stars.

Flashes of little eyes along the roadside hinted at deer and night things, waiting to cross. The drive was so eerily similar to the one I'd made last night that it was difficult to think of anything else.

My thoughts wandered back to Viola with every twist of the country road. Who would kill her? And why? Her house had seemed to be in perfect order, at least the parts of it I'd been in or had peeked into, like the foyer, dining room and study. There weren't any signs of a struggle. The stand beside the door was unmoved, as was the potpourri bowl and frame standing on top. Both would surely have broken if the stand had toppled.

So, what exactly had happened?

Had Viola known her killer and invited the person inside?

I shivered hard and my muscles tightened in response. I wondered idly if Teddy would tell me if anything had been stolen. And if Mama would give me his home number.

When Viola's home came into view, I thought again of Teddy and his evening visits.

My foot moved away from the gas pedal as a light flashed on in the home's front window. I checked the clock on my dashboard. Seven fifteen. "Clyde," I said, hitting my blinker and turning onto the driveway. "We might've just gotten a golden opportunity." Right place. Right time. "If I stop by to pay my condolences, I can ask Teddy whatever I want while I'm at it, and use Mama's name as an icebreaker." I didn't have a casserole to offer him, but I was wearing black. And that was something.

Clyde's ears worked like tiny satellites in the dim glow of dashboard light. "Meow."

"I'm not going to be long," I promised. "I know I said that last night, but last night was a total fluke. It won't happen again." It couldn't.

"Meow," he complained, more loudly. "Meow. Meow."

I rubbed my hand against the mesh door of his carrier, sorry to have upset him.

Outside, crickets and bullfrogs set the score against an otherwise silent night. Ahead of me, Viola's estate appeared, illuminated by landscape lighting and drenched in dignified southern charm. It was strangely unsettling to think a woman who'd lived in this home, for the better part of a century, had been walking its halls yesterday. And tonight she was gone.

I parked, then hurried to the door, eager to keep my promise to Clyde.

Teddy's tweed jacket was hung over the banister on the staircase inside, visible through the window, and a bolt of excitement zipped through me.

He was here, as expected, and this was my chance to get a few answers to my pressing questions.

My shoulders shimmied as I imagined putting the pieces of a puzzle together, and delivering the facts to Detective Grumpy.

The door opened when I rapped my knuckles against it, so I stepped inside, giving a wide berth to the space where Viola had lain. "Mr. Runsford?" I called, closing the door behind me.

The possibility he might be a killer popped quickly in, then out, of my mind. The heartbreak I'd seen in his eyes last night made me sure I was being unnecessarily paranoid.

"Teddy?" I tried again. "It's me, Bonnie Balfour. I hope it's okay that I stopped by. I saw the light on and your jacket on the steps."

I followed the sound of footfalls to an open door in the kitchen, then peered into the basement. The lights were on downstairs as well, and I recalled him telling Sheriff Miller that he kept an office down there.

At least the space seemed to be finished, and not a cobweb-riddled dungeon like the one Gigi had given me. I'd decided when I moved in that whatever lived in the basement could keep it, and I wouldn't go looking. It was a very real case of ignorance being bliss.

I inched down three steps, feeling suddenly, impossibly intrusive, but unwilling to leave when I was so close to getting the answers I wanted. "Hello?" I crooked a knuckle and rapped it against the wall as I descended.

Piles of neatly organized boxes came into view. All labeled with their destinations.

Teddy must've been working all day to have sorted and packed so much.

I opened my mouth to call for him again, but the lights

suddenly extinguished, drowning me in darkness. A moment later, the door slammed shut.

And I screamed.

The door opened fifteen minutes later, and I ducked behind the stacks of boxes, hopeful but unsure. I'd forced myself to find and flip the light switch, then attempt to open the now-locked door, but it'd been no use. Eventually, I'd texted my mama and relayed my predicament. She'd assured me she was "on it," but the footfalls moving down the stairs were heavy and slow. A man's for sure, and not my dad. He would've been yelling my name and running.

When the sounds stopped, I peeked.

Detective Wright stood on the opposite side of the boxes, hands on narrow hips, waiting for me to show myself.

"Hi," I said, straightening to my full height, which wasn't much more than the piled boxes.

"I got a call from your mother," he said, looking more than a little put out.

I let my head fall back a beat before righting myself and moving around to his side of the stacks. "I didn't ask her to do that."

"Why not?" he asked. "You should've called me, or dispatch, yourself."

"I don't have your number," I said, crossing my arms. Plus, I could've done without him ever hearing about the situation.

"You should have called dispatch."

"I wasn't in immediate danger," I countered. "So I decided this wasn't an emergency."

"You decided," he parroted, crossing his arms and mirroring my stance.

I straightened my spine, refusing to be intimidated, but certain my prints were on the front door knob again. Which couldn't look good for me, and I was sure I'd hear about it.

I frowned as another thought came to mind. "Did you find Teddy? Is he okay?"

Detective Wright wrinkled his nose. "Mr. Runsford? Why wouldn't he be okay?"

I considered that a moment. "His jacket was on the banister. I assumed he was here. Which was why I stopped. I wanted to give him my condolences," I fibbed a little, though I had wanted to let him know I was sorry for his loss. "Maybe he locked me in here!"

Detective Wright shifted his weight and hardened his expression. "You saw his jacket on the banister, so you walked inside a murder victim's home and went to her basement? I'm not supposed to think that's suspicious? Or that you're here to tamper with evidence you left behind before?"

"Sure," I said, my apologetic mood beginning to change. "I broke in here to cover my tracks as a murderer, then locked myself in the basement to cover my true intent. So much smarter than just leaving when I finished."

"Not all criminals are smart," he said, feigning sadness. "This is an old house. The door might've swung shut and locked while you were mid-meddle. And you called your mother instead of the sheriff."

I imagined screaming, then remembered I shouldn't let him get to me like he did. "So, Teddy isn't in the house?" I asked.

"I'm not sure," he said. "I came straight to the basement. That was my mission."

I turned and marched up the steps, making a mental note to ask my mama what she'd been thinking.

After a quick trip around the first floor, peeking into the various rooms while Detective Wright cleared them, I gazed up the steps, past the plastic numbered teepees where I'd found Viola.

"Stay here," he said, stepping over the crime scene with his unreasonably long legs, then taking the steps by twos.

He bobbed in and out of doorways, before jogging back to me. "No signs of Teddy."

I tipped my head toward the jacket on the banister.

"Ever think he might've forgotten it?" he asked.

I crossed my arms. "No. He said he came here every night at seven. It was seven fifteen when I arrived. I assumed he was the one who'd turned all the lights on and unlocked the door."

"House was dark when I got here," he said. "Door was unlocked, but you were snooping. Admit it."

I lifted my chin. *Never.*

"That doesn't make you look any taller," he said. "If that's what you're going for."

"I was just alone in this house with a killer," I said, untangling my folded arms so I could point at him. "You need to find whoever it was before he or she hurts someone else. Or me."

He cocked his head and sucked his teeth. "Did you add the 'he or she' in there because you're a feminist or because you're guilty?"

I gave my most utterly blank expression. "Just tell me you have some kind of lead."

"I do. The same woman keeps turning up at my crime scene," he said. "That seems like something I shouldn't ignore."

I threw a hand up, then let it drop as I turned for the front door. "I'm going home now. Unless you plan to haul me off to jail."

"Not tonight," he called politely. "Don't leave town."

I picked up my pace, ignoring the infuriating detective and suddenly remembering poor Clyde was still in the car.

I was a horrible cat mom!

I woke the next morning with a stiff neck and dull headache. I hadn't gotten enough sleep for three nights in a row, and it was wearing on me. I bumbled into the kitchen to start a pot of coffee.

Clyde raced me into the room, then banged his head against the air-tight plastic container where I kept his food.

"All right," I said, nudging him aside. "Let me help." I filled his bowl, then refreshed his water while my parents' hand-me-down Mr. Coffee chugged and puffed on the counter.

My body begged to go back to sleep, but I'd have to slap on some heavy-duty under-eye concealer and a smile instead. I had to prove my innocence and drive traffic to Bless Her Heart, ASAP, before rumors began to form.

I toasted two slices of bread, buttered them and began to eat while I waited for Mr. Coffee to get his act together.

Eventually, I stuck a mug under the drip.

My mood improved when the caffeine took hold.

Birds flitted around the feeders outside my window, as a few golden rays of sunrise climbed the sills. My warm apricot-colored walls seemed to glow in the abundance of natural light. Gigi had used the light to grow flowers. I just enjoyed it for what it was. Warm and bright.

My new home sat at the edge of my parents' flower farm, at the end of a mostly residential street. My little cottage, like my folks' farm, had once belonged to my grandparents. My parents bought the farm when Grandpapa and Gigi built the cottage, no longer interested in caring for so many acres of land. Gigi had inherited the parcel from her folks, who had been more traditional farmers. She'd loved the idea of keeping the property in the family, and had planted flowers everywhere for fun while she lived there. Mama had grown up among the blooms, then earned a degree in botany before marrying Dad.

When Grandpapa passed a few years back, Gigi packed a bag and went to live at Driftwood Bay, a naturalist community tucked between two active tourist towns at the shore. The residents lived as if they were completely off the grid, while enjoying the convenience of quick access to staples such as medical care and prescription medicines. Two major bonuses, considering the average age in their community was around sixty. Most retired folks made their ways there to stretch pensions and pennies. Some were holistically minded and enjoyed the constant commune with nature. A few younger hipsters tried and failed there every year. But the folks like Gigi were completely at home.

She'd been a true flower child, long before the term was invented. She'd raised Mama to be the free-spirited, earth-loving member of humanity she was, and Mama had attempted the same with me.

I was a strong argument for nature over nurture.

Gigi had offered me free use of the cottage and given me the freedom to make the place my own. I'd cheerfully accepted both offers. From the mismatched boho chic furniture and accents, to the abundance of fresh flowers and ultra-feminine décor, the interior now looked like something from the Bonnie Balfour catalogue of style.

I'd painted every room a different color. The furniture was mismatched but perfect, right down to Dad's army trunk, which I now used as a living room end table.

Clyde leaped onto my lap and rubbed his cheek against mine.

"Hello, handsome," I said. "You know, if you wear your

white bow tie with the gold bell today, I can wear my polka dot dress, and we'll be matchers."

He jumped down, and I followed. Time to get moving.

I'd fallen asleep thinking of Viola's basement full of boxes, every one labeled for a new destination. What had happened to change Viola's stance on donations? And the historical society angling for Viola's home—what was that about?

There was only one way I could find out. I'd have to go to the source.

Clyde and I dressed for work. Then I packed a special box of my wildly popular strawberries-and-cream cupcakes and tucked it into my bag. Hopefully gratuitous amounts of sugar and butter could loosen a few lips.

I dropped Clyde off at Bless Her Heart before continuing on to my next destination.

Thankfully, the historical society was only two miles from the square, so I'd be back in time to open sharply at ten. I parked in the visitors' lot, then hurried to the door. The Greek revival-style building looked a lot like Viola's home, if on a smaller scale.

I let myself inside, slightly haunted by two similar moments that had ended poorly.

"Welcome!" A beautiful young woman greeted me from her position behind a small white desk at the base of the stairs. "How can I help you today?"

"Hi." I lifted my fingers in a weak, hip-high wave. "I'm Bonnie Balfour. I run Bless Her Heart on Main Street." I dug into my bag and pulled out the box of cupcakes. "These are for you." I smiled while she pulled the gift nearer, inhaling the sweet scents of strawberries and cream. "I have a few questions about the Abbott-Harrington estate. I was hoping someone here could help me answer them."

She nodded, eyes widening as she opened the box. "Of course. I'll see if Mr. Totoro is available."

The name was new to me, so I made a mental note to see what I could find out about him later.

I smiled at a stack of half-sheet flyers on the desk, all emblazoned with the headline "Shop Bliss" and a subscript encouraging folks to come out and get involved in the town's upcoming events. My gaze stuck on the line about the cake walk, and I recalled with a jolt that I still had to make five pecan pies.

"You're free to look around while you wait," the woman said, freeing me from the foyer.

"Thank you." I turned my attention to a wall of paintings and photos in an adjoining room, then went in for a closer look. Black-and-white images showcased our town in eras gone by. Men and women in fancy hats and dress clothes walked the square, stood on platforms at a train station, long since removed, and cheered for football players dressed in matching team sweaters and baggy pants.

There were photos of a massive evergreen dressed for Christmas at the square, New Year's Eve parades on Main Street, and soldiers coming home from war. The scenes warmed me from the inside out as I examined each of the countless faces and imagined the fingerprints each person had left on our town.

My reverie was interrupted by the sound of approaching footsteps.

A man stopped at the desk, and the woman pointed in my direction. "She's right in there."

I lifted my hand in greeting when he headed my way.

His dark hair was combed back and shiny with product. His three-piece suit was gray, and in my opinion, overkill, right down to the pale-blue shirt and navy-blue tie. "I'm Patrick Totoro," he said, sounding stiff and pretentious, without so much as the offer of shaking my hand. "How can I help you?"

"I'm Bonnie Balfour. I have a few questions about the Abbott-Harrington estate, if you can spare a minute or two of your time."

He checked his watch, then covered it with the opposite hand and rested his joined arms in front of him. "I have another appointment soon, but I'm happy to discuss the matter until then."

"Thank you." I blew out a steady breath and wondered where to begin. I decided to start with the basics. "Viola made a very generous donation of dresses to my store, Bless Her Heart, on the morning she died. It hadn't been something she was interested in doing a few months ago. Then she asked me to come by and pick up more gowns that night," I said. "It was wonderful, but unexpected, and a little odd, to be honest."

Mr. Totoro's expression darkened. His brows furrowed in distaste. "I can't give you anything from the Abbott-Harrington estate until the will is read and legalities are handled. Even if you feel entitled. Regardless of alleged promises made before her death. Otherwise everyone in town would be lining up to say she promised them something as well."

I reared my head back, feeling as if I'd been slapped. "I'm not trying to get anything from her. I only want to know why she'd begun to donate and give away her things before her death."

His frown deepened, and his gaze shifted away briefly before returning to my face. "I'm sorry. I can't say."

I couldn't help wondering if he truly didn't know or simply didn't want to tell me. So, I switched gears. "Rumor has it the historical society was making a play for the Abbott-Harrington estate, possibly before Viola died," I said, feeling a little smug for having the information. I waited patiently while he decided how to respond.

"That was an open discussion, to be pursued, if Mrs. Abbott-Harrington wanted, when she was ready," he said. "Nothing more than an expression of interest until then."

"Was she ready?" I asked.

He checked his watch again, overly blasé. "I'm sorry. That's all the time I have right now. If there are any other questions about the property or its contents, you should check with her estate manager or her attorney."

I nodded, then saw myself out while he waited at the desk, presumably for his alleged upcoming appointment.

A dirty white Jeep wheeled through the parking lot as I stepped back into the day. The now familiar vehicle took the spot beside my car.

I watched as Detective Wright climbed out. He pulled wire-rimmed aviator sunglasses away from his face and stared, in apparent disbelief, as I approached my convertible. "What are you doing here?"

"Meeting with Mr. Totoro," I said. "I guess you're his next appointment." I hadn't learned any new information from my encounter with the historical society representative, but that didn't stop the immense pleasure flowing through me as Detective Wright stared.

Because I'd beat him there.

"Why are you talking to Totoro?" he asked.

"I'm trying to find the truth about what happened to Viola. Because someone has to. And every minute you spend thinking I'm the one who killed her is another minute the actual killer gets to finalize plans to leave town and/or cover their tracks."

Detective Wright's pale-blue eyes flashed with heat, betraying his cool. He pointed his sunglasses in my direction. "You need to take a little pixie step back, and steer clear of my investigation. This isn't a game."

"I never thought it was," I snapped, annoyed he'd taken

yet another shot at my height. "What are you so worried about anyway? Afraid you'll look ridiculous when the woman you suspected of murder proves you wrong and finds the real killer, all while you're here on loan?"

He leaned forward, eyes narrowed and expression seething. "Assuming you didn't fool around and lock yourself in the basement last night, that means someone is out there who knows what you're up to, and they're not going to like it if you keep pushing. Because in my experience, criminals don't want to get caught. This whole doe-eyed Nancy Drew act is entertaining and all, but you're going to have to knock it off before you get hurt. Or worse."

I unlocked my car door and dropped behind the wheel, practically vibrating with indignation at his tone. "Would if I could," I said, "but some long-legged loaner cop from up north has pushed me too far."

I hung my elbow over the door frame as I backed out of the space and zoomed away.

CHAPTER TEN

J parked outside Bless Her Heart, then smiled at Clyde in the window. My trip to the historical society hadn't taken as long as I'd expected, and I had nervous energy to burn. I waved to Cami and her ladies, already busy in the town square, then locked my car and pulled myself together on the sidewalk.

Large baskets of flowers hung from every other lamp post, creating a banner basket pattern around the green. Additional brightly colored blooms and fresh mulch circled the gazebo and lined walkways throughout the square.

I smiled at the number of people moseying among the trees and sitting on the benches, enjoying the lovely spring day. Walking dogs. Holding hands. Pushing strollers. All while Cami's crew hung lanterns from the limbs of several oak trees.

Small town in population? Absolutely. Small town in heart? Not even close. And thanks to the Shop Bliss campaign, we might be seeing more tourists soon too.

I walked past Bless Her Heart, in favor of a quick trip to the store next door, suddenly in the mood for a praline latte.

Blissful Bean was one of the oldest cafes in the area and a staple downtown. The scent of fresh-brewed coffee and warm candied pecans drifted on the breeze in my direction, pulling me down the sidewalk more quickly with each step.

I paused as I reached my destination, distracted by a fancy black car parked outside the bank on the next block. The vehicle reminded me of the obnoxious little beast that had buzzed past me on Main Street at twice the posted speed limit. I narrowed my eyes in disapproval before carrying on with my coffee plans. Hopefully the next time the driver was in such a hurry, he'd pass a deputy's cruiser.

I slipped into the coffee shop on a whiff of vanilla-laced heaven, then got in line.

A long, narrow counter split the area nearly in half lengthwise, making the most of a limited space. Two round tables sat before the window. And a row of square tables lined the wall in front of the service counter.

The line shuffled forward while Dave and his daughter, Daisy, took and filled orders in perfect harmony. Dave's grandparents had been pecan farmers and worked the land next door to my parents' property until I was in high school. His dad had branched out and bought the coffee shop when the previous owner put it on the market, and Dave had followed in his father's footsteps. They might've left the trade, but the heart of the farming community was everywhere I looked.

Signs and ads from the old pecan farm hung on the walls in frames. Announcements of the shop's dedication to using only locally sourced milk and cream were present on the menu board. And fresh-roasted pecans from the same land his grandparents had once tended were proudly sold in bags and by the bushel.

"Hey, Bonnie," Dave said, when it was my turn at the register.

"Hey," I returned, feeling instantly twenty years younger.

He wrapped an arm around his daughter's shoulders and smiled at me over the counter. "You remember Daisy," he said. Their matching white paper hats and aprons bore the Blissful Bean logo. Their matching bright-eyed expressions gave an air of genuine well-wishes.

"I do," I said, feeling suddenly my age again. She'd been a newborn when I left. "You're much bigger now," I told her, with a smile and nod of approval.

"Thanks." She barked a laugh, then shoved away from her dad with a grin. "You wouldn't know it to hear him talk."

Dave chuckled as he turned his attention back to me. "What can I get you today? Still drinking extra-large hot chocolates, stacked high with whipped cream, jimmies and caramel syrup?"

I nearly touched a finger to the corner of my mouth, checking for drool. I'd nearly lived on those drinks my junior and senior years of high school. And when the outdoor temperature passed eighty, Dave would prepare the drinks over ice. The chubby devil on my shoulder said I should go for it. YOLO and all that. "No, thank you," I said instead, choosing to voice what I thought the little angel on my shoulder would say, if I had one of those. For me, it was usually just the devil.

"You sure?" he asked, wagging his eyebrows and wiggling a can of whipped topping.

Considering the last time I'd been to Blissed Bean, I'd had the metabolism and constitution of a teenager, neither of which had stuck with me past thirty, I simply couldn't. "How about a latte?" I said, offering my most appreciative smile. "And a bag of roasted pecans."

"You got it."

Daisy scooped pecans into a bag while Dave went to work on my latte.

He looked up as the foam spewed. "I hear you're donating some of your pies to the cake walk. There's probably going to be a brawl now."

I grinned. Everyone had loved my sweets in high school. And I'd gotten even better over time.

"I think you were in middle school the first time your mama brought one of those coconut layer cakes to a party and told everyone you'd made it. We could hardly believe it. You still needed a chair just to work at the counter."

I offered him cash for the order, then tucked the change into a tip jar. And I refused to think of how Detective Wright would probably suggest I still had trouble reaching the counter. "Gigi taught me well," I said. "Magic happens when you have a great teacher."

Daisy scooted back and bumped her dad with one shoulder. "Agreed."

Pride bloomed on his face as he smiled at her, then me. "Tell your mama and them they ought to come see me soon," Dave said as I lifted my cup and pecans to go. "I can't keep this place open forever, and this one doesn't want to run a coffee shop all her life." He hooked a thumb at Daisy, who wrinkled her nose.

"I'll let everyone know," I said, a fuzzy little thought forming as my gaze flicked to the wall separating our spaces. "Are you thinking about selling?"

"Thinking," he said. "I did all right here, like my old man, but I'm ready to call it enough. Dad died too young, never got to enjoy retirement. I think it's time I go fishing and play cards with my buddies. Have dinner with my wife more than once a week. While I'm still young enough to enjoy it. I don't want to miss out on anything, you know? The trouble will be finding a buyer who'll love this place as much as I do. I can't let it go to just anyone."

"Is it on the market?" I asked, feeling nonsensically alarmed.

"Nah." He swiped a hand through the air. "You know how it is. The right person will come around when it's time."

I grinned, having nearly forgotten how much locals truly saw our town as... I searched mentally for the right word. Enchanted? Blessed? Whatever the terminology, residents of Bliss simply believed things would work out. And I might've missed that most of all.

I waved and stepped away from the counter, heading back to Bless Her Heart and wondering how much money it would take to buy or lease Blissful Bean. I could sell my baked goods and manage both stores if I busted a hole in the wall between them and added a glass door. Then I could still bring Clyde to work with me.

It took another minute for me to remember I was broke.

I hustled into my shop, ready to change my financial status, then flipped the sign to indicate I was OPEN.

"Clyde," I called, circling the space.

I set my coffee and pecans near the register and dropped my bag behind the counter.

A quick search of the store revealed Clyde was asleep in the layers of a petticoat I'd intended to steam. I supposed for now, it'd have to wait until after his nap.

I petted his head and admired my store. Small, but chic, with bits of me woven throughout the collection. I'd spent enough time in Bliss to understand its culture, and enough time in the better parts of Atlanta to understand fashion and style. At Bless Her Heart, I'd done my best to combine them all.

It'd taken leaving home for me to appreciate the skill involved in living frugally, but I'd learned to see the process of preservation as a dying art and a show of respect. Things didn't become disposable when they were no longer new and perfect. Usually, a little love and attention changed everything.

The premise translated well to people too.

"You know," I told Clyde's sleeping face. "We've come a long way in six months. We completely started over. Moved into Gigi's house last fall, then leased this place on a parental loan and a prayer. I'd spent the coldest weeks of the year making the empty storefront fabulous, and I'd hung out an open sign before spring arrived." I sighed. "I might get frustrated by how slow things feel like they're going, but, really, we're doing all right."

Clyde stretched and yawned, flexing his little paws against the crinoline. His long white canine became visible, stuck to his semi-rolled lip.

I smiled. "I've developed a bad habit of not seeing the good, but we're not in Atlanta anymore, and I'm no longer invisible. Don't let me forget it."

Negativity was a bad habit I'd picked up over time in my marriage, but I was determined to change that. Just because Grant had consistently pointed out my downfalls and shortcomings didn't mean I had to. In fact, I absolutely refused to. "Make sure I'm nice to myself," I told Clyde, giving him a few more pets before moving on.

I walked the pretty space, chin up and shoulders back, leaving Clyde to his petticoat bed. And I allowed myself to be proud instead of disappointed for a moment. I accepted the internal praise instead of shying away from it.

It was time to set some serious plans for the grand-opening party. If I wanted to get more people into my shop, and help them fall in love with my products, I had to throw a shindig that would make and keep folks talking. I had to stop focusing on all the things that might go wrong and start accepting all the things that could go right.

My eyes caught on the Shop Bliss banners outside,

hanging from lamp posts around the square, and my heart swelled with hope and anticipation. I drifted to the front door, knowing Cami had been right. And if there was one thing I'd learned to do well during my time in Atlanta, it was how to throw a party.

I nearly hooted from the thrill.

I waved to Cami when she noticed me staring through the glass, then froze as the black car I'd seen outside the bank cruised between us.

Once again, I couldn't see the driver, but Mr. Totoro from the historical society was riding shotgun.

CHAPTER ELEVEN

A few hours later, when my stomach insisted I eat something other than the baked goods on my refreshments table, I placed the plastic clock sign in my window and set the arms to indicate I'd be back in an hour, then I headed out.

I'd sold three more dresses. One for a maid of honor and another pair of prom gowns to direct referrals from the friends who'd been in and made purchases earlier this week. I couldn't help thinking this was the beginning of more good things to come. And the perfect time to harness my forward momentum. So, I'd decided to forgo my prepacked, home-made lunch and go out. "Workaholic and suspected killer" weren't the personas I was going for when I came home and opened Bless Her Heart, so I'd grab food from a café, where people could see I had nothing to hide and was quite friendly, then I'd eat on the square.

The fact that I was behaving exactly like the true killer, pretending nothing was wrong, when things were definitely wrong, was unsettling in a complicated, roundabout way. So, I tried not to think about that.

I'd straightened the modest neckline on my milky-white blouse, then the waistband on my floral chiffon skirt, and put my suede booties into motion, right out the door.

There were a few potential lunch spots on the square, but I headed for Deep South Soups, Salads, and Sandwiches, or the DS for short. I'd eaten there several weeks ago, when I'd forgotten to pack my lunch, and discovered Pammy Banks, an old classmate, behind the counter. It was probably difficult for her to manage the second job, since she'd always worked full time for the gossip mill. But that made her exactly who I wanted to see, and who I wanted to see me. Pammy was the fastest news source in town, if not the most accurate. Seeing me happy, bright, and absolutely not a killer was information I hoped she'd pass around. While I was ordering, I'd also mention my upcoming grand opening and get that news started.

I hurried across the street, then across the square, enjoying the warm southern sun on my skin and the scents of sauces, burgers and cheese wafting through the air. Main Street at lunch or dinnertime was no place to be on a diet. I could practically hear the french fries calling my name.

My mouth watered as I opened the door to the DS and drifted inside. The little restaurant spanned the first floor of a tiny Tudor home built somewhere around the turn of the last century. The pointy tan-and-brown structure was out of place in a town of quaint, colorful cottages and historic white farmhouses. As a kid, I'd thought the place looked like it might contain elves cobbling shoes. Currently, it produced the best burgers known to man.

I smiled at the handful of seated patrons, then made my way to the counter.

Pammy cocked a hip and smiled a crooked little smile at me. "Well, Bonnie Balfour, if I don't have all the luck. I hear you rarely leave your shop." Pammy looked a lot like she had in high school. Still perfectly thin, wearing padded pushup bras and tight V-neck T-shirts that showed off her best features. But the wrinkles gathered in her cleavage were new. Her hair was ironed straight. Blue liner rimmed her eyes. And despite an abundance of sweltering Georgia sun, she still appeared to be getting her tan from a bottle.

I'd never been the most fashionable, thin or popular girl in school, but I'd been happy. Pammy had been teenage perfection, but she'd never seemed happy. Not as head cheerleader, or prom queen or even when she'd married the star quarterback after graduation. That also hadn't appeared to change.

"Hey there." I hiked my handbag higher on my shoulder and smiled as cheerfully as I could manage while being scrutinized. I definitely couldn't order the cheeseburger and shake like I wanted. "I was starving over there at Bless Her Heart and knew I had to come and get a grilled chicken salad before I completely passed out. I've been working so hard getting everything ready." I cut the story short to bait her interest.

Her gaze sliced over my double-digit-sized waist. "Smart choice." She wiped her hands against a dishtowel then swung it onto her shoulder. "Anything else?"

"A bottle of water," I said.

She called my salad order into the kitchen behind her, then set a bottle of water on the counter between us and eyed me curiously. "Your return has made quite a stir these last few months. Almost as big of a to-do as when you left and proclaimed so sweetly…" She pressed a finger to her lips. "Let me see. How did you say it again?"

I cringed inwardly, knowing what was coming and hating that she remembered.

"Oh, yeah." She leveled me with a flat expression. "Goodbye suckers."

I laughed awkwardly. "I was trying to be funny," I said, as casually as possible. I'd seen someone say it in a movie and blurted the expression when my parents had me near tears at graduation, hoping to change the mood. Of course, Pammy had overheard. And taken offense. "I was a kid."

Her expression soured. "You were eighteen. We were adults. I got married two weeks later, before my husband shipped off to boot camp. That's not kid stuff."

This was not how I'd imagined the conversation going.

"Thank Bobby for his service for me," I said, meaning it sincerely and hoping she understood. "Better yet," I tried, "bring him to my party, and I'll tell him myself."

Her brows hitched at the word *party*.

"I'm finally feeling settled in and ready to celebrate my return to Bliss, the opening of my shop and my reunion with the people and place I missed so much. So, I'm having a big grand opening at Bless Her Heart. Food, music, the works." Thanks to budget restraints, I'd be making the food. Music would come from my cell phone playlist, and I wasn't sure what "the works" entailed, but I'd figure that out later.

Pammy worked to control her expression, but it was too late. I'd seen the interest dance in her eyes. "That's right. You opened a little thrift store. I never could understand selling stuff other people threw away. Is it like a yard sale?"

"It's more like a place where everything gets a second chance," I said, straightening my posture. "You might want to try that with people once in a while."

Pammy's eyes narrowed. "Still suffering from Napoleon syndrome, I see. I thought of you as soon as I heard Dr. Phil talking about that."

Napoleon syndrome referred to feelings of inferiority in short people.

And I didn't have it.

I counted silently to ten, wondering how long it could possibly take the kitchen to make a salad.

"I suppose," she went on, "it makes sense you'd lose your cool with Viola. Especially after she called you out in public the way she did at Christmas. Heck, that was embarrassing for me to watch. I can't imagine what you must've been feeling." She performed a dramatic shiver, then grinned.

"I didn't hurt Viola," I said. "The notion is preposterous. Repeating it is shameless, unfounded gossip."

"What if I read it in the paper?" she asked, cocking one too-thin eyebrow as she reached under the counter. A moment later, she slapped a newspaper on top and pushed it my way.

I turned the offering to face me with nervous fingers. A collection of images centered page one. A picture of Viola's home. And several others of me with Detective Wright. At Viola's place. Outside the sheriff's department. At my shop. The headline was short and sweet.

Local Questioned in the Murder of 1945 Debutante

I puffed my cheeks and sighed. Mirabelle's name was on the byline. "This says I'm a suspect?"

Pammy shrugged. "I didn't read it, but it doesn't look good. What with you being questioned all over town. There's got to be some reason that hot detective is following you." She stared me up and down, as if to say, he obviously wasn't following me for personal reasons.

I accepted my chicken salad when it appeared from the kitchen, paid, then asked to take the paper with me.

"Knock yourself out," Pammy said. "Just yourself, though," she clarified as I turned to leave. "Try not to hurt anyone else."

I took my meal and the morning news to the gazebo on

the square and climbed onto the wide wooden railing. I set my salad and water beside me, then dropped my purse to the ground and leaned against one of the support posts.

I read the article twice as I ate. Contemplating how to undo the fact that everyone in town probably now believed I was guilty. Because Pammy was right, based on the headline and photographs alone, it certainly seemed that way. Why would an innocent person be repeatedly questioned by local law enforcement otherwise?

Hopefully a chat with Mirabelle would fix the misconception. She'd been peeping in my shop windows while I'd spoken with Cami yesterday, and I'd avoided her. She was probably trying to get my side of the story.

Cami caught my eye a few minutes later from where she'd been directing her team of ladies. She jogged across the grass in my direction with a smile as bright as the sun. "You came out!" she said, as if I'd been hiding under a rock instead of working in my shop.

I suddenly couldn't help wondering if that was how it might seem to some folks.

"What do you have there?" she asked, eyeballing my lunch.

"Chicken salad." I lifted the logoed bag my meal had been packed inside, just in case she wanted one for herself.

She curled her lip. "The DS is pretty amazing, but it costs a lot to go in there this time of day."

I could tell by her expression she wasn't referring to the menu prices. "True," I agreed. "Pammy made it clear she doesn't like me any more today than she did in high school, so that was fun."

"Pammy doesn't like anyone," Cami said. "Except, maybe, her husband, but that man worships her. For the life of me, I can't figure out why. They're a match set in the stars. Oh!"

She smiled. "That reminds me, I heard you met Gretchen from Golden Matches."

"I did, and Liz from What the Dickens," I said, remembering my new friends fondly. "I hate that I missed Hazel's funeral. Mama didn't even tell me she passed."

"Well, you were going through a lot this time last year," Cami said. "She probably didn't want to cause you any more heartbreak."

I sighed deeply at the memory. This time last year, my husband had filed for divorce. "Gretchen's great-aunt Sutton gave me a plant for protection," I said, forcing my mind on the good and the present. "A couple of hours later someone locked me in the basement at Viola's, so I think the plant is broken."

Cami laughed. "Did you have the plant with you? Because you can't expect a plant to help you when it isn't even around."

"True. And no. Judy was at the shop."

Cami laughed again. "Sutton is too funny, and Gretchen is great. She just moved to Bliss from somewhere in Louisiana last year. She's thirty, single, and a whole lot of wonderful. Liz too. She lived in Virginia until she inherited her grand-mama's bookstore."

I patted the space beside me and tipped my head, beckoning her to have a seat.

Cami joined me on the gazebo railing, looking like a million bucks, even in jeans and a T-shirt. She took a seat opposite my salad, then spun the paper to face her. "Is that you?" She shook the *Bugle* open. A moment later, she peeked at me over the top, eyes wide.

I stuffed my mouth full of grilled chicken and lettuce, then watched as she read, seeming more concerned by the minute. "I'm going to find Mirabelle and offer my side of the story," I said. "That should help."

Cami tented her brows. "Can't hurt."

I snorted a small, indelicate laugh. "You know what's strange?" I asked, running mentally over the few things I knew about Viola's death.

"I'm afraid you're going to have to be more specific."

I grinned. "Mama told me the historical society wanted Viola's house."

Cami frowned.

"Then, I found stacks of boxes in Viola's basement while I was locked down there last night. I'd assumed Teddy had been packing all day, but what if Viola had begun the process before she died."

"Why would she do that?" Cami asked.

"I don't know. Maybe something else was going on." I stuffed my nearly empty salad container back into the bag and turned to face Cami. "Have you noticed a fancy black sedan flying up and down Main Street the last couple of days?"

She shook her head. "I don't think so. Why?"

"I want to know who it belongs to. At first, I was just curious because most folks obey basic traffic laws around here, but I saw it parked outside the bank this morning, then I saw Mr. Totoro in the passenger seat."

"From the historical society?" she asked.

I nodded. "Do you think it could be someone connected to Viola somehow? It's not the kind of car I see in Bliss too often. That car is meant to grab attention."

Cami's gaze pulled away from me, then stuck to something in the distance. "I'll ask around, but right now it looks like you've got company."

I followed her gaze to my store where a woman had parked at the curb and was unloading a stack of very fancy gowns. "Who is that?"

"That is Emma O'Neil," Cami said, gathering my lunch remnants. "I'll take care of this. You go see about that."

"Who's Emma O'Neil?" I asked, hopping down and straightening my outfit.

Cami tracked the woman with her gaze. "She's Viola Abbott-Harrington's personal assistant."

CHAPTER TWELVE

I hurried across the street to catch Emma as she knocked on my shop door.

"Hello!" I called, looking hastily both ways as I crossed the street.

The woman turned, hands full. A mass of dresses lay draped across one outstretched arm. A box with my name on it was pressed against her chest. She smiled as I hustled onto the sidewalk with her. "Any chance you're Bonnie Balfour?"

"Guilty," I returned, then frowned as the unfortunate word choice registered between us. "I mean, yes," I corrected. "Here. Let me get the door." I pressed past her to unlock the deadbolt, then I reached for the box.

We carried the items to my counter, then set them beside the array of vases Mama kept filled with fresh flowers.

I turned and offered my hand, now that hers were free. "Nice to meet you..." I tipped my head, waiting for her to complete the exchange as we shook hands.

"Emma," she said. "I'm Ms. Abbott-Harrington's personal assistant." She paused, then frowned. "I was," she corrected, regret flashing in her deep brown eyes. "Sorry. I'm still getting used to that." She curved thin arms around her narrow middle and worked up a tight smile. Dressed in a black blouse and jeans, with simple black ballet flats, she looked the part of a grieving companion. Her lack of heels brought her nearly to eye level with me, in my two-inch pumps.

"I'm truly sorry for your loss."

"Thanks." She scanned the store, her gaze so distant, I wasn't sure what she saw. "I just can't understand what she was doing on the stairs," she said finally. "I would've gladly carried whatever she wanted. I helped her move the first batch of dresses she brought here. And all this." She motioned to the things on the counter. "I've been working with Teddy for the last couple of days to cancel her appointments and reach out to her contacts about what happened. I completely forgot I had this stuff in my car. She asked me to bring it over on my way home that afternoon, but my mind was on other things, then you know the rest."

"I do," I said softly. "And I appreciate each of these donations more than Viola could ever know." I moved to my refreshments table. "Can I get you something? I have cold water and coffee. I bake to clear my head, so I have plenty of sweets for comfort."

Emma smiled, then brushed a mass of dark hair away from her heart-shaped face. Thick, dark lashes lined her wide-set eyes, and her full mouth pulled gently into a small smile. "When I've got a lot on my mind, I like to eat. We might be a perfect match."

I passed her a small plate and pint-sized bottle of water. "I made vanilla cupcakes with strawberries-and-cream filling."

She raised the cover of my cupcake container, then set one treat on the plate. She carried it to a pink armchair beside a brass-and-glass end table and took a seat. "Thanks."

I pulled a chair onto the braided oval rug beside her, then

lowered carefully onto it. Where to start? I had so many questions, but I didn't want to alarm or worry her any more than she already was. "I didn't know Viola. I grew up at Bud's and Blossom's. It's a flower farm outside of town. I left Bliss after high school, and I just got back a few months ago. I only met Viola twice."

Emma's eyes widened. "She loved the flower farm. I didn't realize that was your family's place. I guess I should have," she said more quietly. "You look just like the woman who works the Petal Pusher flower cart at the Makers Market."

"That's Mama," I said. "She's a total flower addict." And she loved taking her cart anywhere she could mingle and show off her beautiful blossoms and arrangements. The Makers Market was Bliss's largest regular gathering of local artists and craftspeople. "She came across the knowledge and skills honestly. Her mama's the same way. I think my Gigi could revive the most wilted plants with a wink and a smile. I miss her." The last few words had come unexpectedly and in the form of a heartfelt whisper. Being home was great, but it wasn't the same without Gigi. She'd always been my confidant, my playmate and the best partner in crime, much to Mama's dismay.

"Oh." Concern furrowed Emma's brow. "I'm sorry. Is your grandma..."

"No." I smiled, picking up on her presumption about Gigi's possible demise. "She's fine. She moved to the coast before I moved back to Bliss."

Emma nodded. "That's too bad."

It really was.

"I'll have to tell Mama I ran into you," I said. "It's nice to know Viola enjoyed her flowers."

Emma lifted her cupcake, then set it down again. "I

bought fresh arrangements for the entryway, dining room and parlor every Monday morning. Dahlias were her favorites."

I shifted, turning slightly for a better look at her blank expression. "Do you have any idea who might've wanted to hurt her?" She was obviously in pain, but I needed to know. And I wasn't sure when I'd get the chance to ask again.

Emma's eyes snapped to mine, her blank expression reanimating. "No. No one. Why?"

It took a moment for me to realize she didn't know Viola had been murdered. "I just wondered," I said, unable to think of a witty cover. "The *Bugle* had a feature on the investigation this morning. I'm trying to figure out what the sheriff's department is investigating." I stopped to gauge her reaction.

"I haven't seen the paper," she said a bit woodenly. "I didn't know."

"Did you know I found her?" I asked, my tongue thickening with the words. "It was awful, and I'm in all the photos accompanying the article."

"Oh." Emma creased her brow.

"I didn't hurt her," I said quickly. "I'm hoping to find out who did. It's not right that this happened to her." I averted my gaze, feeling nonsensically embarrassed.

The pile of gowns on the counter caught my eye, and I cleared my throat, ready to change the subject. "I really appreciate you bringing all these things here today. Viola's donations will help a lot of people." I turned back to Emma with a warm smile. "I'm thinking of starting a section with only her gowns, and dedicating the space to her. Everything she owned seems so perfectly classic. There's nothing I could add or change to improve them. And since they were donations, I can afford to give them to folks who need them. Do you think Viola would like that? It could be a lovely legacy."

"You'll just give them away?" Emma asked. "No charge?"

I nodded, a wedge of emotion expanding in my throat. "A tribute to one of Bliss's former debutantes."

Emma batted her glossy eyes, suddenly heavy with unshed tears. Her hand, holding the little plate, began to tremble. "She would love that."

"Do you have any idea why she decided to get rid of so many things? She wasn't interested in the prospect at all a few months ago, and now her generosity is almost too much."

Emma bit her lip, then set the plate of untouched sweets on the table beside her. "I suppose this will come out soon enough, so it isn't gossip. Not malicious anyway."

I leaned closer, drawn by the intrigue of whatever would come next. "What isn't?"

"Ms. Abbott-Harrington had cancer. For a couple of years. She gave a good fight, but treatments were tough and they took a toll. Her health was declining rapidly. I think it caused her to reevaluate what was important."

I sat back, caught completely off guard. "She was dying?" That certainly explained all the boxes I'd seen in her basement. She'd been preparing. Saying her goodbyes. "I thought I saw a bed in a first-floor sitting room." I'd caught a glimpse when Detective Wright cleared the rooms the other night.

Emma nodded. "Teddy and I helped her arrange that. The stairs had become too much for her to manage. She was planning to downsize to something smaller, where everything was on one floor."

And that explained why the historical society was negotiating for her house, even before she'd died.

But why hadn't Mr. Totoro just told me? Why give me the runaround and be so intentionally coy? Was he trying to keep her secret, even after she was gone? Out of respect? Something more?

"I should go," Emma said, rising fluidly. "I'm sorry I didn't finish your treats. They all smell and look amazing. My appetite is on the fritz, I guess."

"Understandably," I said, walking her to the door. "Wait." I turned back and folded a small pastry box into existence, then set her plate inside. "For the road. In case you want something sweet later or have a little one at home who might like cupcakes."

She smiled. "I have two, if you count my mother. She lives with me and cares for my daughter while I work. I'm sure they'll both be thrilled. Thank you."

I added cupcakes until the box was full, then closed the lid and passed the box her way.

Emma accepted with sincere thanks, then walked out.

My phone buzzed, and I freed it from my pocket. My attorney's number centered the screen.

I inhaled long and slow, then released the breath the same way, repeating the process my therapist had taught me, before answering. "Hello, Mr. Ross."

"Hello, Bonnie. I'm glad I caught you. Just a little update to let you know I'm working on things."

"Great," I said, hoping to sound more positive than I felt. "You found the missing money?"

"Sort of." My shoulders drooped.

"Grant's attorney has disclosed that Grant has a gambling problem, and that's where the money has gone," he said somberly. As if that were remotely true. "The divorce has pushed him into a state of unrest, which has increased his bets and losses. I've emailed you a copy of the statement."

I guffawed, then hurried into my office so anyone coming into the shop wouldn't hear me lose my mind. "Grant does not have a gambling problem," I said, sliding the door nearly closed behind me. "He's too tight fisted to gamble. Not on cards, slot machines or anywhere else he might not get his money back after he lets it go. He called me reckless for leaving my coupons at home once," I ranted. In Grant's world, money was only spent on things that helped him keep up with the Joneses. Period. "Anytime I pointed out that we had enough money to pay full price for something as innocuous as take-out pizza, he'd say that was only true because he was so careful with every penny. Implying he had to be because I was careless. And I'm the most frugal person I know. So, no, Mr. Ross. Grant Parker does not have a gambling problem." More likely, he'd taken that money out of our account and hidden it. I couldn't begin to fathom where.

"He's enrolled in online counseling for the addiction," Ross said.

I paced my crowded office, considering the possibility. "If he is, then that's new and it's part of his cover to this scheme. I guarantee you this is a setup." I was learning the hard way that Grant would rather give all his money to the lawyers than see me get a single penny of what he perceived as his. Not ours. And certainly not mine. Especially after I'd had the audacity to suggest a temporary separation. He'd practically run straight to the attorney's office to initiate divorce papers. Needing to be the one in control more than he needed to evaluate and remedy whatever had brought me to that point.

"Hiding marital assets is a crime," he said. "I can bring in an investigator, if you'd like. If we find Grant has committed fraud, charges will have to be filed."

My heart sank. How had I gotten myself into this situation? When had Grant stopped loving me and started loving money? Or had it always been that way, and I'd somehow not noticed until it was too late? Why did it still hurt to be abandoned by a man I'd stopped knowing long ago?

"Okay," I agreed, sinking onto my desk chair. "I understand, but I also need to finalize this divorce. Having one foot in the past is making it awfully hard to embrace my future. If that makes any sense."

"It does," he said. "Of course."

I forced myself to sit taller and remember I'd come from a long line of amazing, strong and capable women. If my shop and I were going to succeed, we'd do it on our own. I couldn't let my dreams be waylaid by the circumstances of a life I'd left behind in Atlanta.

I grabbed the nearest notebook and a feather pen, then began scribbling party plans for the grand opening.

The distinct jingle of bells over my front door, combined with Mr. Ross's awkward silence, told me it was time to end the call.

"I'm sure you'll figure this out," I said. "Tell whoever you hire to be thorough and to think outside the box. Grant's very smart, and he's not afraid to break rules." I disconnected with my chin high.

So far, this week wasn't shaping up to be the best one of my life, but it also didn't have to be the worst. I still had free will and self-possession. I could turn my luck around.

The store's door bells jingled again as I opened my office door. I'd make more plans tonight while I baked pecan pies for the cake walk.

Until then, I had at least two customers to serve. Maybe more. Maybe two big groups had arrived. I smiled at the thought. Maybe I'd think back on this moment in years to come and remember it as when I finally took the bull by the horns. The moment that changed my life.

I stopped, confused at the end of the hall, peering into the empty shop.

Apparently, I hadn't heard two people, or two groups, arrive. I'd heard the same person come, then go, because

Clyde stood on the display case near my register, cheerfully licking frosting off the glass.

Someone had smashed one of my cupcakes against the counter, then left me a note in the creamy red filling.

LEAVE IT ALONE

CHAPTER THIRTEEN

I called the main line to the sheriff's department, feeling more annoyed at the inability to clean my counter than afraid. I explained the situation to Janine when she answered.

She assured me she'd send someone over.

I locked the front door to protect my ridiculous little crime scene, then pulled Clyde onto my lap and waited. "I wish you could talk," I told him, not for the first time. Clyde was an excellent listener, but sometimes I needed input. Like now. "I know you saw whoever did this."

He purred and nuzzled his head against my chin, as if to say he had everything under control. And would I please set him back on the counter where he could finish enjoying my crushed treat?

I stroked his fur and examined the message. "At least it doesn't say, 'or else,'" I told him. "Even written in strawberry icing, 'or else' would be unsettling." As it was, I hated that some yo-yo had made a mess on my counter and ruined a perfectly good cupcake.

Clyde stretched a paw toward the icing, and I twisted away, causing him to miss.

"What kind of person does a thing like this?" I complained, feeling my nerves tighten and my edges fray. Why was it that just when I'd resolved to take control of things, something counterproductive happened?

I imagined various people coming into the shop, seeing I wasn't there, then grabbing a cupcake and squashing it on the glass. I started with the faceless human who drove a fancy black car. Then Teddy. Finally, Mr. Totoro. I pictured each with menacing scowls and cruel intentions.

Before I got any further, someone yanked hard on my door, and I screamed.

Clyde dove from my arms and made a run for the nearest clothing rack, like the fierce protector he was.

Outside, Detective Wright waited, hands on hips, frown on lips.

I unlocked the door, then stepped aside as he marched in.

"You okay?" he asked, gaze skating over me before homing in on my counter.

"A little shaken. It's definitely a weird situation."

He examined the message for a long moment, then dropped a small black bag from his shoulder and liberated a camera. He snapped photos from every angle, then tugged on a pair of blue gloves and put the ruined pastry, along with a dollop of filling into a small plastic evidence bag.

"Do you think that's overkill?" I asked, hoping he would agree and suspecting he wouldn't. "I mean, you can't get fingerprints from a cupcake. And I can tell you what's in the filling since I made it."

He dropped the camera and bagged dessert into the duffel. "You made that too?"

I tipped my head in the direction of the table. "Want to try one? For due diligence?"

"Maybe." He turned in a small circle, searching the ceiling. "I don't suppose you have any working security cameras in here."

"I don't have any cameras in here," I admitted. "I didn't think I'd need them." And I couldn't afford them anyway, so it didn't matter.

His frown deepened. "Any idea who might be responsible?"

"Well, yeah," I said, shooting him my most disbelieving look. "Viola's killer." *Obviously*.

"Why would her killer do this?"

"Probably because I've been trying to figure out their identity."

Detective Wright struck his usual aggravated pose. "Hey, here's an idea on the subject. Quit snooping."

"Kind of late bringing that advice, don't you think?"

"No." He shook his head. "I told you when I saw you at the historical society, but you just drove away."

I pointed at his chest. "Because I seem to be your only suspect, and I'm innocent. I told you I was going to look into this. Don't act so surprised."

His eyebrows rose, and he performed a slow blink. "What exactly have you been doing to look into this?" he asked, tossing a few of my words back at me. "Aside from harassing Mr. Totoro at the historical society."

"I did not harass him," I said, bristling at his tone as much as his meaning. "I asked very basic and simple questions. If he felt harassed it might be because he has something to hide. Ever think of that?"

"I'm thinking of it now," he said, staring flatly at me. "You seem to be feeling harassed as well."

"Funny," I said, pursing my lips and letting my lids go heavy.

"Who else have you been bothering about this?"

"Pammy at the DS, my best friend, Cami, my mama," I ticked fingers off as I went so he could see I was serious and that I'd been busy. "You and Emma, Viola's assistant," I continued. "I plan to talk with Mirabelle at the *Bliss Bugle* as soon as possible and also Teddy."

Detective Wright peeled off his gloves, then ran a finger along the edge of his jaw. "That's not going to work for me. I'm afraid I'm siding with your vandal. You need to leave this alone."

Clyde and I called it a day after the detective left, and headed home to stew in private.

I wasn't sure how to feel about the situation at my shop. I was unsettled, but not necessarily afraid, because if the culprit wanted to hurt me, wouldn't they have done that already? I'd been alone in my office. Alone in Viola's home. Why hadn't I been pushed down the steps instead of locked in the basement? Likely because this person wasn't a homicidal maniac. Which went along with my opinion that most killers were regular people who lashed out, then couldn't take it back. I doubted I was dealing with someone looking to kill again.

Not that I won't be cautious, I thought, flipping my cottage door's deadbolt behind me.

I went ahead and checked the window locks while I was thinking about it, just in case.

Clyde barreled into the kitchen and sat beside his food bowl.

"I'll be right there," I told him.

I traded my work clothes for my favorite cotton PJs, despite the fact that it was only four P.M. Then I wrenched my hair into a loose bun and prepared my game face.

Tonight was a double-header baking and sewing marathon.

I moved a vintage swing dress from my shoulder bag to the seamstress form in my bedroom, then carried it with me toward the kitchen where I could study it and think.

My perfectly adorable mint-green-and-cream living room called to me as I passed, beckoning me to take a load off and prop my feet on the overstuffed couch with rose-striped pillows. Maybe make some hot tea and set my cup on the old pine coffee table I'd topped with little piles of my prettiest books. Somedays, I could still feel my grandparents in the space, despite my personalization, and I loved that about this place the most.

I smiled at the large teal-framed photos hanging neatly in a row above the sofa. Each image had been taken at my parents' farm this year. Closeups of tulips in the spring. Bouquets of roses on their market cart. And my parents, kissing behind a straw hat. After forty years of marriage, they were as in love as ever and didn't care who knew it. I envied them that.

"Meow!" Clyde met me halfway to his bowls, then raced back to where he'd begun.

He headbutted the air-tight kibble container until it fell over, then gave me a pointed look.

"Are you starving?" I asked sweetly, setting the dress form near the pantry. "Poor thing. I'd apologize for letting you waste away, but there is clearly some kibble in this bowl from breakfast." I gave him a stern look as I righted his food storage container. "Maybe you don't need more to eat. Maybe you need a pair of little kitty-cat glasses," I suggested, filling the bowl and stroking his head. "You'd look like a grumpy little professor," I mused. "Or a tiny feline Clark Kent."

He ignored me and chowed down.

I washed my hands, then set my baking ingredients and supplies on the counter while sneaking glances at the dress I'd brought home.

I'd found it in one of the donation boxes stacked in my office more than a week ago, and the memory of it had been wiggling in my mind ever since. The eggshell-colored swing dress was sheer perfection. From the simple scooped neckline and box sleeves, to the cinched waist, with its delicate white cross stitching. But what I loved most was the skirt, lined in white satin and designed to flare when the wearer spun. If whoever had owned this gown wasn't a dancer, she'd clearly missed the point, and a golden opportunity.

I planned to replace the skirt's white lining with red, then attach a petticoat made of alternating pink and white layers. The bizarre pastry attack had given me inspiration, and the next time someone spun in this simple eggshell gown, an explosion of color would follow. Paired with red pumps, nails, lips and a matching clutch, the new owner would be a showstopper. I couldn't wait to bring the idea to fruition—as soon as my cake was in the oven.

I prepped a pan and batter for a coconut cake, while running mentally over the things I knew about Viola's death and the people in her regular orbit. Detective Wright's insistence I leave the whole thing alone had only made me want to best him all the more, and turning everyone's eyes away from me on this matter was in my best interest. Also, if Mirabelle planned to do a series of articles on Viola's death, I could provide her with information to turn the eyes and minds of her readers away from me as a possible suspect.

It was a win-win, really.

I was smaller than Detective Wright in inches and investigative experience, but I was big on wits and heart. Two things he would soon find out.

I stirred the batter, thinking of my two recent threats. I

understood why someone had locked me in Viola's basement. I'd shown up unexpectedly and interrupted whatever they were doing. What I couldn't figure out was why that person had taken the time and risk of coming into my shop and smashing my cupcake.

Was it possible I was already getting close to unmasking the culprit and that person was getting nervous? Or was I just irritating a killer with my abundant and vocal interest?

I suspected Detective Wright would vote for the latter.

I poured the finished batter into a cake pan, then popped it into the oven and set a timer.

Next, the dress.

Clyde had parked his adorable self under the hem, and I took a minute to appreciate him, before washing and drying my hands.

"You know," I said, as another idea came to mind. "I thought the article in the *Bugle* made it seem as if I was being questioned in conjunction with Viola's death, but what if that's not the only possible interpretation? For example, I'll bet a guilty person could've seen those images of me with Detective Wright in the paper and gotten a whole different idea about what was going on." The theory firmed in my head as I wiped down my workspace. "In fact, it might've seemed as if the detective was talking with me because I'd found Viola and therefore knew useful things."

Clyde's ears turned, listening for things I couldn't hear, or maybe considering my new theory.

"If the killer knows I've been asking around about Viola's death," I continued, "then I can see how that might be frustrating."

Clyde rolled and stretched, probably considering my words.

"Are you familiar with 'The Tell-Tale Heart'?" I asked.

"The killer went crazy from paranoia, certain his crime was evident."

Clyde slunk from beneath the dress and rubbed against my legs as I opened my sewing kit. He'd always struck me as the sort of wise and street-smart kitty who knew more than he let on. If he hadn't walked into my life and stolen my heart when I'd needed him most, I was sure he could've been the kingpin of the alley cats, frightening rats and keeping the other felines in order. As it was, he mostly chattered at birds and squirrels from the window.

I worked until the dress and cake were finished. Then I took out the evening's trash, feeling like the Queen of Productivity.

My mood changed dramatically when I spotted a familiar Jeep at the end of my block.

CHAPTER FOURTEEN

I frowned, then waved at the distant, filthy off-roader, whose driver had no reason to be on my street, other than to stalk me.

"I can see you, you know," I groused to myself, marching indignantly toward the detective's vehicle.

The Jeep was parked several houses away and facing the opposite direction, not to mention tucked stealthily into a patch of shade. I never would've known he was there if I hadn't brought out the trash.

I imagined him watching my approach in the rearview mirror. When he didn't get out, I waved more wildly, then checked nearby houses for signs of lookie-loos.

"For goodness' sake." I stopped outside his door and rapped on the window.

He had the nerve to look completely shocked.

"What are you doing?" I asked through the glass.

Detective Wright powered down the window, faux confusion on his face. "Bonnie? Is that you?"

"Oh, cut it out," I said, crossing my arms and tapping my

foot. I made my best get-serious face. "Yes, it's me. Who else would it be, outside my house at dinnertime?"

He glanced around, wide-eyed. "I had no idea you lived here. Which one is yours?"

"Get serious," I told him. "You're busted. How long have you been here? And why?"

His feigned innocence melted into the more typical, unimpressed expression I'd come to expect. "I think a better question is, why are you outside in your bare feet and pajamas? Why are you in pajamas at all? It's six-thirty."

I glanced down at my Pretty as a Peach pajamas, the pattern of little fruits polka dotted my T-shirt and matching sleep shorts. My lavender toenails sparkled far too delightfully for the ugly asphalt underfoot. "I was taking out my trash. I didn't expect to find a stalker."

"Sorry. I'm still working out the reason for your pajamas. Is this your bed time?"

"I like to be comfortable. I suppose that's a crime now?"

"No, but those pajamas might be."

I sensed a little heat in his tone and gaze. My ridiculous stomach flipped in response. "I'm not expecting to get any sleep tonight," I said, redirecting the conversation. "I was baking."

"So, the pastry thing did upset you." He caught me in his piercing gaze. "Good to know I wasn't the only one."

"You were upset?" I swallowed hard, the weight of the statement threatening to knock me down.

Originally, I'd only cared about the mess, seeing the whole thing as a petty act of childishness. But as time had passed, I'd begun to recognize the derangement. Whoever had smashed my cupcake could've done anything they'd wanted to me or my shop, but they'd chosen to leave a specific threat. A warning that I was being watched. That they could get to me too, if they wanted. And they were in control. "Do you want to come in?" I asked, without waiting for his answer to the other question. Suddenly, I didn't want to be alone.

He opened his door and emerged. His casual jeans and T-shirt looked great with the ballcap and tennis shoes.

I forced myself not to stare.

"I didn't bring my pajamas," he said, raising his arms overhead and twisting at the waist to stretch. The hem of his shirt rode up, and I nearly swallowed my tongue.

"Shut up." I turned on my bare toes and headed back to my house, attempting to mentally erase the swath of tanned skin from my mind.

Clyde was in the window when we approached.

"You take your cat everywhere you go?" he asked, tapping on the glass as I opened the door.

"Just to work," I said, stepping aside to let him pass.

"And to crime scenes."

I shut the door behind him. "That doesn't count. I was on my way home from work both times."

Detective Wright looked around, tipping left and right without taking a step in any direction. From the space inside my front door, both the living room and kitchen were visible, along with the hall leading to my bedroom and bath.

"Looking for a murder weapon?" I joked, bypassing him to prepare a pot of coffee.

"Just taking it all in," he said. "Looks a lot like your shop, but homier."

"Then make yourself at home. Mr. Coffee takes about twenty minutes to work his magic. Meanwhile, I'll grab a hoodie and some socks, since you didn't think to bring your jammies."

When I returned a minute later, he was seated at my kitchen table, far too large and serious for the small gold-speckled set.

His gaze flicked to mine the moment I rounded the corner. He'd been inspecting the dress on my form. "That was fast, and for the record, I don't wear jammies."

I pushed the idea he might not sleep in anything at all from my mind and doubled down on the banter I'd grown to enjoy between us. "I didn't want to leave you alone too long. Stranger danger and all that."

His cheek kicked up on one side, teasing at a lazy smile. "Smart thinking."

"You aren't going to point out that you're a cop, so I don't need to worry?" I asked, selecting two mugs from the rack.

"Nah," he said, breezily. "I'm a detective, there's a difference. We know how to hide the bodies."

"Good to know." I stood beside the gasping coffee maker, mentally choosing a chair at the table. "Were you really upset by the message left on my counter?" And if so, did that mean he finally believed I didn't hurt Viola?

"I didn't like it. Whoever left that threat could easily have gotten to you instead, and that person has likely already killed once."

I blew out a little breath, feeling the heat leak from my cheeks.

"This is a cute place," he said, crossing one leg over the other. "Bright. Cheerful. Reminds me of you, when you aren't glaring."

"I don't glare."

"Oh, yeah?" He smiled. "You should tell that to your face."

I rolled my eyes. "At least tell me you don't think I'm responsible for Viola's fall anymore. Not after what happened today."

He tipped his head lazily one way, then the other. "You could've smashed your own cupcake."

I pressed my lips together and imagined screaming.

He laughed. "I'm kidding. The look on your face when I

got to your shop told me all I needed to know. You didn't leave the threat for yourself."

"What about Viola? Do you really think I hurt her?"

Tension coiled in the air, tightening my limbs. His gaze darkened and slipped to my mouth before returning to meet my eyes. "I really hope not."

Mr. Coffee chugged, and I gasped, reaching again for my non-existent pearls. "Coffee?"

"Thank you," he said, a small smirk playing on his lips.

I filled two cups, then ferried them to the table and passed one to my guest as I sat down. "Here you are…Detective."

His brows rose. "You don't know my name?"

"Detective Wright."

His eyelids sank shut a moment before reopening once more. He extended a hand to me and waited until I slid my palm against his. "Mason Wright," he said, curling long fingers over my hand. "It's nice to meet you."

I bit my lip and gave his massive hand a little shake, wondering if he could feel the electricity on his skin and down his spine too. "So, you're Mr. Wright," I said, smiling crookedly. "They tell girls we'll never meet you, but here you are."

His lips quirked. "Call me, Mason."

I nodded, then pulled away, tucking my hands beneath the table and collecting my marbles.

I thought about all we'd said since I'd found him outside, and all the unanswered things I still wanted to know. For example, if he wasn't staking out my house because I was a suspect, then why was he really there?

The answer hit like a punch to my chest. "Are you here because you think the killer might come after me tonight?" My voice cracked on the final word. "At my home?"

Mason worked his jaw, a flicker of heat in his keen blue eyes. "I don't know." He leaned forward, cupping his hands around the mug of coffee on my table. "I was FBI for a long while, undercover most of that time, so it could be that I've learned to expect the worst. Or maybe I just have trust issues, but I don't like to let down my guard. Not coming here tonight, after the threat this afternoon, felt like a missed opportunity to protect you and catch a killer."

"Thanks," I said. "For being out there. What happened at the FBI?" I asked, still unsure how he'd ended up in Bliss and why.

He frowned. "What happened with your marriage?"

I nearly laughed. "Touché. Anyway, it was nice of you to be lurking outside, I guess."

He smiled, eyes twinkling with pleasure and mischief. "It was nice of you to invite me inside without even knowing my name."

I crossed my legs and took a sip of my cooling coffee. "I looked you up online. It's like you don't exist."

"I'm a private person."

I pulled my lips to the side, then tried a little transparency, hoping he might reciprocate. "My marriage failed because I couldn't make it work. I tried everything, but after the first year or so, things changed. We wanted to have a baby, but I never could." I dared a look in his direction.

He didn't react, only listened with the same blank expression that both endeared and unnerved me.

"I don't think I ever got past the absence of a child, and he pulled away a little more every year. I tried harder to repair the gap but also realized I resented him for quitting on me. And I resented myself for accepting his neglect. It was complicated and unhealthy. He filed for divorce last summer." I lifted and dropped my palms. "That's my story. You'll eventually hear some variation of that from every gossip in town, so you should probably also get the truth from me."

He rubbed a palm against one lightly stubbled cheek. "You're divorced? Not just separated or figuring things out?"

"The lawyers are still trying to finalize things, but my marriage was over in the mid-2000s, if I'm being honest."

Mason searched my face intently. "I was undercover with the Cleveland FBI so long I thought I'd gone crazy. There were days the lie felt more real than the truth. I knew reality and fiction had gotten twisted in my head, so I called in a personal favor to get me out of there. I needed out of the city so I could regroup and think."

"That's how you wound up on loan to Bliss."

He nodded. "When I asked to leave Cleveland while I regrouped and reevaluated my life and career, I never expected to wind up anyplace like this."

"That's because there isn't any place like this," I said, smiling against the rim of my mug.

"Except that other little place around the bend. Cromwell?"

"Bite your tongue." I set my mug down, expression aghast. "Hasn't anyone told you never to say that word aloud?"

He wrinkled his nose and laughed. "No."

"Goodness," I said, shaking my head. "Someone is failing you. First you ask about bad luck in public, now you went and used the C word."

The doorbell rang as I opened my mouth to fill him in on the historical feud between towns.

I glanced over my shoulder, then pushed to my feet. "Bliss is far superior to Cromwell for about three thousand one hundred and twenty-eight reasons," I said, heading for my door. "Remember that."

"Is that the exact population of this town?"

"You betcha." I unlocked, then opened the door.

A boy I guessed to be around ten years old stared up at

me from the porch. He wore potholder gloves and held a casserole in his hands.

"Hello," I said. "Whatcha got there?"

"My mama said you had a bad day, and she can't come out because she's feeding my sister." He pushed the baking dish at me. "We live across the street. Where the baby never stops crying. Here. It's not hot, I just like the gloves."

I glanced at the blue cottage across the street. Every light in the house was on, and there was a basketball hoop above the garage door. "Oh, okay, well wait a minute." I hurried to the kitchen with the offered casserole, then plated a few slices of coconut cake and carried them back to the boy.

Mason followed for a peek over my shoulder.

I smiled at the child. "How about I trade you? Take these home for dessert and thank your mama."

"Oh, boy!" He took the cake eagerly, then his eyes widened as his attention rose over my shoulder. His mouth formed a little O. "Thank you!" He took one more look at me and Mason, then raced back across the street to his home, cake in hand.

I shut the door and headed back to the kitchen. "I give it about ten minutes before the whole town knows there was a man over here. Twenty before they know it was you."

Mason laughed.

I peeked under the tin foil covering the casserole. "I'm serious. That kid saw you, and I guarantee he's already told his mama, and she's peeking through her curtains right now."

Mason moved to my nearest window and looked.

"She sent spaghetti and chicken. Are you hungry?"

"I could eat." He moved back to my side. "What did that kid mean he heard you had a bad day?"

I got out a pair of plates, knives and forks. "Did you make a police report when you left my shop?"

"Yeah."

"Then Mirabelle saw it, told someone, and they passed it on until it reached my neighbor." Mason wrapped long fingers around his hips and cocked his head. "I thought that kind of thing only happened in movies."

"Nope." I preheated the oven, planning to warm the casserole, then sipped my coffee as I waited.

Mason took another look through my front window. "There is a woman at the window over there." He chuckled. "That's so weird."

The doorbell rang again, and I lifted a finger, indicating he should hold his horses a quick sec. I pointed to the clock on my way to the door. It had been less than ten minutes.

This time a man and woman I recognized as my parents' next-door neighbors were standing on the porch.

"Hello, Mr. and Mrs. Henry," I said. "How are you?"

"We heard about the threat at your shop today," the woman said. "We feel just awful."

"Thank you," I said. "I'm just fine, so there's no need to fuss."

"Well," she said, craning her head for a peek around my door. "We just wanted to bring you dinner, so you wouldn't have to worry about one more thing tonight."

"That's very kind, and I really appreciate it."

She passed me the baking dish and her husband tipped his hat. "You ever need anything, just holler," she said. "We're not much more than a stone's throw away."

"I know it," I said. "Thanks again."

"We heard you have company," she added, smiling as she stepped away, "so don't let us keep you."

I watched with a forced smile until they reached the sidewalk, then closed the door and turned to Mason, standing just out of sight this time. "Hiding?"

"I don't know," he said. "Maybe."

I smiled. "Now we have two selections. This one's hot."

He tailed me back to the kitchen. "How could they possibly have heard I was here already? And baked a casserole?"

"Gossip travels fast. And the Henrys only live a few minutes away. They probably already planned to bring the casserole after they heard about the threat." I set the food on the stove and pulled back the foil cover. Salty scents of cheese and butter reached my nose, and my stomach growled, reminding me I'd only had a salad for lunch. "Looks like hamburger casserole."

He went back to the window, seeming equal parts amused and astounded.

The bell rang again as I pulled the chicken and spaghetti from the stove and set it beside our second option. "Be right back."

"This is nuts," he said, a little breathless.

I hurried to the door, hoping it wasn't my parents. I'd been enjoying my chat with Mason before the casseroles started coming, and I didn't want to make room for anyone else while we ate.

Mason stopped behind the door, and I opened it.

Three women stood on the porch, all with wide smiles.

"Hello," the tallest of the group chimed. "I'm Stacey Melville. This is Traci and Kim. We heard about what you went through today, and just can't believe it. You must be feeling so awful. We thought you could use a little pick me up." They piled their baking dishes and pie tins in my hands. "And a good book." She balanced a paperback on top. "It's about an everyday gal who runs an iced tea shop by the beach and solves crimes. It's a real cute story. If you like it, you should come to book club. I put all the information inside."

"I will definitely check that out," I said, processing the abundance of information. "I appreciate y'all stopping by.

Today was a little scary, but I'm fine, and now I won't be hungry."

Stacey smiled. She leaned closer, eyebrows rising. "You know who else is fine? That new cop you were photographed with in the paper."

I chuckled nervously, hoping she'd stop there.

"Find out if he's single, would you?" she asked. "Then give him my number. It's with the book club details."

The ladies broke into giggles, and I imagined Mason's smug face.

"Will do." I nodded goodbye, then turned and closed the door.

Mason reached for the casseroles, unloading my arms. "They seemed nice."

I followed him to the kitchen.

"What were they saying at the end?" he asked, setting the casseroles on the stove, then unstacking them. "I couldn't quite hear."

"They said you're handsome, and I know you heard them. Don't gloat. It's not as if that's brand-new information."

He turned comically slow in the small space between my counter and island, eyes twinkling once again. "You think I'm handsome?"

I ignored him in favor of peeking under the foil cover on each dish. "I'm not going to have to cook for a week." I stuck a serving spoon into each dish and a pie cutter into the dessert. "Now we also have a cowboy casserole, spoonbread and coconut cream pie."

He narrowed his eyes, confused again. "You're going to have to interpret a couple of those. What the heck are cowboy casserole and spoonbread?"

I turned on him, mouth open in faux betrayal. "Yankee!"

Mason flipped his palms up in surrender. "Just tell me

what the heck it is. I'm willing to try it. As long as it's not made of cowboys or spoons."

I shook my head in faux disappointment. "Spoonbread is like cornbread. It's sweet and you scoop it with a spoon. Here." I put some on a plate and passed it to him. "You know what cornbread is, right?"

"I love cornbread." He added a little from each of the baking dishes to his plate. "Oh, and I love potato puffs," he said, going for the cowboy casserole.

I waved a hand at him. "Excuse me, those are tater tots."

He carried his plate to the table and waited while I caught up. "You always keep a dress in your kitchen?" he asked, eyeballing the eggshell number I'd been working on. "Is that your outfit for tomorrow?"

"No." I laughed. "That's a project for the shop. I spent the last two hours adding a new satin lining and multiple layers of crinoline under the skirt for fullness and pizazz. It wasn't easy. What do you think?"

He grinned around a mouthful of tater tots. "I'd say you had the burden of poof."

I shook my head at his joke. "How old are you?"

"Forty-one. Why?"

"Just curious," I said, not caring at all that he was utterly age appropriate for me.

Mason set his fork aside, then looked me over carefully.

"What?"

He shook his head and shrugged. "I don't know. You cook, bake, sew, live in a little cottage beside a flower farm where you grew up. Are you even for real?"

I stuffed a forkful of spaghetti and chicken into my mouth, suppressing a smile. "I'm not sure which part you're making fun of, but that is my life, so stop it."

"Little blue birds should be following you around." "I

thought I scowled all the time," I said, reminding him of his earlier complaint.

"At me, sure. Otherwise you seem really happy."

I shifted under his scrutiny. "I am."

"Even now? After what happened today?" I shrugged. "I'm enjoying dinner with a new friend." I poked my slice of cream pie with a fork.

He watched me for a long beat. "What are you really thinking?"

I lifted my eyes to his, feeling my mellow mood slip away. "I wish I knew who's going to inherit Viola's estate," I admitted. "It feels important. She had an estranged son in Nashville, and I hear she was sick. What if she'd invited him over to reconcile before it was too late but things went poorly instead."

"I've considered that. How'd you hear about her illness?"

"Her personal assistant."

"Emma?" He nodded. "She's a good resource, but I must respectfully ask you to stop talking to her about this and stop asking questions about Viola in general."

I frowned.

"I mean it," he said, resting his fork on an empty plate. "That smashed cupcake incident today isn't sitting well with me. You've already been locked in a basement. I'm not sure how many more warnings a killer will give before taking serious action."

I opened my mouth to argue, but the implication of his statement sent ice through my core.

Mason stood. He carried his plate and mug to my sink. "I hate to eat and run, but I got a few texts while you were collecting casseroles. I want to check on some things before bed, and it's getting late. Plus, it seems to me the whole town believes I'm here, so it's less likely anyone with nefarious intent will try to bother you right now."

I bit my tongue against the urge to ask him to stay or at least go back to stalking me from outside. I followed him to the door, heart racing and speechless. "Are you sure? You didn't even have dessert."

He turned on the porch and pinned me with a look that curled my toes. "Lock your doors. Call me if you need anything. And thank you for dinner. It was nice."

"Anytime."

He grinned. "All right. Stay safe."

I flipped the deadbolt, then watched from my window as he headed toward his Jeep.

Mason was a nicer guy than I'd originally given him credit for, but he was also off his rocker if he thought I was going to stop asking questions about Viola's killer. I needed that person named and arrested before I became the next victim.

CHAPTER FIFTEEN

I started my day early the next morning, after getting very little sleep. I couldn't shake the fact that Mason had been parked outside my house because he'd been worried about me. Anyone who'd come from Cleveland law enforcement and spent time undercover in the FBI probably wasn't scared of much. So if he was worried, I was worried.

I dressed in white capri pants and an apricot peasant blouse, then cuddled Clyde for as long as I could. After what happened at the shop yesterday, I wasn't ready to bring him with me again just yet. If whoever had smashed my cupcake hurt Clyde to punish me, I'd never forgive myself. So, I kissed his head once more, stuffed him into his carrier, then carried him outside because I definitely wasn't going to leave him alone all day either.

We were going to my parents' place for breakfast, and Clyde would hang out with them today, like the grand-fur-baby he was.

I turned left out of the driveway and motored up the street, away from the bulk of houses and along the wildflower fields on my left, until my childhood home appeared in the distance. I took my time on the long gravel lane to their place, passing under an arching wooden sign carved with the farm's name, and feeling lighter by the moment.

Dad waved as I approached, a water hose in one hand. His jeans were belted above his waist, and his plaid button-up shirt was open, revealing a white T-shirt underneath. His boots were caked in mud, and his ballcap announced he'd Rather Be Fishing.

He extinguished the spray when I shifted into park, then came to meet me at the car.

"Hey, Daddy," I said, wrapping him in a hug. "How are you?"

"Better now. How are you doing?" He peeled the cap from his head, then screwed it back on a few times until he was satisfied.

"Better now," I echoed with a smile.

Dad was tall and broad, but trim from working the land and maintaining a healthy lifestyle. His skin was tan from long days in the sun. His hair and eyes were brown from genetics. The former growing slowly thinner, and the latter perpetually wide with wonder. He and Mama were the happiest people I knew, and I loved that.

Despite my unfortunate marriage, I hoped to find the kind of relationship he and Mama had one day, but for the moment, I'd be happy with breakfast.

"You hungry?" Daddy asked, as if reading my mind. "Your mama's inside fixing something to eat. We're going to sit on the patio."

"Sounds good. I'll wash up, then see if I can help."

Dad kissed my head before turning back to his watering hose.

I lifted Clyde's carrier from the passenger seat and

inhaled the familiar, spirit-lifting scent of flowers on a hot humid breeze.

"Mama," I called, passing through the screen door, then pausing to catch it before it snapped shut on a rusted spring as old as time. "Daddy said you're making breakfast."

I crossed the creaky farmhouse floors, toward the kitchen, where Mama danced to whatever music was piping into her earbuds. She'd filled two dessert glasses with vanilla yogurt and was in the process of layering in granola and berries when she saw me and removed the earbuds.

"Baby," she called, coming for me with open arms. "How are you?"

"I'm okay. It's been a wild week."

"I guess so," she said, her attention lowering to Clyde. "Hello, Clyde. Are you hungry?"

I laughed. "Do you have to ask?"

She turned back to the parfaits with a smile, then grabbed a third glass from the cupboard and filled it too. She'd dressed in her usual overalls and T-shirt, a rolled scarf tied neatly over her wild red curls like a headband. The extra length of material fluttered against her shoulder.

"I hope you'll like the granola," she said. "It's a new recipe of mine. The berries were grown and frozen on the farm, and the yogurt is courtesy of the cows next door."

"Just like old times."

I set the carrier on the floor and unloaded Clyde, then washed up at the sink before helping Mama carry breakfast to the table outside.

Their small patio was surrounded by an array of beautiful blooms and partially shaded by a pergola. Glass windchimes jingled in the breeze, and a white picket fence separated the flagstone from the flowerbeds.

Dad was already there, legs crossed at the head of the

table, a copy of the morning paper in hand. "Anything I can do to help?" he asked, straightening when he saw us.

"Nope." Mama kissed his cheek, then unloaded the parfaits, spoons and napkins from her tray.

I delivered the pitcher of water and glasses that had been set out on the countertop inside. "How's the local news looking?"

"You're not mentioned today," he said. "That's refreshing."

I didn't disagree. "Is there anything new about Viola?" I asked, spreading a napkin across my lap when I sat.

"No." Dad folded the paper, trading it eagerly for his breakfast. "Cami's new campaign has the spotlight today. She's getting folks excited to Shop Bliss," he said. "That girl has a lineup of activities even the biggest hermits can't ignore. From community games to music on the square. A movie night in the park and the usual Shop Hops and Makers Market. She's even got local bands and kids' dance troops coming out to entertain."

Mom sipped her water and smiled. "Several of the shops are putting on sales and dressing up their windows to support the effort. Maybe you want to do that too?"

Dad beamed. "I'm planning to attend all the events. I hear she's got some food vendors from the county fair scheduled."

I smiled as pride for my best friend's work bubbled through me. "Cami is a wonder."

"Always has been," Mama said wistfully. "I just hate that her marriage didn't work out."

"Well, now," Dad said, sliding his gaze from Mama to me, then quickly back. "Those things sometimes happen."

"I just want to see everybody happy," she said. "Whatever that takes."

I forced a smile, ready to change the subject. "Would you consider keeping Clyde for the day? I need to visit Mirabelle before I open the shop, and I hate to leave him in the car again. I don't know how long I'll be at the paper. And I'm a little concerned about having him with me after what happened yesterday. I don't want him to be in danger."

"We never mind keeping Clyde," Mama said. "The more the merrier."

"Thanks." I finished breakfast, then said goodbye to Clyde and my folks. I had a newspaper reporter to visit.

The finished eggshell dress hung from a hanger on a hook above my backseat on the way to the *Bliss Bugle*. I kept the convertible's top up but the windows down to enjoy the beautiful morning.

I'd packed a stack of grand-opening flyers into my purse so I could pass them out everywhere I went. I'd designed and printed them at the crack of dawn, when I'd given up on sleep. Passing them out was a big, nerve-racking step because once they were out there in the world, there wasn't any going back. It was just the push I needed, so I planned to put an announcement in the paper as well.

I smiled at familiar faces in the square as I rolled along the downtown streets, then parked in the narrow side lot between the *Bugle* and a pizzeria that opened for lunch. I hopped out with my bag, keys and cell phone, and left my windows down so the car wouldn't be an oven when I returned.

I hustled my way around the corner and climbed the short flight of front steps.

The door opened as I reached for it, and I smiled at the handsome stranger stepping out.

He smiled easily in return. "Bonnie Balfour," he said appreciatively, running brilliant blue eyes over me from head to toe. His skin was fair, his hair blond and short. "What brings you to the *Bugle*?"

My brow puckered while I tried and failed to place his very nice face. "I'm sorry. Have we met?"

His smile widened. "Not officially." He stepped back inside and held the door for me to pass. "I'm Zander Jones. I write the events column, but I've been keeping up with news of your return."

I suspected he meant news of my alleged homicidal tendencies, but I kept my smile in place. "Oh?"

"Yes, ma'am." He turned, then motioned for me to follow. "I was on my way out for coffee, but that can wait."

I followed him into a waiting area, unsure if his use of *ma'am* was an example of good manners or because he thought I was old. I cringed at the possibility.

A gray-haired woman at a metal desk near the back of the room creaked to her feet as we approached. "Well, if you aren't a sight for sore eyes! Come over here and let me look at you!" she called.

My smile lifted at the sound of her familiar voice. "Hi, Mrs. Beech," I said, wrapping her in a hug. Mrs. Beech had been a high school journalism teacher when I left for college. She'd been the one who convinced me I could travel the world breaking big news stories and shedding light on unfamiliar places, cultures and ideas. She looked so much different than I remembered, heavier, grayer, and her hair, which had been long, was now cut short. A pair of glasses hung from a chain around her neck. "It's so nice to see you."

Zander leaned in an office doorway, watching the exchange with amusement.

"I've been meaning to stop by and check out that shop of yours. Most nights, I'm lucky to get out of here by seven. Makes me wonder why I gave up teaching," she said, posing a hand beside her mouth for the last sentiment, as if it was a secret. "But here you are, looking barely a minute older than when you left."

I blushed nonsensically under her kindness and praise.

"What brings you by?" she asked.

"A couple things, actually," I said, digging into my purse. "I was hoping to talk with Mirabelle, and I'd also like to put a party announcement in the paper. I'm hosting a grand-opening event at my shop."

"That's an excellent idea. Everyone loves a party." She pulled a pencil from the halo of silver hair on her head, then went back to her seat behind the desk. "Give me just a second to find the right form." She rifled through cluttered drawers until she found the pad of paper she wanted, then set it before her with a smile. "Whenever you're ready."

I handed her a flyer. "If you can get this into the paper as soon as possible and run it for a week, that would be perfect."

She lifted the glasses onto her narrow nose, then scribbled on the notepad. "Can do!" She hummed as she wrote, then stole a glance at me over the white frames. "I hear you've made friends with the new lawman. He seems nice. Handsome. Single."

"He's nice once he relaxes a little," I said. "He's only here temporarily, I think. On loan from Cleveland." It occurred to me for the first time that *on loan* meant he would be leaving soon, and I didn't like the way my stomach plummeted at the thought.

She moved her attention back to the paperwork. "He looks just like that actor from *Justified*. Have you ever seen it? A U.S. marshal with a troubled past tries to do right by the law while wrangling with his bad-boy ways?"

I grinned. I was familiar with the show and the actor, Timothy Olyphant. And she wasn't wrong. In fact, now that she'd said it, I couldn't unsee it. Right down to the brooding disposition and general attitude of the character she mentioned. "What have you heard about him?" I asked, curiosity piqued.

"Just that he's a bit prickly. Not one for chit chat. Always on his own. Except when he's with you." She smiled without looking up.

I shifted uncomfortably at the confirmation. Folks were definitely talking about Mason and me. "He was following me for a while because he thought I had something to do with what happened to Viola. He knows that's not true now, which is why I'd hoped to talk to Mirabelle."

Mrs. Beech nodded. "I'm glad he saw sense. You wouldn't hurt a soul." She smiled warmly up at me. "I wonder why he's following you now?"

I turned instinctively, assuming Mason had sneaked up on me, and Zander chuckled. I'd nearly forgotten he was watching. "Detective Wright isn't following me anymore. But I am still interested in what happened to Viola. Do you know if she has any family in town?"

"No one local," she said. "She had a son, Nathan, in Nashville. He's a real pill."

The ancient desk phone rang beside her, and she shot me an apologetic smile. "Duty calls." She slapped the desk, pleased by her clever wording.

I waved, then turned to Zander. "Sorry."

"No problem." He straightened his striped tie against a pale-blue dress shirt that emphasized his cornflower eyes, then stretched an arm into the empty office behind him.

I accepted the silent invitation and took a seat across from the desk.

"Mirabelle tries not to come in these days," he said. "She's partially retired, so I vet and handle as much as I can, then pass the rest on to her."

I smiled. "That's very nice. I don't suppose you know anything about Viola's son?"

He wrinkled his nose. "Sorry, I can't help you there, but I can try to help with something else."

I crossed my ankles and considered the offer, hoping to hide my disappointment that neither he nor Mrs. Beech had any new information to offer about Viola's son. "I'd hoped to talk to Mirabelle about what happened the night I found Viola. I thought the article showing me with Detective Wright gave the impression I was a suspect."

He leaned back in his chair and tapped a pen against the desk. "Weren't you? Mirabelle didn't state that emphatically, but to be fair, she could have. You just told Mrs. Beech the detective thought you were guilty."

I fought to keep the shock off my face. "I'm sure Mirabelle interviewed the detective. If he didn't say as much to her, then it shouldn't have been in the paper."

"It wasn't," Zander said. "It seemed to me she did her best to be neutral, all things considered. Reporting the facts is sticky sometimes."

I frowned. He was right. The article had been accurate and without evident bias, but the facts had not been in my favor. Especially at the time.

"Maybe I could take your side of the story," he said, attempting to dazzle me again with his smile. "Did you say the detective is from Cleveland?"

I chewed my lip, not completely comfortable speaking frankly on the subject to someone I'd just met. "You were on your way out when I arrived," I reminded him. "I should let you get back to that, and I should go open my shop. I think I'd still like to talk to Mirabelle, if you could let her know."

He rose and lifted both palms in surrender. "Of course. Comfort in the familiar. Why don't you give me your number?"

I hesitated, then took a pen from the cup on his desk and

scribbled my cell phone number onto the back of one of my flyers.

He passed me a business card in exchange. "Now that I have your number, it's only fair you have mine."

I took the card, head spinning slightly. Was he flirting with me? Or being professionally friendly?

I scanned his handsome, youthful face, then turned away. I was definitely too old for Zander Jones.

He turned off the office light on his way out, waving goodbye to Mrs. Beech as he passed.

She handed me the paperwork for my ad when I reached her desk.

I paid, and she penciled me onto the printing schedule.

I stopped at a large community corkboard in the hallway on my way out. Event flyers, missing pet posters and help-wanted ads had been neatly pinned to the display. I added one of my flyers to the mix, hanging it near the bottom corner.

Another wave of pride and hope lifted my chest as I pushed through the front door and back into the sunlight. I'd done it. The grand opening was officially happening. Folks were going to visit my shop and hopefully fall in love with it. I had a lot of work to do in preparation, and I couldn't wait to get started!

I nearly skipped around the corner to my car, then stopped short when a confusing sight came into view. My beautiful eggshell dress had been ripped from the hanger inside my car and was lying on the ground. Dirt and gravel marred the delicate fabric, and the skirt had been ripped up the center. Its red and pink crinolines were torn and mashed, as if someone had gutted the poor gown.

I couldn't help wondering if the dress was supposed to represent me.

CHAPTER SIXTEEN

*D*etective Wright arrived a few minutes later with two take-out cups, then handed one to me.

"You stopped for coffee?" I asked, stomach rolling as I sat on the sidewalk, keeping watch of the crime scene. Thankfully no one passing by had noticed so far. A few had stopped to talk with me briefly, then kept going without so much as a glance into the newspaper parking lot.

"I was next in line when you called," he said. "I'd planned to deliver this to you at your store. Do you want it or not?"

I took it with a grumbled, "Thanks."

He offered his free hand and pulled me up.

A burst of electricity swept along my arm to my heart, like last night, and I pulled away with a sharp intake of air.

"You okay?" he asked, cocking a brow as he examined my reaction.

I nodded too quickly, then moved out of his way and pointed to my car. "My dress is another story."

He made a slow arch around my ruined work, sipping his coffee and looking at the big picture before crouching to scrutinize the details. "This is the dress from your kitchen."

"Yeah. Someone really didn't like it," I joked.

He turned sharp blue eyes on me. "What are you doing at the *Bugle*?"

I pursed my lips, recalling his specific request for me to stop asking about Viola's death. His concern following my previous threat. And his willingness to sit outside my house because the danger was potentially that serious. "I put an ad in the paper about my grand opening," I said, voice quaking in betrayal. I pulled a flyer from my bag as evidence, then passed it to him.

He read it, then folded and tucked it into his back pocket. "Isn't your shop already open?" He'd worn jeans and loafers today, along with a white dress shirt and gray tie. The shirt was open by two buttons at the collar, not that I was counting, and the dark-washed jeans had adjusted nicely to his crouch.

Compliments to the designer, I thought, taking a long sip of my coffee. "The shop's open, but business is weak, and I think a party will get folks interested. Or at least talking about Bless Her Heart. If I can impress the attendees, maybe some will become regular shoppers."

"I'm not sure if that's clever or cunning," he said, posing his cell phone to take some photos of the scene.

"It's good business. It's called marketing."

He poked my dress with the capped end of a pen, flipping through the folds of material. "I was never one for shopping. Or business. I like to get dirty."

I plucked the material of my blouse away from my chest and mentally blamed the sun for my reddening cheeks. "It suits you," I said, clearing my throat and my head. "What do you make of this situation? Any chance the wind blew the dress through the open window, or a wild animal got tangled up in it, then tore its way out?"

"No." He twisted at the waist, balancing on the balls of his feet as he gazed up at me, squinting against the sun. "The initial cut is clean, probably made with a knife or scissors, the poofy parts look like they might've been ripped. I'd say someone's pretty mad at you, and they took it out on this dress."

"That's what I was afraid you'd say." I took another long drag from my coffee. Anger and fear warred inside me. Being stalked by a killer was unnerving, but having my hard work destroyed just flat out ticked me off. I'd spent hours on that dress.

Mason stretched to his feet, forcing me to tilt my head back as I maintained eye contact. "I'm going to go out on a limb and say this is the work of whoever left the other threats and probably killed Ms. Abbott-Harrington. While I'm making guesses, I'm willing to bet that person doesn't appreciate you mucking up their perfect crime, and this is their way of saying, knock it the heck off."

My stomach dropped. I'd feared he might say something like that too.

"I don't know if you realize it, but your sheriff's department is small and spread pretty thin keeping this little town fairytale perfect. All of this," he said, motioning to the clean streets, happy faces and beautiful scenery around the square. "Doesn't happen on its own. Bliss's unfathomably low crime rate is practically unheard of anywhere else in this country, and that's not a result of three thousand kind, happy souls who never do anything wrong. It's the result of your sheriff using every man and woman on his team to his or her full advantage. Involving them in high school programs, elementary school field trips, community outreach and about a dozen other things departments ten times this size don't have time for. If I didn't happen to be here, with nothing else on my plate but finding this person, the killer might've gotten away with murder. But I am here, and I've got nothing but time to spend making sure this particular criminal goes to jail. Meanwhile, you're out here poking the bear and raising the odds that this town will have a second need for my services."

I blanched.

"Finally, a normal reaction," he said. "Rest assured, I've got this under control. I'm not letting some small-town criminal ruin a stellar record I've spent decades building."

I bristled and my eyes narrowed. "You're worried about blemishing your record? Your job isn't a competition."

"Your job isn't solving crimes," he rebutted. "And wanting to be the best at what I do isn't dumb, so don't make it sound that way."

The child in me wanted to tell him he was dumb, but since I couldn't argue with his point, I switched gears. "You never told me what you thought about Viola's son potentially being a suspect. You got sidetracked when he came up last night."

"I wasn't sidetracked. You were."

I crossed my arms, careful not to spill my coffee. "Fine. Tell me now?"

"Nope."

"Why not? Have you even spoken to him?"

Detective Wright whistled as he collected my ruined dress and stuffed it back into its garment bag. Clearly done discussing the case with me.

I sighed deeply. "Whatever. I have to get to work anyway. Is my car a crime scene or can I leave?" I took a step toward him.

He swung one long arm out to stop me. "You should probably walk."

I squared my shoulders, suspecting he didn't actually need to keep my car. "Fine."

"Fine," he echoed.

"Do you always have to have the last word?" I snapped.

"Do you?"

I spun around and hightailed it over the sidewalk away from him. "Yes!" I called.

How any one person could be such an enormous pain was beyond me. Especially when he'd been so nice and human last night.

Across the square, Gretchen waved from outside Golden Matches, where she swept the sidewalk. I was certain there was no way she could've heard our conversation, but she could've been there long enough to have seen it unfold. Completely embarrassing.

I considered rerouting to ask her, but I was too worked up to talk calmly. I'd have to stop by her place later. Maybe bring a slice of cake.

The black car I'd noticed so many times this week was parked outside a café two doors down from where Gretchen stood with her broom, and a man who looked suspiciously like the images I'd seen online of Viola's estranged son was exiting the restaurant.

I hurried in the café's direction, cutting across the street then beelining through the grassy square.

My phone rang and Mason's face appeared on my screen. I answered quickly, then proceeded to dart, tree-to-tree, closing the distance between myself and the car in question.

"What are you doing?" the detective grouched. "You were headed down the sidewalk, then you took off across the road like something was chasing you. Jaywalking, I might add."

"Shh," I said, interrupting his pointless rant. I stopped at the last tree before the café. "You know Viola's estranged son in Nashville? Well, he's not in Nashville. He's in Bliss!"

"Now, wait a minute," he began.

"I think he might get into the black car I told you about."

The car's lights flashed, and the locks chirped. Nathan rounded the hood, keys out.

"It's his car," I said. "I should've known. That car is too showy to belong around here."

"Says the woman driving a Mercedes convertible," Mason said. "Leave that guy alone and go to work."

"I wish I had my car. If I did, I could follow him." Then something else occurred. "He was right across the square after someone attacked my dress. He could easily have been the culprit."

I looked down the block to see if Gretchen was still outside. She wasn't.

"Leave this alone," Mason warned. "It's as if you're willfully refusing to learn anything from your daily threats."

I pulled the phone away from my ear, scoffed, then hit the red button to disconnect.

On the street before me, the car's taillights disappeared around the corner, and a shiver ran down my spine.

I'd seen that car on my way to Viola's house the night I'd found her body.

Nathan had been in town when his mother died.

CHAPTER SEVENTEEN

I walked back to the *Bugle* after work and picked up my car, which hadn't been touched. Mason hadn't marked it with crime-scene tape or left a notice saying I couldn't move it, and he hadn't responded to my texts asking if I could drive it home.

I interpreted all that to mean I had permission to reclaim what was mine.

After picking Clyde up from my folks' place, we went straight home, then I gave him a thorough snuggle before letting him go.

I followed him into the kitchen, where he waited patiently as I refilled his bowl with kibble and refreshed his water. "I'm sorry you couldn't come with me today," I told him, sitting cross-legged at his side. He ate as I stroked his fur, wondering if he'd worried about me too. "I've got another full night of work ahead, so I'd better get started."

I pushed to my feet, then went to change clothes.

The low growl of a large truck and distinct backup beeper pulled me to the window. It wasn't time for garbage pickup, so unless a construction vehicle had gotten lost and was turning around, I couldn't imagine what was making all the noise.

Clyde trotted across my room and leaped onto the sill behind the curtains as I parted them. He dropped a stuffed tomato onto the sill at his feet. Clearly stolen from my sewing kit. I sometimes stuck pins in it while I hemmed.

"You're lucky there aren't any pins in that," I said, glancing at the felt fruit.

The noise outside continued, and I scanned the scene on my street outside, deciding someone was likely having something delivered. It only took a moment to recognize the vehicle as a tow truck, once I caught sight of it. I cringed for the unlucky neighbor whose car had likely broken down. Being without a car was the worst. Especially in a place like Bliss, where public transit was practically nonexistent and most folks lived miles from their work.

The driver climbed down from the cab. He looked at his clipboard, then my home.

The hairs on the back of my neck rose to attention and suddenly, instinctively, I knew exactly what was happening. Mason had ordered my car towed when he discovered I'd taken it from the lot outside the paper without asking him first. He'd probably insist it was a crime scene, and I'd contaminated it.

Well, maybe he should've been considerate enough to send me a text with some details on how long I was supposed to go without my car.

I darted through the house on a burst of frustration, before landing indignantly on my porch.

The man with the clipboard glanced up from where he was attempting to hook my car to his truck.

"Hey!" I called, nearly stumbling down the steps between us. "Stop! What are you doing?"

He sighed at the sight of me, then passed me his clipboard and went back to work.

"What is this?" I said, glancing from the paper to him. "I know I didn't ask to pick my car up from the paper, but I honestly assumed Detective Wright was just giving me a hard time. Please don't take it until I talk to him." I pulled my phone from my pocket and swiped the screen to life.

The tow truck driver pressed a lever and the chains between our vehicles tightened. A moment later, my car began to roll onto his flatbed. "I don't know any Detective Wright, lady. If you got trouble with the law, that's none of my business. This car's being repossessed for lack of payment. Read the paper." He reached for the clipboard, and I jerked back, willing my brain to catch up.

I scanned the forms, attempting to make sense of the words. The car was in Grant's name, but it would be mine, officially, at the end of our divorce. "We paid this off last Christmas," I said, staring at the mind-boggling total of missed payments typed on the page. "Grant used his holiday bonus from work."

The man shrugged inside his coveralls and offered me a sad smile. "Sounds like that guy lied. I'm sorry about that, but I've got to do my job."

"I know," I said, returning his clipboard. "I had some makeup and personal things in the glovebox."

He pointed to the ground, where he'd tossed all my things out, as if I was being evicted.

I kind of was.

"Empty now," he said.

I deflated. "Thanks. I'll get my keys for you."

"Appreciate it," he said. "It's nothing personal, you know?"

"I know."

When I returned with the keys, Mason stood hands-on-hips at the end of the driveway, a pitying expression on his brow.

I said my goodbyes to the tow-truck driver, and my car, then turned to the detective. "Come in."

I marched woodenly into my living room, too humiliated to make sure he followed, then I flopped onto the couch and tipped over sideways.

Mason's footfalls echoed across my entryway, followed by the soft snick of my closing door. "That was awful," he said. "Ex-husband didn't pay?"

I groaned in answer. "I'm beyond mortified. Everyone on my street saw that, and now everyone he passes on the way to the highway will know too."

"It's not your fault your ex is a—"

I peeked at him from where I'd smashed my face into the couch cushion.

"Creep?" he asked.

"Sure. Let's go with that," I agreed, forcing myself to a sit up. "Can I get you something from the kitchen?"

He shook his head. "Maybe I should get you something. You want water?"

I frowned. "You're going to bring me water from the kitchen?"

"Unless you don't want me to."

I narrowed my eyes, processing. "Okay. Thank you."

He shook his head, then left. He returned a moment later and passed me a bottle of water. "You look mad. Is it about the car?"

"Oh." I rearranged my expression. "I loved that car. We were friends. And thank you for the drink. I'm not used to people doing things for me. Aside from my folks. They think I hung the moon. I hate to ruin that for them."

A smile lit his face as he took a seat in an accent chair

across the coffee table from me. "So you really did marry a creep."

I took several long gulps of water to help me swallow a bunch of harsh words and hard feelings that didn't matter anymore. "Yep."

Mason's hair was damp, probably from a recent shower, and he'd dressed in a T-shirt and jeans again. He looked youthful, despite the gray in his beard and hair. The mischief in his eyes made him seem a lot younger than forty-one.

As much as I hated to say it, butting heads with him made me feel younger too. "What brings you by, Detective?' I asked, focusing on the present instead of the past. "Were you coming to complain I took my car after you'd told me not to?" I rolled my eyes and groaned.

"I was just messing with you earlier. I thought you'd jump behind the wheel and try to run over my toes or something. I figured you'd realize you could take it whenever you wanted. Nothing inside was touched. Seemed like the dress was yanked through the window."

I pinched the bridge of my nose and worked to settle my heart rate.

"I really only stopped by to see if I could help you with anything," he said. "Maybe dig back into those casseroles."

I smiled, despite myself. "You came over to eat my food? After arguing with me this morning? That's bold."

"Hey," he said. "I brought you a bottle of water."

I laughed. "You did."

"We can make a trade. Let me earn my meal. I'll help you bake, in exchange for some more of that casserole smorgasbord you had going last night."

"Do you bake?" I asked, thinking I could probably use the help tonight.

"No, but I follow orders like a champ," he said, wagging his brows. "And we both know you love to give those."

I grinned, then downed half my bottle of water. I liked the Mason who came to visit. The one who wasn't in hard-nosed cop mode. The one who made me laugh, not scream. "Teamwork makes the dreamwork, in case you haven't heard." I stood, and he pumped one fist.

"What are we baking tonight?" he asked, pushing to his feet behind me.

"Five pecan pies for the cake walk," I said. "My mama promised them to Cami on my behalf. Cami's the woman in charge of the Shop Bliss campaign and most of the events coming up. She's also one of my favorite people."

He paused at the counter, listening carefully, as if my ramblings about pecan pies and childhood friends really mattered to him.

When I stopped talking, the tension between us ratcheted up, and my mind went blank. For a long moment, we were stuck in an odd staring contest of sorts, while my cheeks began to heat and my mind began to wander.

"Where should we start?" he asked, and my gaze flickered to the counter.

"I'll get out the supplies." I passed him an apron, in a hurry to make him less attractive so I could concentrate.

He put it on without question. "What do you think?" he asked, smoothing the small heart-shaped top against his broad chest, and fussing with the layers of ruffles below. "Oh, it's got pockets!" he exclaimed, jamming his too large hand into one of the newly added clefts.

"I made those myself," I said. "Enjoy."

He leaned a hip against my countertop and smiled. "Is there anything you can't do?"

A dozen pithy, self-deprecating things came to mind, but I bit my tongue against the bad habit and reminded myself I had a fresh start. I could do and be whatever I wanted. "Not really," I said, hefting a sack of pecans onto the counter.

"Though moving forward, I'll take better care to understand my financial situation."

"That car thing wasn't your fault," he said, washing up at the sink. "I'm all about knowing your finances, but you can't blame yourself for your ex's actions. He deceived you, and that's on him. You were married, so you trusted him. You did the right things. He did the wrong ones." He dried his hands on a towel, then turned to me with an easy smile. "Sometimes we do everything right, and life still goes sideways. And once in a while, a thing that seems terrible at first turns out to be pretty okay."

"Like coming to Bliss?" I asked, moving into position beside him at the sink to wash up. "How's that working out for you?"

"I don't know," he said thoughtfully. "It's not bad, but apparently I've got to earn my meals around here."

We worked in companionable silence for a long while, prepping the crusts and fillings while the oven heated. When the first two pies had gone in, we took seats at the table and relaxed.

"That's not easy," he said, stripping off his apron and motioning to the flour-covered countertop where I'd rolled out the crusts. "You do that every night for fun?"

"Not every night. But baking helps me think, so I've been at it more often than usual this week."

He smiled. "I hope you're thinking you need to do something else for fun once in a while. Otherwise, I'm going to need to find a gym."

Now I smiled. "I am planning to switch my routines up a little. I'm going to the cake walk tomorrow night."

He patted his flat stomach and groaned. "You do have a gym in town, right?"

"We have a tow path that some folks like to jog on. There's great kayaking in the lakes and at the river. Hiking through the parks is nice. Swimming is good exercise," I suggested, rattling off all the ways I used to stay busy as a kid. "The waterfall is iconic and alluring, but don't go in the water. It's sort of cherished around here. Folks take it very seriously."

"That's a no on the gym, then?"

I smiled again, then chewed my lip, considering my next words. "You should come to the cake walk," I said. "It's a popular event at fundraisers. I'm sure everyone will be at the square to see it done on such a large scale. It'll be a great opportunity to meet more of the people who live here. I could introduce you to the folks I know. And you might even win a cake."

His eyes narrowed. "You're asking me out."

"No," I protested, panicked and looking quickly away. "It's only a friendly suggestion. I'm trying to be helpful."

He laughed. "I'm teasing. I realize you've got your hands full with the car thing, a new business, and that party you're planning. Not to mention healing from the end of what sounds like a pretty terrible relationship."

I released a long shuddered breath. "I'm a mess."

"You and everyone else. Some folks just hide it better."

"You hide it pretty well," I said, assuming he included himself in the same category as *everyone else*.

He fixed me with a look I couldn't quite name. "Then you're not looking very closely."

My breath caught as pain, anguish, guilt and shame raced over his suddenly transparent expression.

For a long moment, neither of us moved.

His phone buzzed on the table between us, effectively breaking the spell. He lifted it, peered at the screen, then stood. "I've got to go."

"What about dinner?" The casseroles were still in my refrigerator.

"Rain check. Maybe I'll see you on the square tomorrow."

"Maybe," I agreed, following him to the door a little shaken and confused. "Hey!" I called as he hit my driveway at a jog. "Wherever you're going, be careful."

A smile split his handsome face, loosening the tight expression. "You too," he said. "Lock up and call if you need anything."

I nodded, then shut the door and twisted the deadbolt. I pressed my back against the cool wood and slid dramatically to the floor.

Clyde climbed over me, sniffing and licking my hair and forehead.

I pulled him to me for a cuddle. "My life has gotten really murky and extremely complicated." Then an unexpected rush of pleasure tore through me, raising a broad and senseless smile. "I don't hate it," I said, a little stunned by the truth. I was perfectly okay with the drama, the intrigue, the danger and the excitement. I didn't even care that my car was gone.

Because for the first time in far too long, I felt alive.

My phone dinged, and I rolled onto my hip to free it from the opposite pocket, embracing the moment of self-awareness.

Mason's name and number anchored a brief message. "Pick you up for work tomorrow?"

And I said, "Yes."

CHAPTER EIGHTEEN

Mason arrived early the next morning in his mud-soaked Jeep. The interior smelled like a concentrated version of him. Newly familiar hints of his cologne, shampoo and shower gel were in full force inside the sun-warmed confines as I climbed inside.

He stole glances at me as he drove, and I stared openly back. "What?" he asked.

I raised my brows. "I'm waiting to hear why you ran off last night. You invited yourself over for dinner, then took off when your phone buzzed. Was it a new discovery on Viola's case? Did someone set up a time to ask Nathan Harrington if he killed his mother?"

Mason slanted his eyes my way. "The sheriff wanted to talk. His shift was ending, and I needed to get over there before he headed home."

"What did he want? It must've been important if it couldn't wait until morning." And Mason had told me this was his only case, so something big had to have happened on Viola's murder investigation.

"It was."

"Important?" I guessed. "Did it have anything to do with Viola's estranged son being in town on the day of her death?"

"No."

Something equally terrible came to mind. "Was it about me?"

"What?" Mason shot me a bewildered look. "What do you mean, about you?"

My shoulders jumped to my ears. "The sheriff is a friend of my dad's. He watched me grow up. I thought maybe he heard you were at my house two nights in a row and wanted to, you know…" I motioned pointlessly with one hand before dropping it to my lap and forcing my shoulders down. "Make sure you weren't taking advantage of my predicament."

He turned to me in horror, then barked a loud laugh.

I jumped.

"What exactly is your predicament?" he asked, blatantly amused.

"I was a murder suspect, temporarily, and trying to convince you otherwise," I reminded him.

He scoffed. "The fact you think it's even a remote possibility that the sheriff would know we've been together after work, and suspect there's anything inappropriate going on, confirms my opinion that this village is truly as crazy as a soup sandwich."

I folded my arms, embarrassed I'd brought it up. "I don't know what the gossips are saying. Or what men think. It was only a guess."

Mason went quiet. He slid the Jeep against the curb outside my store a few minutes later. "Would the sheriff really call me in, hours after my shift ended, because his friend is the father of a grown woman I've been spending time with? What would be the point of that? To see if my intentions are honorable?"

"I don't know," I said, gathering my purse, phone, pies

and keys. I hated how badly I wanted to analyze and unpack the meaning behind the words *spending time with*. "You won't tell me what he wanted, so I assumed the worst."

"Someone is threatening you, and this is your idea of the worst?" He rubbed his eyebrows. "I have a lot to think about. It was nice driving you to work. Pick you up at seven?" he asked, peering through the window toward my shop's hours on the door.

"No," I said, quickly climbing out. "I have a ride home, but thank you."

"At least let me help you with the pies."

"I've got it," I called over my shoulder as I hurried to the door. I marched inside without looking back, then peeked through the window and waited for him to leave.

He stared straight ahead for a long while before pulling away.

Thankfully, Dad had promised to follow Mama to my shop this afternoon and leave a farm truck for me to use until I bought new wheels. For now, I was fine on foot, and without Clyde at my side, I wasn't ready to open up for the day and stay at the store.

I grabbed the pair of extra-large, handled shopping bags filled with pies in boxes, then headed for the tourism office at town hall. The sun was out in full force, but I was far too restless to hang out at Bless Her Heart alone. Sweat trickled along my hairline, and I prayed my deodorant lived up to its claims.

"Hey! Good morning!" Gretchen appeared across the street in black jeans and a tie-dyed T-shirt. She jogged my direction, long dark hair flowing behind her. "Do you need some help?" she asked, hopping onto the curb with a smile.

"Yes." I stopped to catch my breath and thank my lucky stars for a set of helping hands. "You're beginning to make a habit of saving me. Is it awful if I just say thank you? Because seriously. Thank you."

She laughed, then took the bag from my right hand. "I thought you'd be headed this way today."

"You did?" I asked, suspicious but grateful. "How?"

"Tonight's the cake walk." She tipped her head toward the nearest sign announcing the event. "I've heard nothing but great things about your pecan pies for the last few days. Everyone wants one." She grinned. "I love pie, but I'm a vegan, which makes it hard to eat a lot of things."

"Other than plants," I said.

She laughed. "Exactly."

"My folks raise some edible flowers over at the farm. I always thought it was weird."

Her eyes widened. "No. It's not weird. It's beautiful, but don't let my great-aunt Sutton hear you mention it."

I laughed. "I definitely won't."

I scanned the scene around us as we climbed the stone steps of the town hall. Goosepimples raced over my heated skin, leaving me certain someone was watching, but I didn't see any signs of an onlooker, so I hurried inside.

Wide marble floors stretched before us in three directions, as well as upstairs.

I followed Gretchen to the first-floor office marked as Tourism and Hospitality, then held the door as she walked inside.

A familiar squeal split the air a moment later, and Cami appeared. "Hello, hello!" She took the bags from Gretchen and me before hugging us each in turn.

"Holy cake walk!" Gretchen said, taking in the tables full of home-baked donations.

The Tourism and Hospitality suite was small and outfitted with standard supplies. A trio of desks, computers and printers. Framed posters of popular and successful events gone by. Plus a multitude of folding tables topped with pastry boxes in every shape and size.

I smiled at the mass of sugary confections. "This is amazing."

"You should see the refrigerator," Cami said. "I'm testing out my late-twentieth-century *Tetris* skills in there. We're about to host the biggest cake walk in Bliss history. I invited media from state and regional outlets to cover it."

"That's brilliant!" I cheered. "Have any of them responded to the invite?"

"Not yet," she said. "But Zander will be there. He'll get all the details so we can share the story later if other sources want to run a story after the fact." She nearly vibrated with pleasure. "We should meet up after the cake walk and hang out for a bit. I can see if Liz's interested too."

Gretchen beamed. "That sounds like fun. I can tell you about your soul mate if you want."

I laughed until I noticed she was talking to me. "Oh, no. No, no. I'm newly divorced. Definitely not in the market for love. But thank you for a really kind offer."

She shrugged. "Suit yourself, but we don't decide when we find love. Love decides when it finds us. And when it does, it lasts. Because true love is abiding, and it doesn't let go."

"That sounds ominous," I said, sliding Cami a look. "I should go open the shop before it gets any later, though. I just wanted to deliver the pies and say hi. Oh!" I dug into my bag and produced a stack of flyers for my grand opening. "If you think of anywhere to put these, I'd appreciate it."

Cami looked them over and whistled. "How about on my desk and everywhere I go?"

"Perfect." I laughed.

Gretchen opened her palm in my direction. "I'll put some on the counter at Golden Matches."

"Thanks!" I doled out another pile for Gretchen, then said my goodbyes while she stayed behind to visit.

Outside, I looked both ways before donning my sunglasses and heading toward Bless Her Heart. The sensation of being watched rolled down my spine once more, and I quickened my pace.

I crossed the street at the corner, happier to be on the square's side of the road where sidewalks were busier and I was less alone.

The sight of Teddy and an older woman changed my direction, taking me across the grass to a bench where the couple sat, sipping from disposable cups and chatting.

"Hi!" I called, approaching with a broad smile. "I'm Bonnie Balfour. I run Bless Her Heart, the dress shop on Main." I pointed in the general direction of my business without taking my eyes off the couple. "You're Mr. and Mrs. Runsford?"

"That's right," the woman said warmly. "It's nice to meet you."

"Thank you. My mama told me y'all sometimes play cards together. It's always fun to meet a friend of Mama's." I dragged my attention to Teddy then. "I'm sorry we haven't had the chance to officially meet before now. I was the one who found Viola the other night. Absolutely awful," I added, shaking my head to support the statement.

His eyes widened a moment, and he traded a strange look with his wife. "Yes," he said. "It was."

I fought to hold my smile. Something was amiss, but I wasn't sure what it could be. For the second time, I wondered if Teddy was the one who'd locked me in Viola's basement. His coat had been on the stairs after all.

Mrs. Runsford's expression turned sad. "I was very sorry to hear about Viola. It must've been terrible to find her that way."

I nodded. "It was."

The pain in Teddy's eyes seemed to increase. Was it just friendly affection and loss? Or was it guilt and shame?

Maybe I was becoming paranoid.

I dipped my head and leaned slightly closer, creating what I hoped would feel like a private space to speak. "And she was already going through so much."

"What do you mean?" Mrs. Runsford asked.

I glanced at Teddy, wondering if Viola's battle with cancer and recently declining health was still a secret as far as he was concerned. If so, I didn't want to offend him by bringing it up.

"How do you know about that?" he asked.

I bit my tongue against the urge to tell the truth. Emma had told me. "I saw her bedroom," I said instead. "On the first floor."

Teddy's cheeks darkened.

His wife stared at him, then turned to me. "Sorry. We didn't realize anyone knew."

I pressed my lips together. Better to say too little than too much.

Teddy's expression grew grievous and solemn. "She'd just decided to move to a retirement facility with a twenty-four-hour nursing staff," he said. "Her home was in a state of flux. Still is."

"I understand," I said, rolling the information over in my mind. "I'm sure her place was too much to manage. I can't imagine taking care of all that at my age and in good health. Even with a capable staff."

He smiled at the compliment, but the effort didn't reach his eyes. "You're probably right. I just can't see why she wanted to go all the way to Nashville. Aside from her son, who didn't even know her anymore, she didn't have anyone there. Emma and I tried to talk her out of it, but she was stubborn and set."

I shivered at the idea of her moving away from her support system and to a town where her only family was a man she'd lost contact with. The estrangement had to have been for a reason. "How was she doing the last time you spoke with her?" Teddy looked to his wife again, then blew out a breath. "She wasn't herself since she'd decided to move. She thought someone was after her money. I worried about her mental health, but I suppose the paranoia could have been caused by her medications."

I immediately wished I knew if that was true. What kinds of medications was Viola taking? And what were the side effects? How could I find out?

I excused myself when Mama texted to make sure I'd gotten to work safely, but Teddy's words stayed in my mind. He wasn't the first to tell me Viola thought someone was after her money, and I couldn't help wondering if there might've been a very real reason for that.

CHAPTER NINETEEN

*M*ama arrived at lunchtime with a fresh salad. The ingredients were all organically grown and handpicked from her garden. She also brought a fruit smoothie and an eggplant, tomato and basil sandwich. "You're going to love it all," she said, arranging the meal on my countertop. "You can taste the love and sunshine grown right inside."

"Thank you, Mama. For lunch and for letting me borrow the truck." I couldn't imagine having to bum rides back and forth to work at my age, not to mention anywhere else I wanted to go.

"It's no problem," she said warmly. "Your dad and I go just about everywhere together. The truck gets very little use these days. He's right behind me. He made a pit stop on the way."

I hugged her tight and kissed her cheek.

She stroked my hair as I pulled away. "Have you had time to contact your attorney about the car?"

"Yep, and according to Mr. Ross, Grant's attorney claims

this is also a result of Grant's alleged gambling addiction. Coincidentally, he stopped making car payments the same month he filed for divorce."

Her lips pulled into a frown. "I'm so sorry."

"It's fine. I'm where I'm supposed to be, and I'll figure it out."

She cupped my cheeks in her hands. Emotion filled her soft hazel eyes. "You're going to be just fine."

"I know."

The bells over my door jingled, and Dad marched inside with Clyde in his carrier. "Here you are," he said to me, hefting Clyde to my eye level. "I stopped by to check on the little guy, and he looked so sad in the window, I thought you might like to have him with you here."

My folks had a spare key to my place, and I had one to theirs. It was nice to be back in a world where trust was present and mutual. Neither of us had had reason to use the keys before, but I was immensely thankful for them now.

My heart swelled at the sight of my handsome kitty. I'd been worried for Clyde's safety when I'd decided to start leaving him at home, or with my folks, during the day. But truthfully, he wasn't any more vulnerable here with me than he was at the cottage alone. I took the carrier from Dad's hand, then set Clyde free at my feet. He rubbed against me, purring instantly, and I melted a little on contact.

Mama drifted to Dad's side and his arm curved easily, naturally, around her, as if they were meant to be connected that way. Like two pieces of a locket. "Well," she said, resting a palm on his middle. "We're going home to wrap up some things, then we'll meet you here for the cake walk. If you come home first, we can always ride back together."

"Sounds good," I said. "Let's see how much I can get done before Cami comes over here to chase me outside."

I watched them go hand in hand and smiling toward the coffee shop next door. Then, I peeled Clyde away from my lunch on the counter.

He moved on to sniffing my new knick knacks and costume jewelry, fresh from the box Emma had delivered, while I dug into my salad, sandwich and smoothie.

Viola had generously included a number of lovely figurines in the donation box, including ballerinas and brides, angels and cats. A few blown-glass baubles made the perfect accents to my bookshelves. I especially liked a blue stained-glass bowl meant for jewelry and a large leaded crystal vase that was probably worth more than I currently had in checking and savings combined.

Clyde rubbed his face against the spotless surface. "I'll bet that would look perfect in the window display," I said, an idea forming in my mind.

I set my salad aside and went to the front of the store for an evaluative look.

A white shag rug anchored a dress form draped in a poofy pink gown. I'd stacked white leather-bound books on a gold-rimmed glass table, and set a pair of silver heels on a short white stool. "This is where the vase should go," I told Clyde. "Not on the bookcase. Matter of fact, we could create an enchanting effect with a few lights around the window."

Clyde swiped a hoop earring from the box, then trotted away with it in his mouth.

I rolled my eyes. "Be right back." I darted into my office for a spool of white twinkle lights, then carried them to the window. I outlined the entire space and arranged the excess in sweeping boughs along the back of the display for added depth. "Look at this, Clyde." I smiled at the effect. "Now our display looks like the square. And I just need one more thing to complete the look."

I hurried toward the bookcase, where Clyde had reappeared, sniffing and rubbing his cheek on every item I'd unpacked. "Okay. Two things," I said, pulling a shiny gold wrap from a hanger as I passed. I tossed the faux fur over my shoulders, and Clyde leaped onto the floor.

The bookcase rocked under the force of his dismount. "Jeez," I complained, throwing my free hand up to stop the dainty figurines from falling. "You're going to topple this whole thing." I shook my head and thanked my lucky stars nothing had broken. "I thought cats were supposed to be lithe and graceful."

Clyde stared up at me from beneath the rack of Viola's gowns.

I couldn't help wondering what he'd run off with this time.

"You're lucky you're irresistibly handsome." I picked up the heavy vase and grimaced at the deep scratch in my newly repainted teal bookcase. The mark hadn't been there before Clyde's wild leap, and it sparked a fuzzy memory in my mind.

I turned the vase over, examining the slightly cracked bottom, where one edge was jagged instead of smooth. My skin chilled and my heart raced as the memory came into focus. I'd seen the same distinctly shaped scratch on the stand in the foyer at Viola's house. And Emma had told me she brought Viola flowers every Monday for the entryway, dining room and parlor. But there hadn't been a vase in the entryway that night.

I suspected the missing item was a murder weapon—and currently in my hands.

My phone buzzed ten minutes later, with a return text from Mason.

I'm at the door.

I bumbled to the front of my store on numb and shaky legs. I'd locked up and turned my sign to CLOSED after letting him know what I'd possibly found.

He looked me over as he stepped inside. "You okay?"

I nodded affirmatively, but my traitorous mouth said, "Nope." I wound my arms a little more tightly around my center and tried to be as levelheaded as possible. "I could be completely overreacting. The more I think about it, the more I'm not sure what the scratch on Viola's stand looked like. And even if the mark is identical to the one on her entryway table, it doesn't mean the vase was used against Viola. Maybe someone just packed the thing up while they were packing everything else."

"Show me," he said, motioning me to move.

I lifted my chin, then lumbered toward the bookcase. "You've probably already identified the murder weapon," I said, hopefully. "Right? You have it in evidence by now."

"Would I be here if that was true? Now, if you're right about this thing, your prints are all over it. Where is it?"

A shudder rocked through me as I stepped aside and pointed to the crystal vase.

"For an innocent person, there's an awful lot of evidence piling up against you," he said, eyeballing the bookcase shelves. He set his black duffel on the floor at his feet and fished out a pair of gloves. "Let's hope this isn't what you think it is."

"You know I didn't hurt her," I said, stuffing my thumb into my mouth and biting into the tender skin along my nail. "You said so."

"Yes, but that's my gut talking. Not the evidence. I can't

prove you didn't do it," he said. "Can you think of anyone who'd want to frame you?"

"Yes. The killer."

He shook his head. "An enemy of some kind. Maybe someone from your past."

"Of course not."

"Well," he said, snapping on the gloves. "You were at the murder scene, found in the home uninvited the next night, overheard saying you wanted to kill the victim a few months ago, and now your prints are possibly on the murder weapon."

"But I've been threatened," I said, teeth chattering with fear and misplaced adrenaline. "Who would do that, other than the killer?"

"I don't know," he said, lifting the vase for a closer look. "Maybe you faked the threats and are a better actress than I gave you credit for. Maybe you ticked off someone else who's telling you to leave a completely different thing alone." He ran a gloved finger over the scratched paint, then turned the vase on the shelf until the broken edge and scratch matched up. "I'm not saying you're guilty. I'm only saying there's a strong case being built against you."

"By the killer," I snapped, feeling my head go light.

"Probably." He secured the vase into an evidence bag, then took photos of the paint and bookcase. "For now, let's hope someone else's prints are on the crystal when I get it to the lab."

I followed him to the door when he finished.

He paused before leaving. "You going to be okay here? My offer stands to give you a ride home if you want to call it a day."

Cami appeared outside with a smile and a wave.

"I'm okay," I said, waving back to my friend.

He followed my gaze to the woman fizzing with interest and energy just outside the glass.

I unlocked the door to let him out, and confusion wrinkled her brow. Her eyes dropped to the black duffel on his shoulder, still unzipped far enough to see the corner of the evidence bag and the discarded gloves.

"Mason, this is my best friend, Camilla Swartz," I said. "Cami, this is Detective Wright."

Cami's eyes widened with appreciation as she took him in. "Hello, Detective."

He lifted two fingers to the brim of an invisible hat. "Nice to meet you." He stepped aside as she entered, then fixed me in place with a pointed stare. "You sure you're good?"

I pursed my lips and bobbed my head.

He looked from me to Cami, then back, as if he wanted to say more, but didn't.

We watched him climb into his Jeep and drive away.

Cami turned wide eyes on me. "That is the man you've been spending all your free time with?"

"We're trying to solve Viola's murder. It's strictly a professional situation."

"Uh huh," she said, not sounding as if she believed I'd told the whole story. "What brought him over here now? And what was in his bag?"

"I hope you have time for coffee," I said, leading her to my refreshment table.

I filled her in on the crystal vase situation, and everything else she'd missed since we'd last discussed Viola's murder. Then, I emptied a storage container of my leftover cupcakes and ate them all in a fit of nervous energy.

We stared at one another from our seats in accent chairs outside the dressing rooms.

Cami patted my hand. "No one is arresting you for murder," she said. "And it's possible no one is trying to frame you either. At least not the way you're thinking. The killer probably saw the article in the *Bugle* and assumed you're the main suspect. The crystal vase delivery might be his or her attempt to keep things that way."

"That would be smart," I admitted. "Thankfully, Mason doesn't still think I'm guilty."

"Do you mean Detective Wright?" she asked, her voice going high and teasing. "When exactly did you get on a first-name basis? And why didn't you tell me?"

I waved a hand and tried not to smile too broadly. "It's been a crazy week. Wait until you hear about my car."

Cami hugged me at the end of that story.

"And did you know Viola's estranged son, Nathan, is in town?" I told her about his car and that he'd been in town on the night Viola had died.

Cami's mouth formed a little O. "I just heard that from my auntie who works at the bank."

My eyes widened as I slipped to the edge of my seat. "What?"

"I had lunch with her and told her you've been looking into Viola's death. Then she said Nathan's come through the drive through more than once in the last few days. She couldn't say much more than that or she'd be fired, but she said anyone could've seen him in the lineup, so that was okay to share."

"Why would someone who lives in Nashville have money in the Bliss Bank?" I asked.

Cami tented her brows. "Maybe Viola added him to her accounts as part of her preparations for moving?"

I covered my mouth with one hand, processing the possibilities. "If the estranged son had full access to her money, what was the point in keeping her around any longer? I wonder if she also put the house in his name, or at least added him to the deed."

"You saw Mr. Totoro in Nathan's car," Cami said. "And he admitted to wanting Viola's estate."

I dropped my hand back into my lap. "Totoro said he was interested in the house, as soon as she was ready to part with it."

And I was willing to bet her son was more than ready.

CHAPTER TWENTY

I closed up at four, confident I wouldn't miss any sales since the last person to enter my shop had been Cami two hours prior. I took Clyde home so I could change before the cake walk. I couldn't decide where he'd be safer if he had to be alone. At my shop? Or at my home? I eventually decided Clyde was scrappy and smart. There were more places to hide at my house if needed, and he could use those talons if pushed to do so.

I traded my shirt dress and pumps for a pair of comfortable jeans that flattered my full hips and gently rounded middle, then paired that with a loose blue silk tank top that hung by spaghetti straps from my shoulders, and a soft white cardigan in case there was a chill in the evening air.

My folks had some stops to make on their way to the square, and I was eager to get the night started, so I told them I'd meet them there. I smiled at the borrowed farm truck in my driveway. The beast predated my late grandpapa, and had been in my family since it was new. Grandpapa had taught me to drive it on the old dirt roads around the farm. It smelled of pipe tobacco, Old Spice cologne and memories that made me miss him so much it hurt.

I climbed inside and took a moment to appreciate my new life, trials and dangers, then gazed over the fields of wildflowers next door, to my childhood home in the distance. Life was good. And it would get better still if I kept my head up.

I reversed onto the road and set a path toward town, enjoying the way I felt behind the wheel, both young and grown, nostalgic and hopeful. The truck had been repainted in the years I was gone. The faded blue color now shined bright and new. My folks had added the Bud's and Blossom's Flower Farm logo down each side.

It was barely six o'clock when I returned to Main Street, but the square was already busy. Stores, sidewalks and restaurants were peppered with people the way they had been when I was a kid. Most of the parking spaces were already full, but I snagged the last one on the block near Bless Her Heart, before heading across the street.

A heavenly shade of apricot backlit the world as the sun prepared for its nightly rest. An hour from now, the moon would be up, and all of Cami's team's twinkle lights would be in full effect once more. I scanned the square for signs of my parents. I spotted couples walking the paths through the square, friends laughing over ice cream on the sidewalks, and a major change to the village's beloved gazebo. The historic octagonal structure had become a centerpiece, fitted with interior curtains and with large banners hanging from the roof. The air of mystery added to the excitement. Another smart move from Cami. The newly hung banners announced *The Great Cake Walk Coming Soon*, and it was easy to understand that was where the magic would happen. A handful of vendor trucks, normally seen at the fair, had lined two ends of the grassy oval. As a result, the air smelled of lemonade, steak fries and happiness. I hoped Cami was getting plenty of photos to use in her campaign.

Teddy and his wife waved politely as they passed nearby. They rounded the space behind the gazebo, presumably heading for the food trucks. I considered going after them and asking about the vase found in my box of donations but decided to let them have tonight without my interference. Tomorrow would be another story. In the meanwhile, I wasn't sure exactly what to ask.

Gretchen and Sutton were seated on a blanket under a tree. The picnic-style meal spread between them seemed to be composed of mostly veggies, and a row of potted plants made a semi-circle near Sutton's legs. I wondered absently how awkward dinner conversations must be between a woman who only eats plants, and one who talks to them.

"Bonnie!" An unfamiliar voice turned me around on the sidewalk before I could make a move toward Gretchen and her great-aunt.

Emma waved, smiling and headed in my direction while pushing an older woman in a wheelchair. A small version of the grown women skipped along beside them. "This is the dynamic cupcake-eating duo I told you about," she announced once she was near. "Mama, meet Bonnie Balfour."

"How do you do?" the older woman said.

"I'm well, thank you," I returned, my gaze sliding to the little girl, smiling shyly at her grandmama's side.

"I'm Olivia," she said. "I'm nine."

"It's lovely to meet you, Olivia," I said. "I hope you enjoyed my sweets."

She nodded eagerly. "Mama said the strawberry stains, so I had to change my school uniform shirt. It's white."

"It's true," I admitted. "I've ruined more than one nice shirt that way. But it's worth it every time."

Olivia giggled.

Emma wrinkled her brow. "How are things going? Good?"

I nodded, chewing my lip and spotting Teddy with his wife once more. "Kind of," I said. "I was thinking about the bouquets you bought from my folks' farm on Mondays."

Her brows rose with her smile. "Yes?"

"You said you put them in the entryway?"

"Bonnie?" a man's voice turned our heads toward the newcomer.

Zander waved as he crossed the space between us in long easy strides, an expression of distinct pleasure on his face.

Olivia tugged Emma's arm. "Can we sit by the gazebo?" she asked. "Maybe I'll be chosen for the cake walk."

"Sure," Emma answered. She smiled back to me as Zander reached us on the sidewalk. "I'll catch up with you later?"

I nodded, and the three women moved away.

"You came," Zander said.

"I couldn't miss it." I smiled. "I promised Cami I'd be here to support her, and I figured it was about time I started getting plugged back into society."

He nodded. "It took me a while. I didn't grow up here, so there was a lot to learn." He laughed.

"Life here can keep you on your toes," I agreed.

"Where are you from originally?" I asked.

He stared into the distance, and I wondered what he saw there. "Charlotte."

"North Carolina is nice. You miss it?"

He nodded. "Sometimes. The city is nothing like this place. No one is really from Charlotte. Everyone comes temporarily for work or school. They put down shallow roots, so the city is ever-changing. Crime is incredibly high in a lot of areas. Gang violence is on the rise. My family has moved on too. My folks retired to Florida and my sister married a man in Dallas."

I frowned at the thought of my family being pulled apart again, and I hated the idea of being separated from a sibling I didn't even have. "I'm sorry," I said, resting my palm against his arm on instinct. A pitiful attempt at comfort. "Most folks in Bliss are on about their fifth generation here. It's another reason they care so much about everything that goes on."

His gaze dropped to my hand on him, before meeting my eyes with a smile. "I'm glad you're back, Bonnie Balfour. This town has gotten a whole lot more interesting with you in it."

I released his arm and smiled.

Across the massive lawn, Nathan Harrington's car slid against the curb, and he climbed out. I tracked him with my gaze as far as the massive gazebo, then lost sight of him in the crowd beyond.

"Any news on what brought the detective to town?" Zander asked, distinct curiosity in his gaze.

I wasn't sure why he was asking. For the newspaper? Or something else?

The small screech of microphone feedback stilled the gathering crowd and turned all eyes to Cami at a podium erected outside the gazebo, saving me from the question. A line of official-looking people stood shoulder to shoulder beside her. "Welcome!" she said, before beginning to thank the crowd from the mic.

I scanned the nearby faces once more, searching for my parents.

Mason appeared at the edge of the grass as my gaze swept in that direction.

I watched him approach with bated breath, hopeful there would be news about the crystal vase he'd taken from my shop. Confirmation the item wasn't the murder weapon was my first and biggest hope. The discovery of fingerprints on it, other than mine, was a close runner up.

He smiled when he drew near.

"That's him?" Zander asked. "The detective?"

I nodded. "That's him."

Mason stopped at our sides and winked at me. "Hope I didn't miss anything."

My face flooded with heat as Zander looked at me. My furious blush probably lit my freckles up brighter than the twinkle lights around the square.

"Nothing yet," Zander said, swinging his attention back to Mason.

"I don't think we've met," Mason said. "I'm Detective Mason Wright." He offered Zander his hand. "You work for the paper, right?"

"Yeah. Zander Jones. Nice to finally meet you. I've heard a lot of stories." He glanced at me, probably thinking of all the gossip that had been flying from the day Mason arrived.

"That so?" Mason said, turning a small smile in my direction. "All good things I hope."

Zander frowned, apparently noting the brief exchange between Mason and me. "Not from her," he said. "Bonnie hasn't mentioned you at all."

I gave Zander a curious glance, unsure if his words were intended to clear me as a gossip, or if he'd wanted to make sure Mason knew I hadn't brought him up for other, possibly personal, reasons.

We were all silent a long moment before Zander stepped back and lifted a palm. "I'm going to see about some lemonade. Anyone want anything?"

Mason and I shook our heads, then watched as he walked away.

The unnamed friction left in his wake bothered me, but I wasn't sure why, or what I could do about it. So, I inhaled the sweet perfection of the otherwise flawless southern night and turned my eyes back to Mason.

"Friend of yours?" he asked.

"These are all friends of mine," I said, gesturing around the square. "They'll be friends of yours too, if you stay a while. How long are you staying?" I asked, hoping to sound more casual than I felt about whatever the answer would be.

"That depends," he said, expression serious and possibly a little conflicted.

"On?"

Mason peeled his gaze from mine and tipped his head toward Cami, who was wrapping up her speech. "On how the cake walk works, I guess."

I gasped, then smiled. "You don't know how cake walks work?"

"No."

I pressed a palm to my collarbone, and he grinned.

"Tell me about it," he said, nodding again to the gazebo.

I forced my attention to the podium as the head of the Chamber of Commerce stepped up to the mic.

"There are probably tables set up inside the gazebo. The cakes and pies will be lined up on those tables, and each will be assigned a number. There are Xs on the floor made with tape. All the participants stand on an X until the music starts, then everyone walks in a circle until the music stops. Someone will pull a number from a hat, and whoever is standing on the X beside that number wins that pie or cake. The music begins again, and the process repeats until all the cakes have new homes."

He frowned. "So it's not a game of skill?"

"No. It's chance. Like life."

He considered that a moment. "That's less fun."

I shook my head in faux disappointment. "Competitive much?"

"Very much," he said without hesitation. "Which brings me back to why I'm here."

My stomach knotted. "Yeah?"

"The lab called about an hour ago. Your prints were the only ones found on the vase."

I swallowed a brutal groan. "Any chance that doesn't matter because it's definitely not the murder weapon?" I asked.

"Nope."

My mouth went dry as I realized how much trouble I could possibly be in. The lab confirmed my prints on a murder weapon, used at a crime scene where I was found. My ears began to ring with panic.

Applause erupted, and the curtains on the gazebo were opened, revealing the cake walk inside. Contestants jogged forward, along with a regional news crew Cami had persuaded to cover the event. A moment later, everyone stopped. Contestants' expressions changed to confusion and horror. Applause turned to gasps and whispers.

"Oh, my goodness," Cami's voice projected through the nearby microphone. Her eyes sought mine in the crowd.

Mason grabbed my wrist and towed me forward, until the full scene came into view.

Someone had smashed each of my donations to smithereens, utterly destroying the pies and the pie plates they'd arrived in.

CHAPTER TWENTY-ONE

*M*y parents followed me home from the square. They'd arrived with fries from a vendor cart shortly after the cake walk had become a crime scene and Mason had been pulled into sorting the situation.

Dad checked my little cottage for killers before letting me inside. I locked myself in the bedroom with a can of organic pepper spray, courtesy of my mama, then fielded concerned text messages late into the night. Cami, Zander, my folks and Mason had sent words of concern and encouragement until my eyes had become heavy enough to rest.

I kept Clyde close and the curtains drawn until morning because anyone willing to destroy five pecan pies was a true monster in my book and far beyond the point of reasoning.

I rose, fatigued, but thankful for morning at five A.M.

A pair of headlights flashed on as I entered the kitchen, and I was sure I recognized the familiar taillights of Mason's Jeep as it rolled away.

I took my time getting ready for the day, then selected a striped bow tie for Clyde that matched my mint-green blouse and packed him into his carrier.

Together, we made the trip to my folks' house for breakfast. The day was overcast and nearly as gloomy as my mood. The weatherman had called for potentially volatile spring showers, which meant the wind and humidity had swollen my hair into unnatural proportions before I'd climbed into the truck.

With any luck, the only storms I'd see today were literal.

Dad appeared on their porch only moments after my tires hit the gravel lane. He met me at my car door when I parked, then hugged me before carrying Clyde inside.

We ate with Mama, in a strange, charged silence. We'd traded dozens of texts last night and were all visibly and emotionally exhausted, as well as equally worried about what might come next.

None of us finished our breakfast.

Afterward, Mama stacked our dishes in the sink while Dad brought them in from the dining room table. The ominous weather had forced us to eat indoors, yet one more reminder things were off-kilter in our world. "Are you sure you want to go to work today?" Mama asked. "No one would expect you to, and this day could get nasty," she said casting a woeful glance through the window above her sink.

"I need to keep showing up and smiling," I said. Tough as that might be. "Folks need to see I'm not going anywhere, and I haven't done anything wrong."

Mama turned the water off and faced me, leaning heavily against the big farmhouse sink. She'd wrangled her wild hair into a cute messy bun, but I hadn't bothered to fight with mine. The wild ginger mop I'd been born with was fully out of control. A physical representation of my life.

I felt unbidden emotion sting my eyes. "I'm sorry I've worried you and Daddy so much."

She pulled me into a hug. "Come here, silly. You know your father and I adore you completely. We could never be upset with you, and we're not now. None of the things happening to you are your fault, and we've never been happier than we are to have you back in our lives."

"Thank you," I said, squeezing her tight.

Mama released me, and I wiped my eyes as a renegade tear swiveled over my cheek. "I just hate I've caused you so much stress lately. I never meant to do that, and I know your lives were nearly perfect before."

"Only nearly," Dad said, moving into the room with the last of the juice glasses from the table. "But not one hundred percent until you came home." He rubbed my back and looked seriously into my eyes. "You might not remember, but you've always made us worry. It's in your nature. You were born a spitfire, just like your mother. All action and no sense."

"Hey!" Mama protested, snapping a dish towel in his direction. "We have plenty of sense."

He chuckled. "Sure, on practical things, but neither of you can pass up an adventure. It's why Bonnie chose a college in a big city and the reason you married me." He pulled her into an embrace that warmed me from head to toe, even across the small room.

"You have always been my greatest adventure," she whispered to him as he pressed a kiss to her forehead.

I wiped another round of unbidden tears.

"It's no wonder you got tangled in this mess," Dad said, dragging his attention back to me. "You like to be involved. It's like you can't help yourself."

"It's true," Mama said. "You tried out for every school play and sports team. You were the first to volunteer on any community outing."

Dad nodded. "Clean up trash at the campground? Bonnie's on it. Weed the mulch beds around the local retirement community? Call Bonnie. Need teenage chaperones for a preschool field trip?"

Mama pointed to me. "Bonnie's your girl."

"There was a point in your high school career when you knew more folks in this town than we did," Dad said, "because you were out there getting your hands messy anywhere and anytime you could."

"It only makes sense you'd grab onto this," Mama said. "You found Viola. You know she was murdered. You want justice. I think you'd have jumped in head first even if no one ever suspected you."

I frowned, not completely sure I agreed. I'd been forced to get involved. Hadn't I? "You're saying I'm a busybody."

Mama pulled away from Dad and grinned. "No. He's saying you've always been a busy body." She paused between the last two words. "And don't get me started on all the times I had to pick you up from school because you thought someone was being bullied. Pick on an underdog in front of my baby and there was hell to pay."

I laughed. "You taught me that."

"Darn skippy," she said. "I learned it from my mama." Her face lit with a broad smile at that. "I forgot to tell you! Mama called last night, and she's coming home to see you soon!"

"Gigi's coming?" I asked, not quite believing my ears. A thousand amazing childhood memories raced instantly through my mind.

"Yes! She won't let us pick her up, of course," Mama said. "So, she's taking a bus, but she's coming! I didn't get an exact date, but soon!"

Dad signed the cross and received another snap with Mama's towel.

Before I was ready to leave them, duty called, and I packed Clyde into his carrier.

My folks walked me to my borrowed truck, concern on both their brows.

"You know," Dad said, as I strapped Clyde into the passenger side. "We were talking about this investigation of yours before we fell asleep last night, and we really think you should let the sheriff's department handle things. They have training and experience. Word around town is that the detective from Cleveland used to work with the FBI. Let him be the one getting threatened. Not you. Not again."

My chest pinched at his words, proof inside that Mama had lied to me. I *had* stressed and worried them. I didn't want to be the reason they were unhappy, even for a minute, but I couldn't stop looking for the person who suddenly seemed to be hunting me. And I also couldn't lie to my folks.

Dad sighed. "This is one more reason I'm glad we aren't rich," he said to Mama, tugging her under his arm. "Money brings folks a lot of things, but trouble is one of them."

Mama set her head against his chest. "Money isn't bad," she countered. "But it can bring out the worst in some."

I watched them a minute, letting their words settle in. And I thought of Viola's son once more.

I'd seen him at the square last night before the cake walk, but I hadn't seen where he went once the crowd and gazebo obscured him. It wasn't the first time I could place him near the scene of a crime against me.

I climbed behind the wheel, lost in thought, while Mama and Dad waved goodbye.

The trip to town passed in a flash, and I was surprised to see the square roll into view.

The sidewalks and grassy oval were empty as I approached. Only a handful of folks walking dogs were outside, braving the wind and impending storm. Yellow crime-scene tape flapped wickedly on hearty gusts of air through the gazebo.

I parked the pickup outside Bless Her Heart and climbed down from the cab with Clyde in tow. Wind whipped my hair into my eyes and swung Clyde's carrier in my grasp.

A pair of women stood outside my shop's door, watching as I approached.

"Hello," I said, slightly wary. Neither looked especially familiar.

Were they here for details about last night's hubbub? Or seeking the earliest spoonful of gossip? Was it even possible they simply wanted to shop?

"We weren't sure what time you opened," the older one said. "We saw you'd be here soon and decided to wait." She pointed to the posted hours.

"Welcome," I said, stepping around them to unlock the door. "I'm Bonnie Balfour, and this is Bless Her Heart." I let them in and switched on the lights, then freed Clyde from his carrier.

The ladies made soft ooh and aah sounds as the room illuminated.

"Thanks," I said. I tucked Clyde's carrier behind the counter, then went to meet them near the rack of Viola's gowns. "Is there anything I can help you find?"

The ladies pulled excited eyes from the dress rack to me.

The older woman offered me her hand. "I'm Heather Winters," she said. "I teach eleventh grade English at the high school. This is Maria Johns."

The younger, quieter woman smiled. "This is my first year as a freshman science teacher. I moved up from Talla-hassee about six years ago, but I was at the elementary school until last fall."

I smiled. "Are you looking for something special?" I nodded to the gowns. "Chaperoning the prom?"

Heather pursed her lips, seeming a little awkward and unsure. "I overheard a student of mine bragging about the gown she's wearing to prom. She said she got it here, and I know this is none of my business, but that girl and all her siblings have received Blessings in a Backpack for as long as I've known them, which is always."

"Blessings in a Backpack?" I asked, unsure what that was or how it was connected to my shop.

"It's a program for food-insecure children," she said. "The community collects non-perishable donations and assembles selections of staples like peanut butter, applesauce, bread, crackers, things like that, into as many individual bags as needed. While classes are in session, school administration puts a bag into the backpack of any student who isn't guaranteed a meal over the weekend or extended break. During the school year, our cafeterias provide breakfast and lunch, free if needed, but these kids are on their own when they aren't at school."

I pressed a palm to my heart. "That's a wonderful program. I'm so glad you started it."

Heather smiled warmly. "We didn't start it. The program has been around longer than I have. You probably never knew about it because you didn't need it, and most kids who need it, don't mention it because it's uncomfortable for them."

"Oh." I nodded. "Right. Sorry. How can I help?"

"We assemble the bags on the first Tuesday of every month at the bus garage," Heather said. "All are welcome, but we're actually here to talk about your gowns."

Maria nodded. "Lexi Holcomb posted an image of her gown online. It was gorgeous, and if it truly came from here, and she was able to afford it..." She glanced at Heather, who smiled warmly, encouraging her to continue. "We thought we could help some other girls afford their dresses too. The teachers took up a collection."

I stepped forward and hugged them, interrupting her

story. I got the gist, and maybe my emotions were on the fritz lately, but my eyes stung once more.

We broke the embrace with matching red faces and goofy smiles.

"Sorry," I said. "Y'all are just really wonderful. I can definitely help." I stroked a hand down the buttery material of my nearest gown, slowly wrapping my mind around an idea as it came. "What if we set a day that works for the girls and their mamas, or whoever needs to be here, and we meet at seven, when I normally close for the night. I'll ask my mama and my best friend to help. I'll have refreshments, and the girls can take as long as they'd like to choose whichever dress works best for them. I'll take measurements for any resizing that needs to be done, and that's on the house. As long as I don't have to buy anything additional to make the alterations, you can keep your money. Or better yet, donate it to Blessings in a Backpack."

The women came at me, arms wide and hugging me tight once more.

I laughed as my eyes blurred and stung.

Heather stepped away first, then smiled brightly. "I almost forgot. We brought donations."

"What?" I asked, following as they hurried for the door.

Outside, Maria popped the hatch of her small SUV and pulled out multiple laundry baskets piled with dress clothes, gowns folded neatly across the tops. "The teachers have been collecting these since Christmas," she said, squinting against the wind and cold mist that had begun to fall. "Some of the styles are old, but these are all in great shape. Most were only worn once." She handed a basket to me, then stacked two more for Heather.

We hurried inside with them, then lined them on my counter. I marveled at the generosity piled there. "This is amazing. Thank you, and please thank your fellow teachers.

I'll get every one of these items steamed and updated as necessary, then into the right hands."

I gave the ladies some flyers to pass out among their friends and hang in the teacher's lounge, then added my cell phone number and personal email to the back of one. "Hang onto this so we can arrange an evening to invite the girls out to choose dresses."

My heart soared as they walked away, and I was reminded once again how proud I was to be a part of this community.

CHAPTER TWENTY-TWO

The storm came fast and hard, before the sun drove it away. Within hours, the world was dry, all evidence of the rain utterly gone, and I moved on to a new project.

I spent a longer amount of time than expected adding the words Bless Her Heart in large golden script to my storefront window. The result was stunning and deeply aesthetically pleasing with the new white exterior paint. My shop was officially no longer an eyesore. In fact, it now blended with the pertly colored array of shops on the square. It felt a little like putting on a team jersey, and I planned to wear mine proudly.

Clyde shadowed me as I put my supplies away and went into the small restroom near my office to wash up. He followed me back as well, racing alongside my legs and occasionally in front of my feet. I wasn't sure how I managed not to trip over him daily.

The bells above my shop door jingled as I rounded the corner.

Zander strode inside, scanning the space, then smiling

when he spotted me. "I hoped I'd catch you," he said. "Love what you've done with the exterior."

"Thanks." A little thrill ran through me at the realization of all I'd accomplished, thanks to Gretchen's help, Cami's encouragement and my folks' support. Being productive felt so much better than being idle. It was a shame I'd spent the previous few months like a hermit. In hindsight, I'd probably ignored the shop's exterior deliberately, at least on a subconscious level, because it would've been impossible to hide while standing on a busy sidewalk. "What brings you by?" I asked.

Zander moved into the store, approaching me with a gentle grin. "Just checking in. I wanted to be sure you were okay after the big pie debacle."

"I'm good. Better than I have been in a while." I smiled, loving that it was true.

My eyes landed on Clyde, now perched on the bookcase where Viola's murder weapon had once been, and my throat thickened.

"Making any progress on the private investigation?" he asked.

"No." I pressed my lips briefly. "And I'm on the fence about how much I want to keep pushing," I said honestly. "I'd love to know what happened to Viola that night, and I definitely want her killer caught before he or she stops going after my baked goods and starts coming for me."

"But?"

I tipped my head over one shoulder and sighed. "I'm scaring my parents, and I hate that. They're so sweet and kind, and I feel as if my drama is messing up their lives."

Zander's cheek lifted in an amused half smile. "That's very considerate. I shouldn't be surprised that's your reasoning, and not straight fear for yourself."

"I'm more concerned about what it would do to my folks

if I got hurt than about actually getting hurt," I said. "That's not to say I'm unafraid or fearless or anything. My folks just feel like the top priority, I guess. And honestly, I'm kind of mad about my threats. I think whoever is doing this is a rotten human being who killed a sick old lady. They should've come forward by now, done the right thing, and confessed. Instead, they're branching out."

Zander's eyebrow kicked up. "You think a killer would ever come forward and confess? Isn't that going against who they are?"

"I'd like to think most people do the right thing when they can."

He heaved a long breath, then put his hands into his pockets. "I have something I want to tell you, but I don't want you to think I'm gossiping. I hear so much stuff in this town, and at my job, you'd never believe it. I don't believe it half the time, but this made me think you'd want to know. Just do me a favor and don't repeat it, especially not with my name attached."

My brows rose and my stomach fluttered. The devil on my shoulder chortled. "Okay," I said, holding my composure, even as my mind began to splinter with guesses at his possible next words. "What is it?"

"I was putting my kayak in the river early this morning, and I overheard a couple talking on the trail a few yards away. There were a lot of trees between us, and the river is a little loud, but the voices were fervent, and I went up the hill to listen. I'm not proud, but something told me what they were saying was important. If it hadn't been, I would've gone back to my kayak."

"Okay," I repeated, gripping my hands at my waist, reminding myself not to grab him or attempt to shake the story out. "Go on."

"The woman was upset about an emotional affair the man

had been having. She was deeply hurt and thought that what he'd done was worse than if the relationship had been fast and physical."

I didn't disagree, but my interest waned slightly. I didn't know enough couples in town to care about any sort of infidelity. Unless… "It wasn't my parents, was it?" I asked, startled by the idea and the words as they flew from my brain to my tongue.

My mama and dad were the only couple I cared about in Bliss at the moment, enough to have a personal stake in the matter anyway. Enough for Zander to tiptoe around about the information's delivery.

He snapped his chin back. "No, of course not," he said, looking as if I'd lost my mind. "I'm talking about the Runsfords."

It took a moment for the name to register. Then the older couple popped clearly into mind. "Teddy and his wife?" They had to be in their seventies. And Teddy had an emotional affair?

Zander nodded.

I grimaced. "Who was Teddy having an…" The answer registered before I could finish asking the question.

Zander tented his brows. "Yep."

"He and Viola?"

"Apparently," Zander said. "And Mrs. Runsford was livid. She was telling him all about it during their walk. I jumped into my kayak and took off before they saw me, but it seemed like information you would want. I debated going to the police station, in case it was relevant to Viola's case, but admitting to eavesdropping on a couple's private argument in the woods felt a little icky and embarrassing. I know you're focused on Nathan, but this might be important to think about too."

Zander was right on all counts. Nathan had been my

most likely suspect, given all he had to gain by his mother's death. I wasn't sure why Teddy would've wanted to hurt a woman he cared about, but Mrs. Runsford would've had reason to argue with Viola, and to possibly lash out.

"Thanks," I told Zander. "I'm glad you shared that with me. I'm not sure what I can, or will, do with this information, but I promise not to link you to it if I tell anyone."

He nodded, patted my counter, then turned on his heels and left.

I stared after him, imagining sweet Mrs. Runsford as a killer.

***

Before I knew it, the sun was setting, and my workday was done. I'd finalized a number of plans for the grand opening and created a menu of cheap and easy, but impressive, hors d'oeuvres. I'd handle the food and the baking to help with the budget. Mama promised floral bouquets and arrangements that would wow my guests, and I had enough donated trinkets, paperweights and knick knacks to create fifty or more swag bags with thank you cards, tiny treasures, and information on how to contact me if guests had questions or wanted to donate in the future.

Between phone calls and customers, I'd been lost in thoughts of Teddy and his alleged emotional affair all afternoon. The possibility reminded me that everyone needed someone who understood them and who listened. Without a confidant and sounding board, life was tough, frustrating and lonely. I'd gotten a therapist when I'd realized my marriage was one-sided, but I didn't dare judge. My life in Atlanta had come with privilege, opportunity and an excellent healthcare package. I was learning firsthand these days just how easily any situation could go pear-shaped. Honestly, the more I thought about it, the worse I felt for both Runsfords. Mrs. Runsford had been betrayed, and I knew from personal experience, the minute I'd been served my divorce papers, that betrayal was a gutting emotion. As for Teddy, I, too, had felt alone in my marriage, which might be why he'd become attached to Viola. Or maybe I was projecting.

Secondhand news of their rift was upsetting enough. I couldn't imagine what they were going through. I just hoped whatever weird love triangle had formed between the septuagenarian trio hadn't ended in murder.

I ushered Clyde into his carrier at seven sharp, looking forward to my evening off. I had a lot to think about. "I'll bet you're ready for your dinner," I said, scratching his head before zipping the container closed. "We'll call Mason when we get home and tell him what we heard today. He'll know what to do with the info." I flipped my CLOSED sign, then locked up on our way out.

We cruised around the square before heading home. "Let's check out the new window stencil from the road," I told Clyde. "I want to be sure it flows with the surrounding storefronts the way I planned, and catches folks' eyes in a nice way, even in a car."

I smiled as I made the loop and approached once more. The bright white paint and golden stencil gave Bless Her Heart a majorly upgraded appearance. The twinkle lights and pale-green taffeta gown in my display was sure to pull shoppers inside for a closer look.

I stopped at the light, pleased and proud of my progress in making my shop a destination instead of a dive. Nathan Harrington's fancy black sedan caught my eye, and I groaned. He'd parked outside the pub again, and I couldn't help wondering what was so fantastic about the place. There were a half-dozen great locations to eat on the square.

Clyde meowed, and I wondered if maybe I should hop out and place a to-go order for dinner.

From the length of the line, half the town wanted in on the daily special. A baked potato deal with a sign inviting guests to "Come in and get loaded."

"You know what?" I said. "In for a penny. In for a pound." I parked before I could change my mind, then hopped out and unfastened Clyde's carrier. "You can come with me. Try to be still and pretend you're just an adorable wallet in a really big purse."

Nathan noticed me almost immediately from his seat at an outdoor table. He swung an arm over the back of his chair and twisted to face me. "Hey." He smiled lazily, high-end sunglasses propped on his balding head. His motorcycle jacket looked too small, and as if he was trying too hard. His loafers and dark jeans screamed businessman. His ruddy cheeks screamed sunburn, and his general disposition said tipsy.

I hoped that last part would work in my favor because regardless of the recent scoop on the Runsfords, Nathan had always been my main suspect.

I lifted my hand in a little hip-high wave upon approach, and his grin widened.

"I've seen you around town staring at me," he said, his words slurring a little. "Why don't you come over here and let me buy you a drink?"

"No, thank you," I said. "I have dinner plans, but I'd love to chat for a minute, if you don't mind."

He tented his bushy salt-and-pepper brows, then patted the table, apparently surprised I hadn't declined. He pointed to an empty seat across from him, where a glass of water had begun to sweat.

"No, thank you," I said. "I won't take up much of your

time. Do you have company?" I asked, motioning to the drink.

He waved a dismissive hand. "It's fine. We can talk a while. You know, I'm new in town. Maybe you can show me around."

"What makes you think I'm from here?" I asked, stopping at the narrow wrought iron fence separating the café's outdoor seating from sidewalk passersby.

"Isn't everyone?" he asked, chuckling softly. "Who moves here intentionally?"

I bristled, offended by his dig at my town.

"You run that store over there, don't you?" he asked, motioning behind me, presumably to Bless Her Heart. An icy drop of warning rolled down my spine, curling my toes inside my sandals. "You know where I work?" Had he visited my shop too? Perhaps to smash a cupcake?

"Yeah." He smiled. "I told you. I've seen you around. I've noticed you," he added, emphasizing the final three words. "And I've seen you noticing me."

Clyde gave a low, guttural moan, then hissed.

Nathan cut his eyes to my bag, as if just realizing it was actually a cat carrier. "What is that?"

"My cat," I said, and Nathan's lips curled into a slick grinchy grin.

"Your little kitty doesn't like me," he said, before taking another drink of the nearly empty beer in front of him.

I glanced quickly over my shoulder toward his car at the curb, then back to find him, swaying slightly in his seat. "Are you okay?" I asked. "You're not planning to drive when you leave here are you?"

"Maybe. What's it to you? My mom just died. I get a pass."

"I'm sorry about your mama. What happened to her wasn't right."

He didn't look surprised by my statement, so I went on.

"I was the one who found her that night," I said, quietly, forcing the words through a dry mouth and watching for his expression to change.

His brows furrowed and his face reddened. "You're the one asking questions about me."

I nodded, sucking in a shuddered breath. There were no more secrets now. "I saw you here, in Bliss, on the day she died."

Pain washed over his features, and he blinked long and slow. "She asked me to help her make some decisions. She was sick, you know?"

"And moving to Nashville," I added.

He frowned. "Yeah. Not that her staff was any help. That woman tried so hard to keep her here, it was like she was her mother. But she was my mother," he said, beating a palm to his chest like a tipsy gorilla.

"Emma?" I asked.

"Yeah." He nodded. "Emily."

I rolled my eyes. "Emma Lee," I corrected, saying the two names distinctly. Lee must be her middle name.

"That's what I said."

I puffed out my cheeks. It was easy enough to understand why Viola's caregivers wouldn't want to see her leave the state with this guy. Kin or not. "Were you handling the estate's transfer to the historical society?" I took a step closer, and Clyde growled once more. "I saw you with Mr. Totoro."

Nathan raised his brows and examined me again, this time with less physical interest and more unbridled distaste. "Me and Ricky go way back. So what?"

"Curious," I said. "Do you have any siblings? Children?"

His jaw locked and he stood, slow and unsteady, towering over me until the little wrought iron fence between us didn't feel like nearly enough. "Why are you asking?"

I swallowed hard, hating my big mouth and head full of

questions. "I'm just trying to figure out what really happened to your mama. That's all. Someone's been following me and threatening me almost every day since I found her. I'm not sure who else to talk to. You seem like the one with all the answers."

His stance relaxed slightly, and he nearly lost his balance, leaning against his small table for support.

Clyde hissed, and I twisted at the waist, moving him away from the perceived threat.

Nathan's gaze dropped to the bag on my arm. "You ever hear the expression, curiosity killed the cat?" I stumbled back, his words cutting like knives. My cheeks heated and stomach clenched, then I ran away. I secured Clyde in the pickup, then climbed behind the wheel, hating that my parents' flower farm logo was painted brightly down both sides.

I jerked the truck into Drive and pulled away, daring one last peek in Nathan's direction.

He'd turned back to his table, where Zander was taking a seat.

CHAPTER TWENTY-THREE

I made the final turn away from the pub when a commotion at the bookshop drew my attention.

The front door had swung open, and Liz had stormed out, her curly brown hair looking especially wild, and her expression matching. She dropped her arms to her sides and peered back through the window of What the Dickens, as if something inside had really peeved her off, and she'd needed a minute to regroup.

I pulled up at the curb and hollered through my open passenger window. "You okay?"

She turned slowly, smoothing her hair and shirt, then breathing easier when she seemed to recognize me. "No," she said with a small laugh. "This store makes me crazy."

I shifted into park and smiled. "So, there's no one in there that I need to have a talking to?"

Liz tipped her head slightly left then right. "No one who'd listen," she said, sounding as defeated as she suddenly appeared.

I climbed out, curiosity piqued, then rounded the hood of

my borrowed truck to meet her on the sidewalk. "What do you mean?"

Liz pressed her lips together, obviously contemplating what to say. "I'm trying to make the store more accessible for people. Less cluttered. More organized. Someplace folks can find what they want without spending an eternity wandering around, or ideally, some sort of system I can use to help shoppers find what they want."

"I can help with that," I said. "I'm kind of an organization nut."

Liz began shaking her head before I'd finished talking. "Not here," she said. "Normal things don't work here. I put things in order, but they don't stay that way."

I felt my brow crumple as I glanced at her store. "Maybe you need to clear out some old stock to make it easier to navigate the new."

She hooked her hands on her hips and gave an exasperated laugh. "I'd wondered why no one protested when I inherited Grandmama's bookshop. Now I know. No one else in my family could put up with this."

I set a gentle palm on her shoulder. "I really think I can help. Let's take a look."

She slid her attention from me to her store. "All right. Why not?"

I grabbed Clyde from the truck, then followed Liz into What the Dickens, a crowded space, overrun by books, complete with a second level, railing and loft. "I used to spend hours up there," I told her, "getting lost in books like *Through the Looking-Glass* and *Anne of Green Gables*, while Mama and Gigi attended a book club down here with Hazel."

"Yeah," she agreed. "I loved the loft as a kid. It felt twice as big back then and filled with mysteries waiting to be uncovered. Now it just feels like a mess I can't clean. The book club is still happening monthly. I'm pretty sure they just come to drink wine and eat cheese, but they come." She turned her eyes to me. "You should come. The ladies are a hoot."

"I might. I'll ask Mama too." I trailed my gaze over the room, then up a wooden staircase on the far right wall. Books were stacked everywhere, including on top of and in front of large over-burdened shelves. The light was dim, despite large storefront windows, which were mostly blocked by piles of tomes. Dust motes twinkled and cartwheeled through the air like sparkling silver confetti, and I immediately felt drawn back in time.

Liz bent to swipe a few toppled books from the floor, then sighed. "I tried to make a tidy romance section, and this is what happened."

"The stacks fell?" I guessed, setting Clyde's carrier on the ground, then collecting a few more books near my feet.

Clyde made a small chattering sound, like the one he saved for squirrels and birds.

Liz cast him a look, then continued cleaning. "Something like that. I tried to take pictures of the overall effect. Didn't work." She pulled her phone from her back pocket. "It looked great for about five minutes," she growled, eyes scanning the store.

I followed her gaze, but saw nothing more than endless books.

She turned the little screen to face me, but a series of light streaks and colored blurs were all that centered the screen. "Darn it." She put the phone away. "And this is why the people of this town think I'm nuts." She collapsed onto an old rocking chair and let her arms fall over the rests.

"No one thinks you're nuts. My pictures don't always turn out either. It's not a big deal."

She laughed, then smiled and shook her head. "You really are a nice person. Everyone says so."

"They do?"

She nodded. "Yeah. I'm glad we met."

"Me too." I matched her smile with one of my own, then turned to place the books I'd gathered onto a pile at my side.

They fell immediately to the floor.

"They don't go there," she said, leaving her rocker to pick the books up once more. She placed them at the top of a pile several inches taller than her head. "Don't ask me how anyone is supposed to find them there."

I looked at the pile, then decided Liz needed support rather than an organizational system, at least today. "Maybe you can play up the beautifully organized chaos theme. Like the wand store in Harry Potter."

She laughed. "Maybe. The most I've been able to change in three years are the window displays."

"They're really nice displays," I said, recalling the beautiful setups on either side of her store's front door. "Readers can't help but come inside, I'll bet."

"We do get a lot of foot traffic." She sighed.

I wondered who she meant by "we" but decided not to ask. Instead, I headed down one of the overcrowded aisles. "Did you say there's a romance section? I'm a sucker for happy endings and a man in uniform. Doesn't have to be military. Firemen. Doctors. I don't discriminate. I just love when a hero has devoted himself to a higher calling."

"Detectives?" she asked.

"No," I answered too quickly, immediately suspicious she'd bought into the gossip about me and Detective Wright. "Why?"

Liz frowned. "You said you might come to the mystery book club, so I thought…"

I relaxed and tried to look less accusatory. "Sorry. I thought you had someone in mind."

"Perry Mason?"

I laughed. "I prefer female investigators." *Maybe I should be reading some of those,* I thought, *to figure out what I'm missing on my current amateur investigation.*

"Oh, well, the romances are scattered," she said, pulling me back to the conversation. "That's the problem I was trying to fix, but the one you want is probably right there."

"Right where?" I asked, turning to look at her.

She shrugged, then flopped back into the rocker. "Usually what people want is right in front of them."

I glanced around, and noticed a tattered paperback with a man on the front. His rigid stance and brooding expression told me he was an honorable protector of justice. The badge and sidearm helped. My goofy heart fluttered. "I see one," I told her, lifting the book to learn more. I turned it over in my fingertips, skimming the back cover for details.

When an undercover FBI agent finds an irresistible woman at the center of his new investigation, he's soon falling hard and fast for the beautiful witness. He'll do anything to protect her from danger, but who will protect his heart from her?

I set the book down. "Maybe not this one."

I wound my way through a few more rows of books, then smacked my toe into something on the floor. "Oops." I bent to retrieve the book and stilled.

It was a copy of the same book I'd put down in the last aisle.

"Do you stock many copies of each book?" I asked, carrying the paperback with me to the front of the store. "I just saw this one in another aisle."

She stretched to her feet, then headed for her register. "I

don't know for sure. It's hard to keep track of inventory around here, as you can probably imagine. But honestly, that's probably our only copy."

I glanced back at the cluttered aisles and considered backtracking to the place where I'd seen the first copy of the book, nonsensically curious to see if it was where I'd left it.

But Nathan's cold words returned with the thought.

"You ever hear the expression, curiosity killed the cat?"

I shivered, then set the book on the counter. "I guess I'll take this one."

Liz rang me up, took my money, then walked me and Clyde to my truck. The sun had set, and twilight colored the world as we parted ways. "Come back anytime," she said. "Enjoy your romance, and don't forget about the book club!"

I smiled, then waved goodbye as Clyde and I rolled away, my new paperback on the bench seat between us.

Nathan's car wasn't at the curb outside the pub when I checked my rearview mirror at the corner. I could only hope Zander had driven him home.

Clyde growled and chattered at the book as I drove, then gave a pained "Merowl" as we turned onto my street.

"Poor kitty," I said, pushing my bottom lip forward. "You're probably starving. How about I add a little shredded chicken to your kibble to make up for delaying your dinner?"

I slowed as my cottage came into view, then used my turn signal out of habit, despite the fact that no one was behind me or in motion anywhere in sight. Sadly, I didn't see Mason's Jeep either.

The pickup's headlights flashed over my front windows, then slid along the cement driveway before landing on the closed garage door.

I reached for my cell phone as a ragged two-word threat came into focus, smeared in mud across the white vinyl door.

FINAL WARNING

———

Mason arrived about twenty minutes later with a white logoed take-out bag from the pub where I'd spoken to Nathan. "Thought you might be hungry." He passed the food to me with a frown.

Delicious deep-fried aromas wafted up from the bag, distracting me, briefly, from my panic. "Do you know how long I've been waiting?"

"About fifteen minutes?" he guessed, shining a light over the garage door.

"Twenty," I corrected. "What if the killer was still here? I could be dead," I grouched, hating the quake in my voice as I spoke.

"Nah," he said, moving carefully across my driveway, snapping pictures of the mud message and surroundings. "If you thought you were in danger, you would've gone to your folks' place or called nine-one-one. Besides, why would a perpetrator with ill-intent warn you they were here?" he asked. "If a killer was waiting for you to come home, he or she would've hidden, not announced their presence. Now, if you'd called me with news of a busted porch light or an open window, I'd have sent a cruiser straight here."

"But you would've stayed and waited for your burger," I accused.

"I was already in line. I'd just placed the order. There's a burger in there for you too."

I rolled my eyes and ignored the happy dance in my stomach. I'd been too panicked to notice before, but I was starving.

When Mason finished processing the crime scene, he sprayed my garage down with the garden hose. "Let's eat!"

I set the bag onto my kitchen table, then pulled out a chair and motioned him to sit. "I'll get us some waters."

Mason unpacked our meals while I filled two glasses with ice, then flooded the cubes with cold water from my fridge. "I wanted to repay you for the casserole buffet the other night," he said. "Especially after I had to run off before dinner last time."

I ferried our drinks back to the table, then took a long, appreciative look at the foil-wrapped burger and paper basket of fries. "You didn't have to do this, but it's perfect. Thank you."

He stuck a finger into his mouth and sucked a dollop of ketchup off the tip.

I averted my eyes and stifled a moan. I was clearly starving.

"Any chance you have security cameras?" He tented his brows in question. "You asked about them outside Ms. Abbott-Harrington's place."

"That's because she has a ginormous estate. This was my grandparents' place. It didn't even have the internet before I moved in." I tucked a salty fry between my lips and sighed with contentment. "These are absolute heaven."

He grinned. "I'm glad you like them. I tried to get a couple of those loaded baked potatoes everyone was waiting on, but they were out. The guy at the counter said it would be another half an hour before they had more."

"I'm glad you didn't wait. I'm more frightened than I appear right now. I'm just distracted by the food."

Mason smiled, then started when Clyde's fuzzy black paw appeared on the table, reaching toward a loose fry from Mason's bag.

"No, no." I shooed my kitty, then promised him cat treats after I finished my meal. I'd already fed him shredded chicken while I waited for Mason. He was going to get chunky if my life stayed in danger much longer.

Mason tossed his burger wrapper and empty paper fry boat into the logoed bag a few minutes later, then wiped his mouth and stretched his long legs beneath the table. He watched me as I nibbled my cooling fries. "Any idea what instigated tonight's warning?"

I considered all the possible answers. Then I took a steadying breath and relayed the news Zander had come to deliver.

Mason chewed on the information a moment. "Emotional affair? That's rough."

"Yeah," I agreed. "I wish I didn't know. It feels too personal."

"Uh huh," he agreed. "And you heard this while you were kayaking at the river?" I nodded, hating the fib, but determined to keep Zander's secret.

Mason sucked his teeth and watched me. "What kind of kayak do you have?"

"What?" I asked, stunned and utterly off guard. The delicious seasoned fries turned to mud in my lying mouth.

"Your kayak," Mason said congenially. "What kind is it? Where do you keep it?" He glanced around my small cottage. "Where do you launch it?"

"Uhm." I forced myself to chew and swallow the mush in my mouth. "At the river."

"Uh huh," he said again. "You know, it's funny because I've started jogging on that trail you mentioned. And I've seen Zander Jones putting a kayak into the water just about every morning since I started. I've never once seen you. I'm not even sure how you work it into your schedule. You leave for work at nine and don't leave there until after dark. You must have to start getting ready every morning by eight. Doesn't leave a lot of time to get over to the river and back after sunrise."

I shrugged, unwilling to tell any more untruths.

Mason watched me squirm. "Is there anything you want to tell me?"

I pressed my lips together.

Mason clasped his hands and set them in his lap, piercing me with his blank cop stare.

"Maybe one thing," I said.

"Great." Mason motioned for me to go ahead.

"Nathan told me he was in town to discuss some things with his mother. When I mentioned seeing Nathan and Totoro together, he said the two of them go way back. Then I saw him having dinner with Zander, who's made it clear he thinks I shouldn't be looking at Nathan as the culprit."

"Zander told you about the Runsfords," Mason said.

I performed a long, slow cat blink, hoping to convey something I wasn't ready to say.

Mason shifted forward, resting his forearms on the table. "Are you telling me you spoke privately to Nathan Harrington about his mother's murder?"

"No. I saw him at the pub. He was sitting at an outdoor table, so I stopped to talk to him. Zander showed up as I drove away."

The detective's gaze darkened, and his jaw set. "So, you spoke publicly to Nathan Harrington, on the sidewalk outside a busy restaurant, about his mother's murder."

I cringed. "Yes?"

He made a low throaty sound and grimaced. "Keep talking."

I recapped the entire chat for Mason, while his face grew slowly redder.

"Half the town could've heard every part of that discussion," he complained.

"Maybe, but Nathan's car was gone when I left the bookstore a little while later. He had time to come over here and leave that message on my garage if he left the café soon after I did." "The same is true about every other person who heard you pressing on about his mother's murder." Mason wadded a napkin then shot it into the paper bag.

"I didn't think of that," I admitted. "I was focused on him, not the crowd. No one seemed to be paying any attention to us." My stomach flipped, and I pushed the rest of my food away, lifting my glass of iced water instead. "I know I need to find a way to let this go. I can't believe someone came up to my house like this. It's terrifying."

"Agreed. You're sort of a big pain for such a little package."

"Gee, thanks."

"But…" he said. "You didn't let me finish."

I crossed my arms and narrowed my eyes.

"But I'm getting used to all your troublemaking," he said. "I never thought I'd say this the day we met, but I'd kind of like to keep you around a while, Bonnie Balfour."

I rolled my eyes, fighting a small, unintentional smile.

"How about we make a deal," Mason said. "You stick to your job and steer clear of mine. I'll double down on my end and wrap this up in a day or two."

I snorted an indelicate little laugh. "Oh, okay. Confident much?"

His cocky smile appeared in answer. "You do your part, and hopefully the next murder scene I'm called to won't feature you as the victim."

I cringed. "You have a real way with words."

"Maybe, but I never mince them," he said. "So, is that a deal?"

I nodded, my stomach twisting violently at the thought of becoming his next case. "Deal."

CHAPTER TWENTY-FOUR

I packed Clyde into the carrier and drove to my parents' house after Mason left. His comment about me becoming a murder victim was more than enough to keep me squirming through the night, and I knew Mama and Dad would understand if I didn't want to be alone.

They met me with open arms. Mama poured three glasses of dandelion wine and ushered me to the dining room table. Dad arrived a moment later with a stack of new puzzle boxes and a smile.

"I've been waiting for a reason to break one of these out." He wagged his eyebrows as he fanned the options. "What will it be? Antique Toy Store? Enchanted Library? Or Kaleidoscope Kitties?"

"Cats," Mama and I answered in near unison.

Did he even have to ask?

It was long after midnight when we finished the puzzle, a large charcuterie tray and two bottles of wine. My eyelids were, thankfully, heavy. I attributed that fact to the wine and the company. Whatever was happening in my life, I was safe and at ease with my parents.

I followed Dad through the house, checking window and door locks, then climbed the steps for bed. I pushed away worrisome thoughts, focusing instead on the lighter conversations of the evening. My folks, for example, were looking forward to taking Petal Pusher, their flower cart, to the Makers Market on the town square tomorrow morning. I couldn't help but get a little excited along with Mama. Fingers crossed, my storefront's recent facelift would be enough to pull a large amount of market patrons across the street and entice them inside.

I slid beneath the covers of my childhood bed with happy, hopeful thoughts, then drifted to sleep in an epic shrine to my youth, complete with boy-band posters, hot-pink walls and a lacy canopy overhead.

I woke early the next morning to the muffled, cheerful sounds of my parents' voices in the kitchen and the blessed, blissful scent of brewing coffee. I showered, then dressed for work as quickly as possible, eager to see my folks and dig into breakfast, which smelled unmistakably like Dad's blueberry pancakes when I opened my bedroom door. Dad had given me the recipe as a gift when I married, and though I'd tried to recreate his magic many times, my version never compared.

I twisted still damp locks of hair into a tight chignon, then secured it with bobby pins from my vanity, in much too big of a hurry to blow it all dry.

My phone buzzed with an incoming text as I finished, and I flipped the device over to see who'd sent the note.

Shockingly, there were five unopened messages. Apparently I'd missed four while I was in the shower.

The first was from Zander.

Zander: Detective Wright just called me to the station. Any ideas?

It was nearly eight-thirty A.M., and Zander's message had arrived at 8:04 A.M. Had Mason called Zander first thing this morning because I'd told him I saw Zander having dinner with Nathan last night? Or was it because he knew it was Zander who'd told me about the Runsfords?

I chewed my lip, then my fingernail, before responding with the only answer I could.

Bonnie: No clue. Keep me posted?

The next two texts were from Emma, and they'd arrived with photos of vintage heels, wraps and clutches.

Emma: Nathan and Teddy said I can have these

Emma: I'd like to donate them to your section honoring Viola. I think that's wonderful, what you're doing.

I nearly squealed at that stroke of luck and generosity, especially with the high school girls coming to look for prom dresses soon. I responded immediately, hoping to get my hands on the offerings sooner rather than later. If anything needed to be touched up or repaired, I wanted plenty of time to get the work done.

Bonnie: Amazing! Thank you!

Bonnie: When can we meet?

I scrolled to my newest message while I waited for Emma and Zander to respond. The fourth and fifth texts were from Mason. I ignored the flutter in my stomach at the sight of his name. The reaction was clearly a result of my inflamed curiosity, caused by his early-morning call to Zander. I read the texts quickly, then backtracked and read them again.

Mason: Making progress on my end of our bargain

Mason: Meet me at the station for lunch?

It took a minute for the meaning of his first text to settle in.

According to our bargain over burgers last night, I was

supposed to stay out of the killer's way, and in turn, Mason would find and arrest the guilty party. A chill ran down my spine as I processed that. Was I right about Nathan as a killer? Or was it possible that what Zander had overheard from the Runsfords had become relevant to the case? Could Mrs. Runsford have lashed out at Viola for her emotional affair with Teddy?

Then another thing occurred to me. If Mason told Zander he'd gotten the information from me, after I'd told Zander I'd keep his name out of it, then Zander wasn't going to be very happy, and I'd look like a terrible friend.

A knot of guilt and panic twisted in my core. I hadn't been thinking clearly, thanks to the threat left on my garage door. I hoped Zander would understand I wasn't myself, after I had a chance to explain.

Bonnie: Sure. Noon?

I accepted Mason's offer, eager to sit down and talk with him. I wanted to know what was going on. And how much he would tell me.

I headed out of my room in search of coffee and pancakes without waiting for his response.

Mason sent a single thumbs-up emoji before I reached the staircase.

I kissed my parents goodbye after breakfast, then swapped Clyde's bow tie for a navy polka dot number that matched my cream-colored sleeveless blouse and navy-blue pencil skirt marvelously.

We climbed back into the borrowed pickup and headed into town right on schedule. I liked to open my shop at ten, take an hour for lunch, then close up at seven. It was the first morning in weeks that I wasn't bringing any baked goods for the refreshment table, and it felt strangely like the ending of an era.

My mind raced as I drove, mostly with questions about why Mason had wanted to see Zander first thing today and why Zander hadn't given me an update. I could only assume he was upset I'd let Mason figure out he was the source of my Runsfords' story. And I hated that it was true. With a little luck, I'd get the details from Mason at lunch. Then I'd know exactly how everything had gone down and could craft a better apology.

The square was busy when I arrived, loaded with shoppers and colorful displays. Local crafters, bakers and artisans hustled around the grassy oval and along the little paths, toting wares and setting up booths to showcase their goods. I recognized a few of the farmers with produce stands and Sutton yammering away at a table of succulents, apparently talking to the plants. I'd put Judy on my office bookshelf the day I received her and had accidentally left her there every day since. I made a mental note to read up on succulent care.

I pulled into the only available parking spot outside my shop, then took a minute to savor the scene before unfastening Clyde's carrier.

Liz waved from her position a few doors down. She'd set up a pretty book display beside a sign announcing a sidewalk sale. Her floppy hat and large white-framed sunglasses made her look like a movie star. The free-standing Shop Bliss sign at her side made her look like the posterchild for Cami's new campaign.

I waved back, then let myself into Bless Her Heart. Once the lights were on, and Clyde was free, I dropped my things in my office and checked the time. I had more than an hour before I needed to leave for my lunch appointment with Mason but enough nervous energy to blast me through the roof long before then.

I put myself to work being a good shop owner. First, I

dragged a pretty accent chair, small table and the large flower basket Mama had most recently dropped off, onto the sidewalk. I arranged the items in an appealing group, then placed a marble clipboard with a stack of flyers for my grand opening on the table.

I waved to Liz again as she chatted with a group of ladies, then scanned the controlled chaos across the street. If my folks had arrived with Petal Pusher, I could flag them down or hop over to say hello.

The sun warmed my cheeks as I stared, and scents of icing-drenched cinnamon rolls mixed with coffee on the breeze.

No signs of Petal Pusher, but a familiar gray-haired woman in a maroon velour track suit moved into view. A severely overweight Pekinese trotted awkwardly on a leash at her side. They seemed to be headed for Peter's Pupcakes, and I'd recognize the woman anywhere.

"Mirabelle," I whispered.

I glanced at Clyde, seated lazily among a cluster of plush throw pillows in the window display. Then I turned back to the square. I wanted to talk to Mirabelle, but I hated to leave my shop. I couldn't afford to miss a customer or a chance to make a good impression. Still, Mirabelle hadn't been easy to pin down.

No one on the sidewalk seemed headed in my direction, and I told myself I would be quick. My feet were in motion before I'd fully made the decision to catch her.

"Excuse me," I called, darting across the street on a mission. "Mirabelle?" I weaved between slow walkers and bypassed a stalled family with a fussing infant. "Pardon!"

Mirabelle handed money to the man at the Peter's Pupcakes booth, then bent to offer something to the log-shaped pooch on her leash.

"Hello!" I called again, finally landing at her side. I pasted on a smile and pressed a palm against the stitch forming in my side. "It's me, Bonnie Balfour. Gigi's granddaughter. Do you have a minute to talk?"

Mirabelle creaked upright and frowned. "If this is about the paper, I'm off-duty. If it's a casual howdy-do, then it's very nice to meet you."

I chewed my lip, deciding how to proceed.

She grunted, then started walking.

"No. Wait," I said, matching my pace with hers. "You didn't include my side of the story in the article about Viola Abbott-Harrington's death, and I feel I was unfairly portrayed as a result. You probably know I just moved back to Bliss a few months ago. I opened a new shop, and I'm trying to create a new life for myself here. I can't do that if half the town suspects I'm a criminal."

She stopped short and her dog sat to pant. "I printed the facts as I had them."

"Absolutely," I said, nodding emphatically. "I know you did, and I was just hoping you'd consider a follow-up piece that included the facts as I saw them."

"Are you saying you saw things differently than the uniforms on site that night?" she asked, curiosity clearly piqued.

"Probably," I said with a chuckle. "I was a mess. I'd never experienced anything like that. Add in the series of unfortunate events that followed, and I think it will be clear to everyone I had nothing to do with what happened to poor Viola."

Mirabelle's head tipped slightly over one shoulder. "What events?"

I laughed humorlessly. "I've been threatened. At my shop and at home. I think it's because I've been trying to find

Viola's killer. Maybe I've gotten close, and the guilty party is trying to silence my investigation. I don't know, but it's scary, and I think folks should know."

She smiled. "Your investigation?"

"Unofficial," I said, fluttering a palm between us. "It's the reason someone had all those opportunities to take pictures of me with Detective Wright. He pegged me as a suspect, and I wanted to provide him with other, more realistic suspects. He's not from here," I said, with a dramatic eye roll. "Cleveland."

Her mouth turned down at the sides, and she shook her head.

"Anyway," I went on. "He wanted me to stop asking questions. He thought I was getting in his way, so he kept coming around to say so. Then the killer must've agreed with him because the threats began."

Mirabelle's brows tented. She fished in her bag and unearthed a pen and paper. She turned to her panting dog. "Sit. Mama's going to be a minute or two."

The dog collapsed onto his side in the grass, tongue lolling.

"Now, you," she said, swinging her gaze back to meet mine. "Tell me everything."

I unloaded the whole shebang, the facts, the feelings and the unnerving scares in between. I'd opened my mouth with the intention of being brief, but the words came like a flood, and I felt surprisingly lighter when I'd finished.

She thanked me with an approving nod, then helped roll her dog back to its feet.

I hurried to my shop, a little guilty for being away so long.

A pair of women exited Bless Her Heart as I hit the sidewalk with a smile.

"Thanks for stopping," I said. "Sorry I missed you. The

square was so enticing. I couldn't help sneaking a peek over there."

They nodded and offered their complete agreements.

"Were you looking for anything?" I asked, lifting a finger toward my store.

"Just browsing," one woman said.

"It's all beautiful," the other added. "We'll definitely be back."

I handed them each a flyer before thanking them again. Then I made my way inside.

I sold several hats, a pair of heels and a lot of costume jewelry before the place grew quiet once more.

The door opened, and Emma bumbled inside, a load of dresses draped across her arms, and hats piled three tall on her head. "Help."

I laughed as I made a run for her. "Oh, my gosh. You weren't kidding."

"No, and there's more in the car."

I glanced around, then motioned her to the back. "Let's put these in my office." No reason to clutter up the clean counter when shoppers had been stopping by.

Emma passed the gowns to me, then placed the hats on my desk with a smile. "I'll get the rest. Be right back."

My phone buzzed as she spun to leave, and I eagerly checked the screen.

The message was from Mason.

Mason: Change of plans. On my way to bag a killer. No lunch. Dinner to celebrate?

I guffawed. Offended both by the last-minute cancellation and for being left hanging.

The screen indicated he was typing again, but I wrote back before his second message appeared.

Bonnie: Who is it?

Mason: Stay at your parents' place. And lock up.

"I'm not at my parents' place," I grouched. Then I sent another message to let him know I was at work. I stared a long moment at the bouncing dots, waiting for his next message to appear. Then, frustrated, I turned to the donations I'd just received.

I admired an elaborate and lovely hat, fit for the Kentucky Derby, and recalled the way Viola had looked when she'd delivered her first big donation to the store. She'd been brusque, but polite, maybe even happy, when she'd asked me to stop by that night for the rest.

Something about the thought itched in my mind.

Was it odd that Emma had arrived after Viola's death, claiming she'd also had donations in her car for me? And one of the boxes had contained the murder weapon?

The vase couldn't have been packed until after it killed Viola, so how had it gotten into the box, which was allegedly already in Emma's car?

My phone dinged, and I jumped, pressing both palms to my collarbone. "Glory!"

My small office seemed suddenly too warm.

I lifted the phone to examine my new text.

Mason's message had finally arrived.

Mason: Emma O'Neil

My world spun, and my ears rang. I pressed the call button on his number and forced my wooden legs toward the half-open office door as the call began to ring.

"Wright," Mason barked, the sound of wind and an engine roaring in the background.

I tried to work my suddenly swollen tongue inside my utterly parched mouth, but the shock had addled my brain.

"Bonnie?" he barked again.

"Emma O'Neil is Viola's killer?" I asked, voice cracking and far too soft. "The one threatening me?"

"Yep. I'm headed over to her place now with a pair of offi-cers," he said proudly.

"Emma's not home," I told him, croaking out the words.

A moment of silence passed, with only the sounds of wind and his Jeep's racing engine. "How do you know that?" he asked finally.

"Because she's here."

CHAPTER TWENTY-FIVE

*M*y office door burst open, and I screamed as Clyde flew inside. The phone toppled from my grip, and I nearly cried in relief. I captured him in my arms, then spun back as the door slammed shut.

Emma stood inside the office, my pretty pink desk between us, a women's golf club in her hand. And a look of resolution in her narrowed brown eyes.

I swallowed hard and felt my eyes go wide. "Emma!" I gasped. "What's wrong?"

I'd never been a good liar, and I was an even worse actress, but any shock she saw on my face was one hundred percent real. I'd been so sure Nathan was at the center of this mess, I hadn't thought too long or hard about who else it could be. Maybe I was as guilty of narrow-mindedness as I'd accused Mason of being when we'd first met.

And look where that had gotten me.

My traitorous gaze dropped to the floor at the thought of his name. The device had bounced out of sight beneath my desk. I could only hope the line was still open, and that she hadn't heard me say her name.

Emma shifted silently, widening her stance.

"Any chance that golf club is another donation?" I asked, a nervous chuckle bubbling free.

Suddenly my small, rectangular office felt like an obstacle course. A door at one, narrow end. Behind my assailant. Bookshelves on one wall, donation boxes on the other. A fabulously refinished desk and two perfectly reupholstered chairs between us.

I needed a way to reach the door without losing my head in the process.

She swung the nine iron onto her shoulder, probably preparing to knock my head off.

But I wasn't an old lady, and she wasn't going to take me by surprise.

Emma wet her lips. "Things were never supposed to come to this," she said quietly, her tone sad, but resigned. "I tried to be your friend. I wanted you to see this isn't who I am." She wiggled her weapon. "I'm kind and happy. I'm a protector and a caregiver. I thought you would see that."

"I do," I agreed quickly. "I've been saying all along that whatever happened to Viola that night was probably an accident. One unfortunate moment that couldn't be taken back."

She nodded stiffly, then adjusted her grip on the club.

"You don't have to do this," I said, taking one baby step to my right, keeping the full width of the desk between us. "I don't know what happened between you and Viola, and I don't have to," I offered. "It's none of my business, and I can stop asking questions right now." I mimed pulling a zipper across my mouth.

Emma's expression went so dramatically blank, it might've been comical in another situation.

I raised my brows in question, lips pressed tight.

She shook her head. "You've already proven you absolutely cannot be quiet. I tried everything to make you stop. I tried to scare you. Tried to warn you. I've even threatened you, but you just kept coming for me." She released a long, frustrated breath. "I can't let you tell anyone what you know."

"But I don't know anything," I yelped. "I thought Nathan killed his mom for her money! Ask anyone. He's the only one I've put any real suspicions on from the start. Never you." I remembered my vow of silence, then pretended to zip my lips again.

She rolled her eyes. "Don't bother lying. That detective I see you with every day and night," she said, tacking the final two words on salaciously, "called me to see if I was free to talk at lunch. I need to know what you told him, then I need to shut you up, permanently. With you gone, and my story straight, I can still survive this."

"Unlike Viola," I said, forgetting my zipper and the fact that I was talking to her killer.

"I didn't mean to do that!" she yelled. "I was just so frustrated." Emma took a step to the side, and I matched her move, stepping away as she stepped nearer, keeping the same amount of distance between us. "My mother and daughter mean everything to me. They are my world, and they count on me to keep them safe. I can't do that if I go to jail."

The idea of a daughter's love for her mother wasn't lost on me. Emma's mama was in a wheelchair, visibly older than my mama, and likely in worse health. I couldn't imagine the vulnerability there, but I knew there was no limit to what I would do to protect my mama. And though I'd never had children, I'd seen my mama's love in action for thirty-nine years.

Mama had faced off with softball dads who got too riled in the stands when I was present or on the field. She'd taken on teachers when I'd struggled in school or just needed an advocate, and when a black bear had wandered onto the farm from the woods when I was six, she'd come running full speed to save me. I'd watched in stunned silence as she'd grabbed, then thrust me behind her without missing a step. She'd screamed for me to go inside while she'd banged a pot and pan together over her head, and she hadn't stopped until the bear had retreated. Even at that age, I understood the danger, knew she could die. I wasn't much older when I'd first realized if her noise assault hadn't worked, she would've traded her life for mine.

Now, ten feet away, I faced another mama determined to protect her family. And I wasn't even remotely equipped for the challenge.

She moved forward and I stepped back. "Turn around," she demanded.

I scanned the stacks of boxes, then the contents of my bookshelves. I had a thousand things to throw at her, but none were as efficient as her weapon. "Let's talk about this," I said. "Why don't you take my cell phone and go? You can lock me in here. I don't have a landline, can't call for help. Meanwhile, you can run home, grab your mama and your little girl, then be out of town before the police come looking for you. Even if you don't trust me not to tell, you'll have a good head start."

Emma blinked and a fresh tear fell. "Your detective is on his way to my place," she said, voice flat and eyes hard. "He's probably already there, with mama and Olivia," she muttered, mostly to herself. "I knew I should've driven that vase to the shore and thrown it in the ocean. It was supposed to seal the case against you, but you found it before I could report it missing from Viola's entryway. I'd counted on Teddy to report it, but he didn't even notice it was gone. He didn't even remember it being there," she snapped.

"Men," I said.

She narrowed her eyes. "The police were supposed to

come here looking for it, then think you took it from the scene to cover your crime, but you messed that up too."

A well of indignation rose in me at her complaint. I was well-past tired of being told I'd messed up or done something wrong, when I'd been trying to do things right. Grant had pushed me to my limit with that, and I wasn't about to start accepting it from anyone in Bliss. "None of this is my fault," I said, feeling my backbone strengthen. "I didn't do anything wrong. You did, then you kept trying to cover it up. Piling on more crimes isn't going to erase the first one and blaming me for your behavior doesn't make you innocent. Have you considered you're just a terrible criminal?"

She gaped. "I'm not a criminal."

"Then stop acting like one," I said a little more gently. "Is this really the kind of mother and daughter you want to be?"

"No," she said. "I want to be the kind of daughter who's around to care for her ailing mother. And the kind of mama who gets to see her little girl grow up. I don't care about the rest." Her lips trembled, and I felt a bud of hope in my core.

Clyde leaped onto a box near my shoulder, and I stifled a shriek.

I'd forgotten he was in the room with us. I had no idea where he'd been hiding, but he gave me a long, slow blink before rubbing his cheek along a brown box marked HEELS.

His luminous green gaze met mine, and I wondered for a moment if he could read my mind.

If there were enough pairs of shoes in that box, I might be able to use them in our defense. I'd never attempted to hit a moving target with a projectile before, but the room was small and crowded. The odds, for the first time in too long, seemed to be in my favor. Emma could still take a swing at my head, but her accuracy would surely suffer if I was pelting her with cast-off Manolos. I scooted carefully toward the box, hoping she wouldn't see my move coming.

"Maybe you can confess and ask for leniency," I suggested. "Tell someone what really happened that night. A court might understand if you give them a chance."

She barked a deep, angry laugh. "Viola Abbott-Harrington was dying," Emma said flatly. "She was packing up her life and preparing for her death. I was doing all the work to make certain everything happened exactly the way she wanted, and that was fine. Doing her bidding was my job. I knew my time with her was coming to an end the minute she'd confided her condition to me. I'd been the one scheduling all her appointments, then making sure she got to them. I continued to do everything I could for her all day, and at night, I worked on my resume. I thought I would take some additional classes when hospice came, but I would've stayed by her side until the very end. Then she announced she was moving to Nashville."

Emma's cheeks flamed red, and her eyes went wild. "Nashville," she repeated. "To be near Nathan, the son who hadn't spoken to her in the seven years I've been around. And she wanted to leave in two weeks. She said she'd give me a nice referral and my last paycheck. That was it. Goodbye, Emma!" She worked her fingers around the golf club's grip, agitated and vibrating slightly, like a shaken soda ready to blow. "I can't find a job making the kind of money she paid me in two weeks! I need time! I had a plan!"

I took another step in the box's direction, and my illuminated cell phone screen came into view. Detective Grouchy was written across the screen. Mason's picture and number were still visible. Our call hadn't disconnected.

"I begged her to take me with her," Emma went on, her voice coming louder and more fervent with every word. "Or to at least allow me to stay on staff until the house was sold, but she refused. Then, she caught me taking something from one of the boxes meant for the historical society. Some jewelry I thought I could pawn or sell to keep my family afloat while I looked for work. It was a desperate, stupid idea, and I regret it now. I apologized, but she realized I'd done it once before, when my mama first got sick. She went to call the police."

Emma stilled. Her eyes glistened with unshed tears.

"That was when you hit her with the vase from her entry table?" I asked.

"She fired me," Emma said. "For stealing. I never would've been hired by anyone after that. I begged her to understand or to at least hear me out, to listen," she dragged the final word into two long syllables. "I'd always planned to buy the things back and return them without her knowing, as soon as I could afford to. But no. One mistake on my part, after seven years of dedicated service, and she was willing to ruin me."

"I'm sorry," I whispered, truly meaning the words.

She inhaled deeply, then stalked around the desk in my direction.

I grabbed the box of shoes and screamed. "Help!"

The golf club sliced through the air with a whoosh before I was ready, and collided with a box of fancy picture frames. The sound that followed was calamitous and ear-splitting. My scream made it worse.

She swung again as I clutched the box of shoes to my chest, panic swelling in my heart and head.

I jerked back, then stumbled as wind from her club passed by. "Help!"

Emma raised the club overhead, prepared to bring it down on my head, and my fight or flight instinct dramatically changed gears.

Anger ripped through my limbs, and I stuffed a hand into the box in my grip. I wasn't going to die at the hands of a selfish women in an office filled with donations made by generous people.

I yanked a stiletto from the box, then chucked it in Emma's direction.

She lowered the golf club several inches, ducking the heel.

The second one hit her in the chest. "Hey!"

"Help!" I screamed again, repeating the word at the top of my lungs, while I kept the shoes flying.

Emma dropped the golf club in favor of blocking the onslaught of shoes.

Clyde leaped from his box when she came near, and landed on Emma's back as she passed.

Her eyes widened before she cried out in pain, his talons likely shredding her shirt and digging into her skin. She screamed and swore, then caught her hip on my desk and careened into my bookshelves, knocking books and trinkets from the top.

I lunged for the door and wrenched it open.

Clyde darted past me into the hall as the bookcase rocked roughly and fell.

I raced down the hall toward my shop's front door, a wild calamity of sounds echoing behind me. And I was met with the sights and sounds of late-arriving law enforcement.

$\mathcal{I}$ hurried to pack Clyde into his carrier for the official Bless Her Heart grand opening, then headed toward to the door. There had been some debate over whether or not to bring him to the party, due to the buffet, but in the end, I couldn't leave him. He'd saved my life.

Cami and my parents had volunteered to hold down the fort while I ran home to change, just in case I was late or guests arrived early. I'd closed the shop promptly at seven, but the party was set for eight, and I'd needed a fresh dress and heels.

I'd borrowed one of Gigi's dresses from a zippered garment bag in her closet. The material was pale blue with a slight shimmer and felt incredibly perfect for tonight. The cut was tight at the waist, snug across my bust, and flared at the hips, perfect for hiding the extra pounds I'd gained from stress-baking. And eating. I deeply approved of the designer, who'd clearly understood women's bodies. I paired the dress with nude pumps and a white petticoat, then let my wild red curls run free. I wished Gigi could be with me tonight, but since she couldn't, the dress would at least make me feel closer to her.

Maybe I could even absorb a little of Gigi's natural grace and confidence because I was about to hold a party at a shop where the town's first murderer in a decade had tried to kill me. And my spoonful of courage had run out in my office when faced with Emma and her ladies' Callaway club. In all the chaos and shock that had followed my attack, I hadn't had time to prepare food for the party, so Mama had promised to take charge.

Clyde meowed from the carrier as I took a cleansing breath, probably sensing my anticipation.

"I'm okay," I promised. "Just nervous." I shook my hands out at the wrists, then headed for the mirror in the living room. "What if no one comes?" I asked, slipping small diamond earrings into my lobes.

He rolled onto his side in the carrier and waited, looking like a feline James Bond in his natural black fur and white tuxedo tie.

My cell phone buzzed on the coffee table, and I started, then chuckled. I was still a little on edge, even days after my run-in with Emma. I checked the time, then the phone. I was officially running late, and I didn't recognize the number. "Hello?"

"Bonnie Balfour?" a familiar woman's voice asked.

"Yes."

"This is Mirabelle Morris. I'm planning to attend your party tonight, and I'm hoping to get a few moments of your time while I'm there."

"Of course," I said. "That would be fantastic."

Mirabelle's article providing my take on the events following Viola's murder had run the day after my attack, and she'd incorporated all the facts quite well. More than that, she'd painted me in a gracious and exceptionally kind light, except for the fact that she'd dubbed me the "Queen of Curiosity," then made a reference to Bless Her Heart, where I "sold the gowns, tiaras and scepters to go with the title." I didn't sell scepters, but I didn't hate the nickname. Mason, on the other hand, definitely had.

I smiled at the memory of his sour face.

Then something curious registered.

"You're covering events again?" I asked. "Not Zander?"

"Zander's out of town," Mirabelle said. "But I will be there. I have to walk Mr. Dinky, so I'll see you in about an hour."

The call disconnected, and I had a quiet laugh at poor Mr. Dinky's unfortunate name. If memory served, her dog had been more like a tiny tank.

Not every pet could have a perfect name like Clyde, I supposed. Clyde had come with his name, and we'd made a daring duo from the moment we'd met. In hindsight, choosing him had been the first in many steps to reclaim my identity in a life and marriage where I'd become invisible, even to myself. Clyde and I might not be outlaws in a traditional sense, but his companionship had helped me become the rebel I'd forgotten I once was. And we'd made a great team, taking down a killer. It was something I wouldn't mind doing again.

I could never admit it to anyone, except Clyde, but I'd enjoyed the drama of what we'd been through. Not specifically the part where a woman swung a nine iron at my head, but the thrill of the chase. Using my brain to collect information, to decipher clues and to piece together facts. I was glad it was over, but I was also thankful for the role I'd played, and that Viola would get justice, even if it had come too late.

A set of headlights flashed over the front window, and I ran to get a closer look.

A filthy white Jeep sullied my drive.

And my silly heart rate kicked up a notch.

I made my way onto the porch as Mason climbed down from the vehicle, all long legs and swagger. His dark jeans blended smoothly into a navy dress shirt he'd unbuttoned at the cuffs and rolled to his elbows. I lifted my hand in greeting. "Hey."

"Hey," he echoed, taking the steps slowly to my porch. His sharp gaze travelled over me from head to heels, and his grin heated my cheeks, chest and core. "You look nice," he said. "Are you going somewhere?"

I bit my lip, suddenly wishing I wasn't, and wanting to sit and chat a while with him instead. We hadn't seen one another for more than a passing moment since I'd watched him arrest Emma outside Bless Her Heart. "I am," I said. "How about you? Are you on your way back from the courthouse?"

"I am," he said, using my words with a grin. "I met with Judge Sweeney about Emma O'Neil and the case we're building against her. Sweeney was exceedingly patient and generously compassionate with regards to Emma's situation." His tone seemed trapped between frustration and exhaustion. "No big surprise there."

The last part was definitely sarcasm.

I narrowed my eyes. "Is that a knock on the judge or my town? Because I'm only inviting you inside if you answer correctly."

Mason pulled his chin back, a distinct get-serious expression in place. "You're going to complain no matter what I say, so I'm not answering that. Anyhow, I'm here to pick you up, so I don't even want to come in. But I will say that if you had more crime down here, the judge wouldn't be so willing to listen to a killer's sob story."

"It's a legitimate story. I've been trying to think of how I can help her mom and daughter, but I'm at a loss, unless they can live on baked goods."

Mason moved in close and I sucked in a breath. He grinned at the response. "Pardon me," he said, pushing the door open behind me and scanning the floor. "I figured." He lifted Clyde in his carrier. "All right. Let's go."

"Where?" I asked, momentarily befuddled.

"To your party," he said slowly, returning to the porch, brows puckered, as if I was in possession of a low IQ. "I stopped at your shop first to see if there was anything I could do to help you get ready for tonight, and your mama sent me over here. She said to tell you to get a move on. There's a line around the block, and she's not holding them off past eight. The food will get cold."

I laughed at the idea of a line to visit my store.

He stared. "What's funny?"

"Food," I said. "And it's not funny. It's a mess. I forgot to order catering, but Mama said she'd figure it out. I can't imagine what there is to get cold."

He tented his brows. "There was a ton of stuff being delivered when I was there. Something from just about every place on the square as far as I could tell."

I blinked, stunned again, as I followed Mason and Clyde to his Jeep. "Really?"

He shrugged, then strapped Clyde into the backseat before climbing behind the wheel.

"You knew I was going somewhere when you got here," I said. "I thought you really didn't know."

He scanned my face with searching blue eyes. "It hurts that you doubt me. I set an alert when I saw the party announcement."

"An alert?" I asked, climbing carefully into the Jeep without accidentally giving my neighbors a show.

"On my phone. You never use your calendar feature? I'd think you'd love that one."

"I do," I said, hurrying to fasten my seatbelt as he reversed out of the driveway. "Okay, now tell me everything about your meeting at the courthouse. In what way was Judge Sweeney compassionate? What was said? I need details, and talk fast because I also need to focus on being a good hostess once we get to Bless Her Heart, and it's a short drive."

Mason blew out a long breath. "Judge Sweeney was moved by Emma's position as primary caregiver for her mom and daughter, so she's willing to entertain any kind of plea bargain. Apparently Sweeney has a granddaughter in Emma's daughter's class at school, so it's complicated."

"Olivia," I supplied. "Emma's daughter is Olivia."

Mason slid his eyes my way. "Right."

"Keep going," I said, eager to hear the rest.

"Emma will do some time, regardless. She confessed to all her crimes, from killing Viola and threatening you, to all the minor counts of vandalism at your shop and home." He rubbed the back of his neck. "Sweeney appreciated her willingness to cooperate. Still, it's unlikely Emma will be home for several years at minimum, and I'm pushing for mandatory counseling while she's incarcerated. Even a few years of regular sessions with a decent therapist will make a difference."

I nodded. "I agree. I like that. She really seemed to think she was doing what she had to do to protect her family."

"Sure. Protect them by killing you." Masons' knuckles whitened under his grip on the steering wheel. "You were smart that day. I haven't told you yet, and I should have. Keeping the line open was priceless. I was able to patch you through to dispatch, who recorded every word of your exchange. I knew your location and your situation before I arrived. It was too bad I'd made it so far in the opposite direction before I realized what was happening."

"I'm just glad the line didn't disconnect. I didn't do that on purpose. I dropped the phone when I jumped." I slid him a self-deprecating smile. "I wish you would've called me to tell me it was her as soon as you knew. That could've changed everything."

"I did call," he said, defensively. His shoulders and pitch rose with the words.

I crossed my arms. "Yes. To cancel our lunch plans."

"I didn't know you were in danger. I was on my way to save the day."

"Nice job."

He flashed a bright smile in my direction but didn't comment.

The town square came into view a little while later, complete with a million twinkle lights and folks out enjoying a beautiful evening.

Mason wheeled his Jeep in a wide U-turn at the intersection, then bounced over the curb outside Bless Her Heart. "What do you know? We got the last parking space."

"This isn't a parking space," I complained, gripping the dashboard and shooting him a pointed look. "This is the sidewalk. Where'd you learn to drive?"

"Cleveland."

I rolled my eyes, then caught sight of the crowd inside my store. "Whoa."

"What?" He climbed out then reached for Clyde while I gaped at the storefront window.

"Do you see all those guests?"

He grunted. "So? That's good, right? I mean, the fire marshal might disagree, but you're happy. Aren't you? I told you they were lined up around the corner."

"I thought you were joking," I hissed, concern tamping

my excitement. "What if they're just here to see the place Viola's killer held me captive?" My limbs locked, and I wasn't sure I wanted to get out of the Jeep anymore.

Mason stared back at me through the open door, then snorted. "You mean the place where you crushed a killer under the weight of unanchored bookshelves? And knocked her out cold with a little green plant?"

"Clyde knocked her into the bookshelf," I said, offering my kitty a warm smile. "He saved me. Judy did the rest."

"That's the plant, right?" he asked, though we'd been over it before.

I nodded.

"Well, the cat might've started it," Mason said, "but you put that plant exactly where it needed to be when it mattered most. So, there's that."

"That was a fluke."

"Was it? I met a lady the other day who says she gave you that plant for protection." He shrugged. "I'm just saying. It's a strange town."

"Stop." I laughed. I'd felt terrible taking Judy's remains back to Sutton the next morning, but she'd seemed proud. Apparently it wasn't Judy's first broken pot.

Mason leaned back into the Jeep, stretching an arm under his seat. He pulled out a portable emergency flasher, then stuck it on the dash. It was small and plastic, like something a child might play with, and he'd wrapped a Bliss Sheriff's Department bumper sticker around the base. "Now, anyone who sees this will know I'm the law, and they'll keep moving. No need to give me a ticket for taking the last parking spot."

"It's the sidewalk," I repeated. "And you're only the borrowed law," I said, opening my door and forcing myself out. "I'm pretty sure you're not above a Bliss parking ticket."

Mason met me at the front of his Jeep with a mischievous grin. He tapped a long, tan finger to the badge on his belt.

"That's another thing that changed today. I'm not on loan anymore."

I peered at the badge, recognizing the familiar logo and insignia. Exactly like Sheriff Miller's.

Mason took a step toward my shop, and I snaked an arm out to grab him.

"Wait a minute!" I latched onto his wrist and gaped. "That badge says sheriff."

"Miller's retiring." Mason winked. "I came for one reason, but it looks like I'm staying for another. Miller will be leading my campaign in the fall election because ultimately the role of sheriff is still up to the people. I'm more like an interim."

My jaw dropped. "You're the new sheriff?"

"Interim," he said, setting a big hand against the small of my back and hustling me toward the party. "But yes. Now, come on, before your mama starts to worry. She's got a surprise for you that won't keep."

CHAPTER TWENTY-SEVEN

"*T*here she is!" Cami called, instantly rushing toward me as Mason ushered me inside. "Look at this turn out!" she gushed. "Can you believe all that food was donated? And there's more in the back!"

I tried to take in the scene, the food, music and faces, while trying not to appear as stunned and emotional as I suddenly felt.

"Everyone!" Cami called, projecting her voice like the professional attention-grabber she was.

The room quieted.

I looked for Mama in the crowd, then spotted her behind my counter, where rows of logoed boxes from local restaurants, pubs and cafés were lined and stacked.

Cami slipped her arm around my shoulders and smiled. "Thank you," she called. "I'm so glad you're all here. Most of you know Bonnie Balfour or have certainly heard of her by now."

The crowd chuckled.

I blushed.

"She's been a part of the fabric of this town for many

years now. Since her birth and even during the years she was away." She turned to me and smiled. "I'm really glad she's come home, opened this beautiful store and is working hard every day to make sure each shopper can afford something special and beautiful. Because that's the core of who she is. Someone who makes everyone else feel special, and tonight, I hope this incredible turn out will show you, Bonnie Balfour, just how special this town thinks you are too."

Mason's arm went up, a disposable cup in his hand. "Cheers."

"Cheers," the crowd echoed.

My folks paraded around from behind the counter, wide, proud smiles on their faces. They hugged and welcomed me, pride oozing from their pores.

Mama gripped my arms and smiled. "Your Gigi made everyone feel special too. You remind me of her every day."

"Thank you." Being compared to Gigi was a high honor. She and Grandpapa had been staples in the community. She'd taught me to bake, and she'd often taken me on her morning trips throughout the town, to schools, churches and homes, just popping in and dropping off a little sugar. Those trips were probably the reason I cared so much for the families in my town today. I'd seen the struggles outside my happy, flower-infused bubble, and I'd seen how far Gigi's kind words and baked goods had gone to brighten dozens of days. I wanted to carry on that legacy. "I really miss her," I said.

Mama stepped away and my mouth dropped open. Gigi appeared, manifesting from the crowd. "That's good to hear," she said, in the deep, scratchy voice I loved so much. "'Cause I'm back."

I squealed and crushed her in a hug. I hadn't seen Gigi since Grandpapa's funeral, and I hadn't realized how profoundly I'd missed her since my return. "You made it!" I said, easing away to look at her. Her strawberry-blond hair had all gone gray, and her skin was impossibly fair, despite living at the beach, but her hazel eyes flashed with mischief, the way they had when I was young, and it made me feel youthful to see it once more. "I'm so glad you're here," I whispered.

She smiled warmly as she studied me. "I couldn't stop thinking that your grandpapa would've given anything for one more day with you, your mama and Bud. Yet, there I was, with the chance to make more memories and be part of your return to Bliss, but I was off living with the naturalists. They were nice, but they weren't family. So what was I doing, wasting precious time on them, when you were right here?"

I wrapped her in another hug.

"I don't want to miss anything else," she whispered.

Mama and Cami made a series of soft aww sounds, and Gigi broke our hug with a chuckle. We wiped our tears, then smiled at one another for a long moment, before her eyes rose over my shoulder, then narrowed.

I turned to find Nathan Harrington behind me, and I nearly fell over from shock. Knowing Nathan wasn't a killer didn't stop the familiar sense of unease that rippled through me. Then I saw his extended hand.

I accepted the shake, and the tension in his expression relaxed a bit.

"Thank you for helping the detective find the woman who hurt my mom," he said. "From what I hear, you played a big part in that, and I'm grateful. Mama and I didn't see eye-to-eye on most things, and she was a tough person to get along with, but she was my mama." He paused to collect himself, and his Adam's apple bobbed. "I wanted you to know I set up a trust fund to help Emma's mother and daughter get by until Emma can get back home to them. It wasn't her family's fault she did what she did."

My heart warmed just a bit to him. "That was very kind."

He nodded, then grinned. "I'm sure Mama would've hated it."

I laughed. Giving money to the family of a woman who'd stolen from her? Then killed her? "Probably," I agreed.

Nathan raised a palm and turned to leave.

"You don't have to go," I said, stalling his exit momentarily. "You can stay. Be with other people who knew Viola. Get something to eat and drink."

He scanned the crowd, then shook his head. "Nah. I've got my hands full over at the house. Mama left a lot of instructions to be carried out."

"If you need any help," I offered. "I think I can round up a hand or two."

Nathan smiled, nodded, then walked out the door.

A moment later, his black car rolled past the window.

Then Sutton and Gretchen appeared.

Gigi nearly ran me over getting to the door to usher them inside. "My stars in heaven! Get in here. What on earth are you doing back in Bliss?" she asked Sutton, wrapping her in a warm embrace. "I swear you haven't changed since bell bottoms were in style."

"Bell bottoms are in style," Sutton said, glancing down at her floral silver muumuu, as if she might be wearing a pair as an example.

Gretchen smiled, then motioned to the older women beside us. "I guess they know one another."

"Seems that way," I said, a thousand questions forming in my mind.

"That's your grandmama?" Gretchen asked, reminding me I hadn't introduced her.

"Sorry." I cringed. "Yes. That's Gigi."

Gretchen eyeballed her appreciatively. "Sutton's got a lot of stories about her."

"Really?" I asked, shocked and impossibly more interested than before. "I'd love to hear some of those."

"Oh!" Sutton froze, then dug into her big quilted bag. "All right. All right," she said, pulling out a pink pot the size of an orange. One small succulent was planted neatly at the center. "Judy won't shut up about her heroics over here, and none of the others can stand it, so I'm afraid you're stuck with her," Sutton said. "Either that or my aloe vera plants are going to pack up and leave."

I accepted the offered pot and plant with a broad smile. "We can't have that," I said, admiring Judy's new digs. A small wooden sign had been stuck into the dirt on one side. The name, Judy, was painted neatly on the stick in pink and purple paints. "I'll take better care of her this time," I promised.

Sutton puffed air into her long sideswept bangs. "Good luck with that."

"Bonnie?" Mason's voice turned me around. His expression removed my smile.

"What's wrong?" I asked.

He stopped at my side, then glanced cautiously at the little crowd of women around me. "Something's come up, and I can't stay. Do you think your parents can drive you home?"

"I'll get her home," Cami said, speaking up before I could get my head around the request. He was leaving me here? And going where? Why? "No worries," Cami continued.

I frowned and bit my tongue against the fact that I was worried, disappointed and maybe a little irrationally mad. "What happened?" I asked, nearly repeating my previous question, which he'd blown off.

"Nothing that concerns you," he said with a teasing grin,

but something in his tone said he wasn't telling me the whole truth. "I'll check in with you later," he promised, already moving toward the door. "I gave Clyde's carrier to your dad. Clyde's roaming free around here somewhere, soaking up all this attention."

Mason walked out, and I turned back to my party. If he didn't want to tell me things, he didn't have to, and I couldn't control that. But I didn't have to let it bother me either.

I made a loop through the room, mingling and thanking folks for coming. I set Judy on my counter for safe keeping.

"Ms. Balfour?" A woman I didn't recognize approached with a young woman who I did.

I smiled and waved to Lexi, the young lady who'd accepted a prom dress in exchange for a few hours of work at my shop.

The older of the two woman, who was still clearly younger than me, extended a hand for me to shake. "I'm Tina Holcomb, Lexi's mom. I want to thank you for what you did. It's not always easy making ends meet with a large family, and I wasn't able to find a dress for her. She wouldn't have gone to prom if it wasn't for you, and quite a few other girls can say the same thing. I don't know if their moms are here tonight too, but I'm going to speak for all of them and say that you gave our daughters gifts that were so much bigger than a bunch of dresses." She turned her phone screen to me and showed me a photo of Lexi in the gown. With her mom. With her siblings. With her friends. Her smile was a mile wide, and she looked like she felt like a princess.

My eyes stung with gratitude for the photos. "Thank you for showing me these," I said, trying not to look as sappy as I suddenly felt. "I'm so glad you had a great time," I told Lexi.

Her mom wrapped an arm around Lexi's back and tugged her close. "You gave her a life experience that I couldn't, and one that I never had. You made so many wonderful memories possible for her. You have no idea what that means to me. To all of us moms."

"It was my pleasure," I said.

Lexi smiled, looking a little embarrassed, and a little thankful too. "Care if I come in tomorrow and do a little work?"

My smile widened and I nodded. "I think that would be amazing."

The Holcombs walked away, revealing Gigi and Dave from the Blissful Bean, chatting behind them. An image of Gigi selling her cakes and pies from the shop next door flashed into mind, and I headed in their direction to propose the idea.

I paused my progress when I noticed Mirabelle, seated on an accent chair, pen and paper in hand. Her track suit was yellow tonight, her orthopedic tennis shoes white. And she was scribbling with an enthusiasm I'd never known, looking up frequently, then back down to where she was writing, presumably documenting the party's details.

She stilled her pen when she saw me. "You've become quite a story," she said, moving her glasses to the end of her nose, then peering up at me over the top.

"Not this time," I told her. "This is about our unbelievable community." I scanned the crowd around us. "A family that comes out to support one another as needed."

Mirabelle chuckled. "Mind if I quote you?"

"Not at all." I gave the guests another long look and realized who I hadn't yet seen. "Do you know if Liz made it tonight? She runs What the Dickens bookstore."

Mirabelle removed her glasses. "I know Liz. She's probably over there with her nose in a book. She can't tell time any better than her mama or grandmama before her. Though she hosts a lovely book club."

"Thanks," I said. "I think I'll run over and invite her to come down."

I waved to a few smiling faces as I laced my way back through the crush of bodies to the door. I paused on the sidewalk when Mason's Jeep came into view. Where had he gone in such a hurry without it? And why?

Across the square, a willowy woman in black approached a motorcycle, then climbed aboard. Her bulbous black helmet did little to hide her long golden hair,

A man in a matching black helmet and motorcycle jacket climbed on behind her.

She revved the engine, and the pair cruised around the square in my direction.

The door to What the Dickens opened as the motorcycle approached, and Liz stepped out, locking up behind her. "Hey. What are you doing there?" she asked. "I was just on my way to your party."

"I came to see if you'd forgotten," I said, eyes glued to the motorcycle as it passed by.

Neither rider looked in our direction, their black visors impossible to see through.

But the license plate on the back had been issued in Ohio.

"Did you know them?" Liz asked, pulling my attention back to her as curiosity ignited like a flame to gasoline inside my veins.

I followed her gaze to the motorcycle, vanishing in the distance. "I'm not sure," I told her, as we turned in the direction of my shop.

But I was going to find out.

———

THANK YOU SO MUCH FOR READING BONNIE & CLYDE'S FIRST
MYSTERY ADVENTURE! THESE STORIES HAVE BEEN A DREAM OF

MINE FOR A VERY LONG TIME, AND I'M BEYOND THRILLED TO FINALLY SHARE THEM WITH YOU. I HOPE YOU'LL ENJOY EACH NEW STORY MORE THAN THE LAST AND THAT YOU'LL KEEP IN TOUCH BETWEEN THE BOOKS!

Don't forget to pick up your FREE copy of
When Bonnie Met Clyde (A Prequel),
exclusively at:
https://www.julieannelindsey.com

I HOPE YOU'LL TAKE A MOMENT TO LEAVE A REVIEW IF YOU ENJOYED THIS STORY. REVIEWS ARE AUTHOR-GOLD AND SO APPRECIATED!

And if you're ready for the next Bonnie & Clyde adventure, you can order Seven Deadly Sequins now!

ABOUT THE AUTHOR

Julie Anne Lindsey is an award-winning and bestselling author of mystery and romantic suspense. She's published more than forty novels since her debut in 2013 and currently writes series as herself, as well as under the pen names **Bree Baker**, **Jacqueline Frost**, and **Julie Chase**.

When Julie's not creating new worlds or fostering the epic love of fictional characters, she can be found in Kent, Ohio, enjoying her blessed Midwestern life. And probably plotting murder with her shamelessly enabling friends. Today she hopes to make someone smile. One day she plans to change the world.

Bonnie & Clyde Mysteries

Seven Deadly Sequins (Book 2 of 8)

Patience Price Mysteries

Murder by the Seaside (Book 1 of 4)

Seaside Cafe Mysteries

Live & Let Chai (Book 1 of 7)

Cider Shop Mysteries

Apple Cider Slaying (Book 1 of 3)

Christmas Tree Farm Mysteries

Twelve Slays of Christmas (Book 1 of 3)

Kitty Couture Mysteries

Cat Got Your Diamonds (Book 1 of 4)

Printed in Great Britain
by Amazon

27030645R00144